THE BLACK MASK LIBRARY

THE EARLY YEARS (1920–26)

The Man in the Shadows: The Complete Black Mask
Cases of Terry Mack *by Carroll John Daly*

Zigzags of Treachery: The Complete Black Mask Cases of the
Continental Op, Volume 1 *by Dashiell Hammett*

THE SHAW YEARS (1926–36)

Blood on the Curb *by Joseph T. Shaw*

Black Harvest: The Complete Black Mask Cases of Jules Tremaine *by Norvell W. Page*

Boomerang Dice: The Complete Black Mask Cases of Johnny Hi Gear *by Stewart Sterling*

The Case-Hardened Samaritan: The Complete Black Mask
Cases of Dal Prentice, Volume 1 *by Roger Torrey*

Dead Evidence: The Complete Black Mask Cases of Harrigan *by Ed Lybeck*

Laughing Death *by Raoul Whitfield*

Luck: The Complete Black Mask Cases of Oscar Sail *by Lester Dent*

Murder Maze: The Complete Black Mask Cases of Jerry
Tracy, Volume 2 *by Theodore A. Tinsley*

The Price of a Dime: The Complete Black Mask Cases of Ben Shaley *by Norbert Davis*

Somewhere in Mexico: The Complete Black Mask Cases
of Jerry Frost, Volume 1 *by Horace McCoy*

South Wind: The Complete Black Mask Cases of
Jerry Tracy, Volume 1 *by Theodore A. Tinsley*

That's Hollywood: The Complete Black Mask Cases of
Bill Lennox, Volume 1 *by W.T. Ballard*

White Talons: The Complete Black Mask Cases of Tex of
the Border Service *by Katherine Brocklebank*

THE LATER YEARS (1936–51)

Dead and Done For: The Complete Black Mask Cases of
Cellini Smith, Volume 1 *by Robert Reeves*

Dog Eat Dog: The Complete Black Mask Cases of Cellini Smith, Volume 2 *by Robert Reeves*

The Hound with the Golden Eye: The Complete Black Mask
Cases of Luther McGavock, Volume 2 *by Merle Constiner*

It Happened at the Lake *by Joseph T. Shaw*

Let the Dead Alone: The Complete Black Mask Cases of
Luther McGavock, Volume 1 *by Merle Constiner*

Murder Costs Money: The Complete Black Mask Cases
of Rex Sackler, Volume 1 *by D.L. Champion*

Murder on the Midway: The Complete Black Mask Cases of
the Human Encyclopedia, Volume 1 *by Frank Gruber*

Murder Pays 7 to 1: The Complete Black Mask Cases of
Rex Sackler, Volume 2 *by D.L. Champion*

THE CASE-HARDENED SAMARITAN

The Complete

BLACK MASK

Cases of Dal Prentice

1933

ROGER TORREY

---

illustrations by Arthur Rodman Bowker

cover by Jes Schlaikjer

BLACK MASK

2023

Table of Contents

Police Business

The police of Magna City might have had an eye for opportunity, but they weren't afraid of their job

"GO ON! KEEP talking," Prentice said dourly.

"S'help me, Mr. Prentice, tha—" a big fist took him squarely in the mouth and he fell to the floor, crashing through the chair he was seated on, as he dropped. Prentice stood over him rubbing his knuckles.

"—— sake! Take it easy, Dal," someone warned.

"He ain't hurt," the detective said briefly.

The man on the floor stirred, felt his bruised lips, picked out a tooth and looked at it dazedly.

"Hell! I know he's not," the same man said. "If he's out, he can't talk, can he?"

The man looked up at the ring of detectives in vain search of sympathy.

Prentice snapped: "He'll talk!" He picked the man up by the lapels of a once natty suit and growled, punctuating his remarks by slapping his victim's bloody face. "Listen you—*CRACK*—who was with you—*CRACK*—who was with you—*CRACK*—come on Vitori—*CRACK*—spill it—*CRACK*—who was with you—*CRACK*—tell me." He shook him methodically for a moment, stopped, then growled sullenly: "Aw, hell! He's out again." He turned to the man in uniform behind the desk, and complained: "If he'd keep from passing out, Cap, I know damn' well he'd talk."

"If he knows," the uniformed captain said mildly.

"Of course he knows," Prentice argued. "He was with those guys when they stuck up Roth, wasn't he?"

"He says he don't know," said the captain dryly.

"Listen, Cap! Four guys stuck up Roth and gunned Johnny out when he busted in, ain't that right? Three get away and we get one, don't we?" He nudged the prostrate man with his foot for emphasis and added, *"This* one. He's been identified by a dozen people as one of them."

"I know, I know!" the captain said wearily. "But Roth didn't identify him and we didn't get him at Roth's place." He added bitterly. "No! We got him an hour later and a mile away—and he's clean."

He spoke to one of the men looking on, his voice rasping harshly: "That's your work, Peterson, you dumb cluck."

The man on the floor stirred again, sat up, whimpered— words coming from his bleeding mouth with difficulty.

"He says he don't know a thing," one of the detectives translated. He laughed sardonically and told Prentice: "If I got a working over like you gave him I could make something up."

"It was my partner that got gunned," Prentice reminded him. He swore viciously and turned to the prisoner: "You rat ——!"

"That's enough, Dal," the captain said wearily. He told one of the others: "Put him away, Allen, and come right back. I want to make a speech."

Allen jerked the prisoner to his feet and threw him towards the door. "Git, you! You're getting a break." The man, still dazed, turned and looked stupidly at Allen, who seized him by the shoulder and half carried, half dragged him through the door, and down the hall.

They waited for his return.

The room was big, so big that three desks and a bench along the wall seemed scanty furniture. Over its entrance a worn sign read *Homicide Dept.* It was decorated fulsomely but monotonously by reward notices and police dodgers—by the door a bulletin board with vacation notices and citations, all this at eye level. Higher, circling three walls and part of the fourth, were pictures of former police detectives, under each a brass plate giving the name and some descriptive data. In a few days another framed picture would be there, with the plate saying— *Lieut. John H. Means. Killed by holdups Aug. 8, 1932,* and this knowledge made the dozen men in the room understand Prentice. They were the homicide squad in its entirety—with the exception of Means, who lay in the Police Morgue.

Prentice said: "Listen, Cap—"

"Wait till Allen comes back, Dal," the man behind the desk told him gently. "I think I've got a plan."

They waited in silence.

When Allen returned, the captain asked him sharply: "Did anybody see you take him down there?"

"No one," Allen answered.

"Good!" He opened a drawer in his desk and took out a padlock. "Put this on the corridor door that leads there. It's not a jail lock and I've both keys."

"But, Cap!" Prentice exclaimed. "When they feed him they'll—"

"He ain't booked, is he? He's in a cell block by himself, ain't he?" He told Allen: "Put the lock on and come on back," turned to Prentice and said: "If he has to eat, by ——! *I'll* feed him. He'll see nobody back there and nobody'll see him."

"I see!" Prentice smiled mirthlessly and the captain smiled back.

When Allen returned from barring the corridor door, the captain asked: "Fixed?" and at Allen's nod slowly got to his feet. He stood slightly leaning over his desk, gray haired, bulking, big, his hands flat on the desk's scarred top, his head thrust forward.

"Listen, men! You all know what's happened. Four men attempted to hold up Jack Roth, and Johnny Means stopped it and got killed doing it. Lieut. John Means—your brother officer. We've got the man or one of the men that did it." He struck the desk with his fist. "We've got him, but how long can we keep him? You know the law in this State. You know and I know that we can't hold him fifteen minutes after his lawyer knows he's here. He'll be out on bail, and when he does come up there'll be twenty witnesses that'll swear him an alibi. Twenty—hell! Fifty if he needs 'em."

He paused, cleared his throat. "Outside of this room there isn't anybody knows he's here except the three that was with him. They'll get somebody to spring him and as soon as we know who they cry to we've got a chance of tracing them. Outside of them and somebody here talking there ain't a way of this getting out, and if you're smart it won't get out. If Commissioner Richards hears about this, I may be back on a beat, but I'll have company. You know the orders about no third degree. Protect yourselves even if you don't protect me. That's all. If anybody asks why the meeting, tell 'em we were trying to figure where to put the finger on the heist guys—you're not lying."

He sat down wearily at his desk and watched the men file from the room, said: "Stick, Dal. I want to see you," in a tired voice.

Prentice pulled a chair in front of the big desk and sat down, staring at his bruised hand. Hallahan looked at him in silence for a moment, carefully unlocked a drawer in his desk, pulled out a bottle and two glasses, and said gently: "Have a drink, Dal. You need it." He slid the bottle towards him.

"I hope I do," Prentice assented heavily. He poured the glass two-thirds full, lifted it halfway to his lips, set it back on the table and completed filling it. He waited until the captain had filled his own glass, then repeated, spacing his words carefully: "I—should—hope—I—do." He brightened a little and said: "Over the river—"

Captain Hallahan finished it mechanically: "and through the woods." They both drank.

Prentice set his glass down and resumed his contemplation of his knuckles.

Hallahan, idly drawing circles on the desk top with the

bottom of his wet glass, finally broke the silence that had fallen between them. "Listen Dal! Vitori won't talk. He's too smart."

Prentice said sullenly: "He'll talk or he'll never talk to anyone else."

"If he talks he'll be spotted fifteen minutes after he's out ——! Dal, you know it. Have some sense. I tell you he's too smart."

"Maybe you're right," Prentice agreed heavily. He reached across the table for the bottle.

Hallahan looked up from his aimlessly weaving glass squarely at Prentice, and asked: "Dal—how did Means get rubbed out?"

PRENTICE, CAREFULLY POURING from the bottle into his glass, answered slowly: "He must of walked into Roth's office, seen it was a heist, and tried to stop it. At least that's what Roth says."

Hallahan said softly: "Roth's office. What was Johnny doing there, Dal?"

Prentice set the bottle down. He was a big man, at least two hundred pounds, stoop shouldered and with a florid face. He seemed to shrink in weight—his shoulders sagged—he looked suddenly twenty years older. He muttered: "Well—" paused. "He and Roth was always friendly. He might of stopped for a drink or—" His voice trailed.

"And walked in on a stick-up. Too pat, Dal. He wasn't friendly enough with Roth to drive out there for a drink with as many joints as he knows in town." He continued mercilessly: "What was he doing there?"

Prentice looked at him, exploded: "Oh, hell, Cap! I don't know. Roth says—" He looked at his right hand again, flexing it, rubbing the puffed knuckles in the palm of the other.

Hallahan looked at him in silence, finally said gently: "I know." He shoved the bottle towards Prentice and suggested: "Take another drink." He continued: "Roth says these four hoods walk in on him just as he's putting the take away. He says they stick him against the wall and just then Means walks in. He says Means goes for his gun and they pop him, then they take the dough and lam. That right? Ain't that his story?"

Prentice said miserably: "Uh-huh, that's right."

Hallahan struck the desk with his fist violently. "By ——! it *ain't* right. *I* say, Roth and Means were in the office together. I say these hoods walk in—rub Means out—shake hands with Roth—and walk out. Roth gives them a start and *then* calls copper." He leaned across the desk challengingly. "*I* say that." He waited. "Ain't I right, Dal?"

"Maybe," Prentice flushed.

"You know I'm right." Hallahan continued softly. "Vitori and these other three guns were hired for this job. You know that, Dal. You know Roth hired them. He proved that when he didn't identify Vitori. He'll have a lawyer here for Vitori just as soon as those three can get him on a phone and tell him we've gathered Vitori in."

Prentice looked up from his knuckles.

"I don't think Roth did. They were brought in all right but not by Roth. He was in it all right, but I don't think he was the one."

Hallahan asked sharply: "He was the one that was crying about Johnny, wasn't he? If he wasn't the one, who'd he cry to then?"

Prentice answered sullenly: "I don't know." He repeated slowly: "I—don't—know."

Hallahan said bitterly: "You—don't—know. The next thing you'll be telling me *your* nose is clean." He leaned across his desk, striking it for emphasis. "What d'ya mean you don't know? You know that Means got the cut from Roth. Where'd he take it? I suppose *his* nose was clean, too."

Prentice leaned towards him. "I don't say that. I know he collected there—" He hesitated a moment. "But I don't know who for. Johnny had only been in on this racket a couple of weeks." He added violently: "D'ya think I'd be here if I did? Johnny might have been getting his, but by ——! I've sided him four years and I won't stand for a cross like this."

"I know, Dal! I know." Hallahan leaned back in his chair. "Listen, Dal! I don't give a damn. Means was on the make and you were with him. I know that. All I want to know is, who put the cross on him." He paused, added: "——! Dal, I'm not trying to make it tough for you, but I'll not have a copper outta my bunch spotted like this without finding out who did it—" He shoved the bottle towards Prentice. "I'll tag some —— for this."

Prentice poured a drink, and said sullenly: "You won't have to. Johnny was a good partner." He drank and stood up to leave.

"Wait a minute, Dal." He looked at him a moment, said slowly: "It won't be a secret long; we've got Vitori." At Prentice's nod, he continued: "Somebody'll spring him." He laughed bitterly. "Probably on the way now. They'll spring him in a couple of hours, see if they don't. There'll be a beef and we—you and I—'ll be up before Richards tomorrow on it."

Dal said: "Maybe."

"No maybe. Cinch." He laughed and said: "He slipped and fell downstairs. We all saw him do it."

Dal grinned and turned to the door.

"Where you goin'?"

Prentice turned, still grinning. "To find out where Johnny was going after he left Roth's. Roth might slip and fall downstairs, too. I don't know."

Hallahan, smiling, watched him leave—reached for the bottle, shook it gently, poured a drink, then carefully put bottle and glasses away. He locked the drawer, grumbling to himself about "man ain't safe from robbers even in a police station." He thought a moment, pressed a button on his desk, and told the uniformed clerk who appeared: "Send Allen and Peterson in." To them he said briefly: "Dal's going to get himself in a jam. He'll show up at Roth's and you boys be around there. Take out a squad car." He considered a moment, and added: "If he don't need you for —— sake don't butt in. If he does, follow his lead."

Peterson bewildered, asked: "But, Cap! How'll we—"

Hallahan interrupted, grinning: "Don't be a dumb cop all your life. You'll hear him if he needs you."

Allen said: "Come on, Pete. Don't be a dumb Swede. Let's go."

Hallahan watched them leave, still smiling.

The clerk put his head in the door to announce: "Commissioner Richards and Jack Bruner. They want to see you about some guy named Vitori."

"Show 'em in," Hallahan said wearily.

MAGNA CITY WAS big—with its police and detective force split into departments, as is usual in most big cities. As in most big cities also, these same departments were honeycombed with graft, this overlooked by a complacent public, so accustomed to racketeering in its many manifestations that graft seemed a small, an accepted thing. Complacent, yes, yet still able to be stirred at intervals out of its apathy. It was stirring now, the leavening agent being a reform newspaper out for circulation, satisfying an old grudge against police heads in its course. Its slogan was: *Down With Police Graft*, its war cry, *Down With Police Cossackism*. This, helped by some few proved instances of police brutality and venality, had forced the harassed mayor to appoint one of the leaders of the reform party, one Arthur Richards, as police commissioner.

Richards, although handicapped by a total lack of their cooperation, was yet a force feared by the police. Bigoted, fanatical, they ridiculed him by calling him Deacon Richards (he was an elder in his church) yet he was strongly supported by that part of the public which refused to realize he hindered the work of the police—that public which would not concede that even an admittedly venal police force is more protection than a force composed of men afraid of their jobs—men afraid to enforce law and order with the only weapon left them by dilatory and equally venal courts—*FEAR*.

RICHARDS, BRUNER, AND the released Vitori, sat in Richards' private office.

Jack Bruner looked like an idealized portrait of a college football hero. Perfectly conditioned, standing slightly over six feet, he carried his two hundred pounds and over like a heavyweight prize fighter.

Actually he was in his forties, was the most successful criminal lawyer in the state, owned the *Record*, the reform paper (a fact known only to the managing editor) and was in everything but name, head of the reform party. He had cold-bloodedly taken that blunted tool and forged—sharpened—it into a formidable weapon, a weapon, however, used solely in his own interest. This had been done so adroitly that the nominal heads of the party considered him only an earnest fellow worker, a man dominated only by a sincere desire to help the public. It pleased him, followed his carefully built up pose of innocuous playboy, to manage by hint and indirection the power he had created.

He had forced the Mayor to appoint Richards as police commissioner—knowing the man was scrupulously honest—knowing the public believed this—and knowing that he could handle the man through his overweening vanity.

Richards, slight, spare, his nondescript features only redeemed by deep-burning fanatical eyes, was plainly excited—a sallow flush mottling his thin cheeks.

He complained: "You see, Mr. Bruner, it's as I told you. That man Hallahan has absolutely no respect for either law or decency." He ran his hand through his thinning gray hair. "I tell you, Mr. Bruner, these things—" he paused for emphasis, "this high-handed disregard of the public and the public's rights must be stopped. I've given orders that there was to be no third degree but those orders are constantly broken. Mr. Vitori claims he was abused and I believe him. And Hallahan denying this outrage—" He purpled and stopped, his shaking hand pointing at Vitori.

Vitori whined: "Well, you can look at me and see I'm not lying."

Bruner shook his head at Vitori, and declared: "Mr. Richards, when this man comes up for trial on this ridiculous charge, I am going to ask you to testify as to his condition and the position in which we found him. I am going to prove to the jury that he was maltreated by those officers. There is no doubt in my mind, that, realizing they had nothing against this man, they deliberately and maliciously abused him."

His vulpine face, a mass of court plaster and surgeon's tape, Vitori interjected: "They sure did. I told 'em I didn't know nothin' about—" He stopped at Bruner's warning look.

Bruner continued smoothly, getting to his feet: "Well, Commissioner, I certainly want to thank you. My client would probably either have died or gone insane under that torture, if you hadn't stepped in the way you did. It's a fortunate thing that Magna City has you as police commissioner."

Richards visibly swelled. "I'm always glad to be able to remedy an injustice, Mr. Bruner. Feel free to call on me at any time." He walked with them to the door. "I intend to investigate this outrage very thoroughly." He smiled at Vitori. "That won't hurt your case, will it, young man?"

Vitori replied hastily: "They haven't got a thing on me. There ain't any copper—" Bruner, concealing the action from Richards by his body, gripped Vitori's arm—slightly pushed him through the door and down the hall. He turned to Richards, shook hands, and apologized. "You understand, Mr. Richards, I'm sure. If it seems necessary, I'll appear before the Board and state my client's side of this unfortunate affair. However, I'm a practicing attorney, and if it can be avoided, I'd really rather not—" His voice trailed. He hesitated a moment and added delicately: "I'm afraid the police would—"

Richards told him heartily: "I quite understand, Mr. Bruner.

I'm sure it will not be necessary. The police would undoubtedly resent it if you were forced to soil your hands in this deplorable mess." He added pompously: "Of course, as a public official I feel that my duty is plain."

Bruner said suavely: "Of course, if it's necessary—thank you again for this help."

"Not at all! Not at all! I'm always glad to be of assistance, you know that, Jack." He turned back in his office.

Bruner joined Vitori who had waited a few feet down the corridor for him, and they walked together to the elevator. Bruner punched the button, commented reflectively. "The dumb b———!"

"That's right, Mr. Bruner," Vitori agreed eagerly. "He sure swallowed that story you gave him, all right."

Bruner looked at him coldly: "You keep that flannel mouth closed, d'ya hear me? He may be dumb, but if you had kept on talking in there he'd have known there was something wrong." He continued critically: "You look all right, but you talk like a mug. You had better—"

The warning light above the elevator flashed, they entered, and were silent during the trip down. On the street, Bruner resumed: "You had better go over to Dora's like I told you and stay there. And I mean stay in the room. I'll send for you when I want you." He added warningly: "If you spill your guts when you get tight, better stay on the wagon."

"I don't talk, Mr. Bruner. You don't have ta worry."

"You're the one to worry—you'd only talk once. I'll get an appearance for you and get this thrown out, but you watch your step. Stay out of sight."

"Okey! I'll be at Dora's when you want me." He walked away

from Bruner to a taxi stand down the street; people turning to look with curiosity at his bruised and bandaged face.

Bruner shrugged, said: "Heel," and walked to his car.

ON LEAVING HALLAHAN, Prentice had gone directly across the street to a shabby office that flaunted the sign: *"Magna City Bonding Co. Bail Bonds a Specialty."* Underneath in smaller letters it stated that Hyman Lefkowitz was manager. Prentice entered, grunted: "H'lo, Babe," at the languid young lady seated at the corner desk, and asked: "Hymie in?"

The young lady said: "Uh-huh. Gee, Dal! I'm sure sorry to hear about Johnny."

"I'll tell him you were sorry when I see him."

"Gee, Dal! He's dead, ain't he?" Babe widened her eyes. "They told me."

He grinned at her. "I won't live forever—will I?" and walked past her to the partitioned cubicle that bore the sign "Hyman Lefkowitz—Private." He asked the man seated back of the flat desk: "How's things, Hymie?"

Hymie was very dark, short and broad. A broken nose, once extremely hooked, betrayed his Semitic ancestry. It was set wryly between sad, black eyes, widely spaced. He wore incongruous horn-rimmed glasses, a candy-striped silk shirt with attached collar of the same shade, and a violently patterned suit, obviously cut by a good tailor. Pomaded, freshly barbered, he offered a decided contrast to Prentice, who looked as if he had slept in his clothes. He said: "H'lo b——"

Prentice said: "Mr. b—— to you," and sat down on the corner of the desk.

Hymie removed his glasses and polished them with a handkerchief apparently cut from the same material as his shirt. "How's crime?"

"There's a wave on. Ain't you heard?"

"——! Dal! I was sure sorry about Johnny getting rubbed out like that. He was a good guy."

"He was at that. I want to get his slice of that Skouras bail."

Hymie peered nearsightedly up at him. "Why, Dal! I can't give it to you. That was Johnny's pinch. I'm a good guy though, and I'll give you half of it—your cut. You know me, Dal—I'm right."

"Johnny was an orphan, Hymie. His will left everything to me and I'm collecting." He added softly: "Don't think I ain't."

Hymie grumbled fretfully: "As soon as a man gets a dollar, you wolves got your hands in his pockets after it." He rose and went to the big safe decorating one corner of the room, twirled the combination, opened it and came back to the desk with a flat packet of bills—Prentice watching him in silence. Hymie counted out fifty dollars carefully, handed it to Prentice—who handed it back. Hymie argued complainingly: "Be right, Dal! Be right! I only got five hundred outta that and I gotta send some in."

Prentice said gently: "Come on, Hymie—you know I gotta eat."

Hymie said bitterly: "And I gotta feed ya, I suppose." He counted out another fifty, added it to the first, handed it to Prentice who gravely thanked him and started to leave.

At the door as he turned to go, he stopped. "Listen, Hymie! I got a case of honest-to-—— good rye. Want half of it?"

"How much?"

"Twenty to you—it cost forty."

"If it's good, Dal—sure."

"It's good. Johnny got it from Roth just a couple of days ago."

"Up to the apartment?" Hymie asked, and at Prentice's nod said: "Okey! I'll phone before I come up."

Prentice said: "You do that. I'll be seeing you then," and left.

From the bonding office he went to the Magna City National Bank, where he and the defunct Means had a joint safe deposit box. He removed from this box a .25 caliber vest-pocket automatic, a weapon that, knowing the identifying numbers had been removed with a file, he had thoughtfully forgotten to turn in at the station, some time ago. Unlike his big police revolver, this little gun could not be traced back to him—this fact being responsible for its concealment. This vicious little arm he slipped into his coat pocket, its meagre weight causing no apparent sag in that already almost shapeless garment, that also effectually concealed the heavy .45 he carried in a spring holster under his left armpit.

So equipped he left the bank, signaled a cruising taxi, told the driver: "*Rex Arms*—on Maple Avenue," and settled back with a grunt for the ride to his apartment. There, he took apart and thoroughly cleaned the little automatic—wiping the betraying fingerprints from each part as he reassembled the gun. Police experience had taught him that in any question as to ownership, police experts had the annoying habit of taking fingerprints from the inside of the gun as well as the outside.

This done, he replaced the gun in his coat pocket, called another cab, and told the driver: "Roth's place, out on the Midland road." He had no plan in mind—always an opportunist, he was certain that something would occur that would dictate his actions, after his arrival. It was yet early in the afternoon, which pleased Prentice. He had a presentiment that too many witnesses of his contemplated talk with Roth might be an awkward thing.

ROTH'S PLACE, WHEN analyzed, was merely an overgrown speakeasy. Its sign read: *"The Golden Slipper—Dining and Dancing,"* and truly enough, it was possible to both dine and dance there, though the majority of its customers believed that such modest amusements were a waste of time better devoted to either drinking or gambling.

It was presided over by Jack Roth, who undoubtedly possessed more than a modicum of genius, having successfully kept open and operated *The Golden Slipper* for several years— and through several administrations. He was a big man, very affable, a hearty laugh and boisterous manner concealing the cold clear brain he possessed. He had the chameleon-like quality of changing political affiliations so as to coincide with the party in power—yet so smoothly that the deserted side would yet consider him a loyal henchman. Prentice, knowing him for years, had no illusions, and a real respect for him.

As he entered *The Golden Slipper,* Carlo, the only waiter on duty, came bustling up all smiles and attention—too smiling— too attentive, Prentice thought.

"Hello, Mr. Prentice. Your friends they wait this hour for you." Suspicious, Prentice asked: "What friends?" at the same moment seeing Allen and Peterson at a table close to the door leading to Roth's office.

"The gentlemen they wait for you—eh, Mr. Prentice?" Carlo led the way across the dance-floor to the table occupied by the two detectives.

Prentice, with a vicious look at Carlo, asked: "You guys been waiting long?" To Carlo: "Rye highball."

Allen said: "Same for me. Not long Dal—What held you back?"

"This and that. What for you, Pete?"

Peterson told him: "Highball, I guess."

Carlo left them, and Prentice queried: "Hallahan send you?" At Allen's nod, he grumbled: "He would! Y'seen Roth?"

Allen jerked his thumb towards the door at his side. He volunteered: "We brought one of the fast wagons out if you need it. Hallahan said you're papa."

The Golden Slipper made no attempt to cater to a matinee crowd—the orchestra being on duty only in the evening. With the exception of a young couple, obviously engrossed in each other, and the three detectives, the big room was empty. Dissatisfied with this, Prentice walked over to the pair, displayed his badge and growled tersely: "On your way." The man muttered some remark about his bill and the big detective told him shortly: "That's okey! Beat it." Plainly awed, they left. Prentice walked back to Allen, said: "Stick around, Al—will ya," walked to Roth's door and knocked.

Carlo, coming back with the ordered drinks, hurriedly set the tray down, stepped to Prentice's side and complained: "Mr. Prentice, Mr. Roth told me he would see no one."

Prentice jerked his head at Allen, who gripped Carlo by the shoulder, whirling him around.

Startled, Carlo cried out: "Hey—"

Allen gripped Carlo by the jaws with one hand, by his jacket with the other, and forcibly sat him in a chair. He told him: "Shut up, mug! Sit down!"

Prentice smiled faintly, said to Roth who had opened the

door at the slight commotion: "H'lo Jack," and walked in—his hand in his pocket—forcing Roth back in his office. Inside, still smiling, he said: "I knew you'd want to see me, Jack. That monkey didn't seem to think so."

Roth answered heartily: "I'm always glad to see you, Dal—you know that. Sit down and have a drink."

"You sit down, Jack—this chair though—away from the desk."

Roth hesitated, said: "Why, Dal—" and Prentice, still keeping his right hand in his pocket, hit him in the face with his left.

Roth stepped back and put his hand to his face. "Why, Dal! You crazy ——!"

Prentice struck again at his face, but unbalanced by his concealed hand, missed. "You hear me, Jack. Sit down!"

Roth retreated to the chair, repeated: "You crazy ——!" and sat down.

Prentice remained where he was, his face showing white lines around the nostrils. He took his hand, holding the .25 caliber automatic, out of his pocket, said in a dead, expressionless voice: "I don't think you'd talk, Jack—but Johnny did. He talked too much."

"Is it a pinch?" Roth's voice was steady.

The detective considered a moment, and in the same flat voice answered: "It started out to be, but halfway back you resisted and got the works."

"Hell, Dal! You can't get away with it. It's too raw."

Prentice without answering him, backed to the door behind him, opened it slightly, still watching Roth, and called: "Al—let Pete watch your boy friend and you come here." When Allen entered he said: "Frisk him—he might be heeled."

Allen looked curiously at Prentice, and obeyed, carefully keeping out of the possible line of fire of the snub-nosed little gun Prentice held so carefully. Roth was unarmed.

Prentice explained, still watching Roth: "Listen, Al! Jack here was one of the guys that hired those hoods to rub Johnny out. He's one of these hard guys that won't talk, so I'm going to take him back to town and when he tries to get away, I'm going to give him the works." He added thoughtfully: "In the belly I think—I never liked the —— anyway." Allen caught the almost imperceptible droop of his eyelid.

Roth said persuasively: "Now, Al! You boys can't get away with—"

Prentice interrupted him. "I don't think we'd better tell Pete the angle—he's so dumb he'll make a better witness if he thinks it's on the up and up. Tell him to take Carlo outside and wait—I want Roth to walk outta here, and it's no use taking a chance on his saying anything to Carlo."

Allen opened the door and told Peterson: "Take that mug outside, Pete, and wait." He turned back to Prentice and asked: "Where'll we take him? It's too crowded back towards town." His saturnine face seemed only concerned with the business at hand—he avoided looking at Roth.

"That's right!" Prentice agreed thoughtfully. Brightening, he exclaimed: "How's this for a gag. We'll go right out the road here away from town. Roth here, is showing us where to put the finger on the hoods that were with Vitori. On the way out, he makes his play. The gun ties in it too—it was in Roth's vest-pocket and we missed it when we shook him down. How's that sound?" He added mournfully: "I wish I knew where those three guys were, at that."

Allen said: "Well, I'd believe a story like that myself and I know *I'm* smart. Let's get it over with."

Roth laughed uneasily: "You guys got a good act, but I'm not going any place with you. A joke's a joke. If this is a pinch—say so."

Prentice exploded: "I'm sick of this ——'s lip. Look and see if Pete's gone."

Allen opened the door and peered out. "Okey, Dal!"

Prentice took a step towards Roth and raised the gun. His face had turned a grayish white.

Allen spoke warningly from the door. "Get close enough so it'll show powder burns."

Roth cried out chokingly: "Dal, don't! I'll talk if—"

"You'll walk to the car and talk there."

The three men walked to the car, Allen half supporting Roth, whose knees seemed unable to bear his weight. Peterson was stolidly leaning against the car watching Carlo, who at Roth's appearance began talking excitedly. Prentice walked to him and took him to one side, out of earshot of Roth. "Listen, Carlo! There's trains outta here all night long and you want to be on one of them. I'm taking Roth now, and I'm coming back. Get me? If I've got to take you in I'll throw the book at you."

"But Mr. Roth, he said—"

"He ain't saying much now, is he?" Prentice asked reasonably. "I'm giving you a break."

"But Mr. Prentice—could I ask Mr. Roth—"

Prentice hit him fairly on the chin, his whole strength and weight going into the blow. Carlo dropped like a log. Prentice walked back to the car and spoke quietly, so Roth would be unable to hear: "Pete, you drive. Straight out the Midland road. I'll tell you when to stop when we get out there."

Peterson replied: "Sure." He nodded at Carlo, who lay unmoving: "What about him?"

"Oh, he'll come out of it all right. We don't want him."

He put Roth in the back seat of the police car, an open Buick, said to Allen, who was starting to sit on the other side of Roth: "Jump seat—will ya, Al?" and seated himself by Roth, twisting his big body, so as to half face him. He told Peterson: "Drive pretty slow, Pete. Jack wants to talk and he's gotta lot to say." The car rolled smoothly away, he prodded Roth roughly with the muzzle of the little gun, and said: "Well! Commence!"

Roth twisted desperately away. "What do you want to know, Dal? Is the safety on that thing?"

"Where Vitori's gang is holed up and who put 'em on the job. Don't worry about the safety—I'm holding the gun."

"What are we going out this way for? You're not—"

"You ain't talked yet, have you?"

Roth's condition was pitiable. The muscles of his stomach quivered spasmodically, his face had assumed a yellowish cast, he was sweating profusely, and his shaking hand and trembling voice betrayed his evident fear. Till the present, he had always a firm faith in his ability either to talk or bluff his way out of any unpleasant situation that might occur, but that faith had left him completely. The scene in the office, combined with Dal Prentice's somewhat unsavory reputation, had broken his nerve to such an extent that a jail cell seemed a welcome haven.

"You ain't talked yet," Prentice repeated.

Roth said sickly: "Vitori and the others are at Dora's *Commercial Club*. She's keeping 'em outta sight in one of the rooms there. Dal! You got to get me out of town after me telling you this. I won't last a day."

"Who put Vitori on the job? You and who else?"

"Jack Bruner did—honest, Dal! I didn't want to go for it but Bruner said Johnny was only giving him part of the dough I gave Johnny for Bruner, and that Johnny was shooting his mouth off about him running the commissioner. Honest, Dal! I didn't want to go for it. I always liked Johnny."

"How come you were paying Bruner off? How's he rate?"

"Bruner said he'd have Richards squawk and have me closed up. He's working the same angle with everything in town. He just started since he got Richards appointed." He asked eagerly: "That clears me with you, don't it, Dal?"

"Like hell! You could have tipped Johnny."

"But ——! I couldn't—" Roth fell silent, staring with fear stricken eyes at Prentice's impassive face, and from there to the tiny gun pointed so unwaveringly at his stomach.

Prentice said thoughtfully: "Bruner, eh! Well, that explains a lot." He turned slightly to Allen, seated across from Roth, and said: "Johnny told me Bruner was the big shot and I thought he was stall—" Speaking to Allen, he had looked away from Roth and his hand holding the little gun had sagged, the muzzle drooping towards the floor. The desperate Roth, certain in his own mind that Prentice meant to kill him in cold blood, seized what looked like a fighting chance, grasped Prentice's wrist with both hands, and tried to wrench the gun away while keeping it still pointed at the floor. There was a brief commotion, the gun barked spitefully, and Roth sagged back in his seat, both hands gripping his belly.

Peterson half turned in the front seat and cried out: "What's that?"

Prentice said: "Nothing, Pete. Turn and go back to town, will ya?"

"He thought you meant it." Allen stared at Roth. "Else he'd never have tried to make a break."

Roth suddenly doubled over head first on to Allen's lap, still holding his belly.

"Where'd it get you, kid?" Allen asked, and tried to straighten him up.

Prentice answered for Roth: "In the belly." He added: "I did."

"Did what?" Allen asked.

"Mean it," Prentice told him.

They drove back to town to the police hospital, siren wide open. The police surgeon, looking at the moaning Roth on the operating table, growled to the nurse: "Ranged up and to the side and punctured the kidney. With that and the shock he'll last maybe an hour—not much more. Can't do a thing." He went out to the waiting Prentice and said: "You should've taken him to the morgue. Why bother me?"

THE THREE MEN went directly to the station where, leaving Allen and Peterson in the outer office, Prentice went in to report to Captain Hallahan. That Hallahan was in was no chance happening. He had been busy all afternoon with newspapermen trying to get a story about Means' murder and the reported shake-up in the department. Also worried about Prentice, he had grimly determined to stay in his office until he had heard either of or from him. Prentice's ability to find, or if unable to find, to start trouble, was well known to him. He gave a sigh of relief when Prentice walked in but concealed it by asking: "Don't you know you're supposed to keep in touch with the office? Where in hell you been?"

Prentice said, his face solemn: "Well—I've been busy."

"So've the newspapers!" Hallahan told him tartly. "Richards hasn't been sitting on his hands all day, either."

"No?" Prentice pulled a chair across from the desk. "What's he been doing?"

"Well, first he called a meeting of the mayor and the Board for tomorrow. This was after I wouldn't fire you. Then he gave out a statement to the papers that you and I damn' near killed some poor —— in here just because we were mad we had him on a bum rap, and Richards he was going to fire us. He didn't say that but that was what he meant."

"And then?" Prentice made motions with his hands like a man pouring a drink.

"And then—hell! Every newspaper bum in town was here and they all went back and wrote something different. The only thing they agreed on was that you and I were both —— —— They put it in such a way that, by —— I believe them."

"Vitori got out then, huh?"

"Yeah! Bruner got him out on bail. I'll say one thing for the —— he picked a smart damn' lawyer."

Prentice gazed fixedly at Hallahan, and continued his pouring motions.

Hallahan grumbled: "I don't suppose you'll talk till I do," and opened the drawer of his desk.

Prentice looked injured. "Why, Cap! I haven't had a chance. You been telling me about Richards." He poured a drink and passed the bottle back.

Hallahan said: "—— knows where Vitori is now."

"I know where he is," Prentice told him.

"Yeah!" Suspiciously.

"Yeah! He's with those other three hoods."

"And I suppose you know where they are."

"I know that, too."

"Don't be so —— damned wise, Dal. What *did* you find out?"

Prentice set his glass down and leaned over the desk. "Plenty! Those guys are holed up at Dora Madison's. How's that?"

"I don't believe it, Dal. Somebody's giving you the run-around. Those guys are on fire and Dora'd be smart enough to know it. She's never been mixed in any hot stuff yet."

"She didn't have an out. These guys were sent there and she had to take 'em."

"Who give you this song and dance?"

"Roth—and that ain't all he told me. He told me who spotted Johnny."

"No!—Dal!"

"He did, you know."

"Well, you could fool me," Hallahan said slowly. "I never figured Roth would rat. Who was the guy?"

"Jack Bruner!"

Hallahan leaned wearily back in his chair, then picked up the bottle and scrutinized it closely. He began: "I thought you were crazy when you told me about Dora hiding out that bunch of red hots. Now I *know* you are."

"It's a fact, Cap. Johnny told me and I thought he was stalling."

"Roth's stalling you too, Dal. Now see here. If you really believe Roth, I'll get him over here and we'll figure this out."

Prentice said easily: "Well, I guess they'll bring him over here if you want him. It's a hell of a way to treat a stiff though, I'll always say."

The bottle dropped with a crash. Prentice cried out: "Jeese!

Look out, Cap! You'll spill it."

Hallahan picked it up and set it back on the desk. He exploded harshly: "Damn you, Dal! Quit clowning."

Prentice said, his face a mask, his eyes never leaving Hallahan's face: "Well, it was like this. Roth spilled his guts and Al and I started to take him back to town. He went screwy and pulled a gun that Al and I had missed when we shook him down, and when I tried to take it away from him he shot himself. You can ask Al. He's outside." He added virtuously.

Hallahan exclaimed slowly: "Well— I'll—be—damned. Where did all this happen?"

"Out on the Midland road. Just past his joint about a mile."

Hallahan looked up quickly. *"Past* his joint. What the hell were you doing past it?"

Prentice answered cheerfully: "Well, I hadn't figured an answer to that one yet. Can't *you* think of something?"

"I can think of plenty. What'll Pete say?"

"He still don't know what happened. He was driving and Al and I told him what he saw so often he thinks he saw it."

"This'll be up at the meeting, too. Richards'll walk on his hands, when he hears this one."

Prentice argued earnestly: "Well, let's give him something to work on. Al and I'll brace Dora's, pick up these hoods, and go on from there and get Bruner. He won't have time to get a tip-off if we work fast and then we got everything our own way. If we got the whole bunch in soak, Richards can't talk about us working Vitori over, can he?"

"But Bruner, Dal. Are you sure about him?"

Prentice said softly: "Roth didn't lie."

"But can you prove he's in it?" Hallahan persisted.

"You leave me alone with those hoods, one at a time, and I'll prove Bruner killed both Garfield and McKinley. It'll stick at the meeting tomorrow, anyway. Of course, Bruner'll claim we got the confessions under duress and maybe beat the rap, but it'll show we weren't shooting at the moon."

Hallahan assented thoughtfully. "We can't really lose. We got to pick these guys up anyway. You'll be out tomorrow unless we get a break, it's a cinch. Well—how'd you figure to work it?"

"It's a cinch. Al and I'll brace the joint, and when we're in all we got to do is take 'em out."

"Just you and Al, huh. What about Pete?"

Prentice said disgustedly: "Oh, what the hell! We'll be too busy to bother with Pete."

"You might at that. —— damned busy," Hallahan agreed. "Now this is better. First pick up Bruner—there's less chance of a tip-off from his end. Then we'll *all* go and grab the hoods."

"Al and I can get 'em all right," Prentice protested. "We don't need a squad."

Hallahan replied disgustedly: "—— Dal! You are dumb. Haven't you ever heard of advertising?" He reached for the phone and asked the operator to get him the District Attorney's office. He said: "Hallahan speaking—oh, yes, Gardner. Can you come over for a little while—okey, I'll be seeing you." To Prentice he explained: "It's young Gardner. He's going with you when you pick up Bruner."

Prentice exploded: "That punk! What in hell for?"

Hallahan didn't look at him. "Bruner's a lawyer. I'd rather have someone from the D.A.'s office along just in case he makes a howl to Richards about brutal treatment, constitutional rights, and the rest of the hooey."

Prentice complained: "Why, Al and I got it all figured out. We won't have any trouble."

Hallahan told him, shortly: "I know you won't. Gardner's going with you. Tell Al to come in and I'll buy a drink." The three men drank and chatted until Gardner's arrival, when Hallahan said: "You boys mind waiting in the other room—I want to talk to Mr. Gardner."

They waited a few minutes, and Hallahan came out with Gardner and walked with them to the car. Hallahan told him: "You go with Lieutenant Prentice and Lieutenant Allen. You know why you're going."

The young man said in a scared voice that he understood, that he was going so that everything would be perfectly legal. Prentice grunted disgustedly. They piled into one of the police cars, the young man sitting in front with the driver, where Prentice had gruffly ordered him, and Prentice and Allen quietly talking in the back.

Bruner's arrest was disappointingly easy. Unable to get in touch with Roth, he had known that something was wrong and rather expected it.

The police car drove to his residence, the three men got out, Prentice rang, a butler opened the door and told them Mr. Bruner was at dinner. They were asked to wait in a small reception room.

When Bruner appeared, Prentice said bluntly: "You're under arrest—here's the warrant."

Bruner read the warrant, appeared puzzled, and said: "Why I'm sure there's some error. I'll go with you boys and we'll get it straightened out."

It was as simple as that. With the eyes of the District Attorney's young assistant upon him, Prentice was as silent as the rest, on the trip back to the station, where Bruner was carefully put in a cell by himself.

"Too easy," Hallahan commented to Prentice. "He won't stay put long."

"Well," growled Prentice, "he's where we want him now, and that's something."

DORA MADISON, STARTING as a humble practitioner in what is theoretically the oldest profession in the world, was living proof of the fallacy "the wages of sin is death." She owned and operated the *Commercial Club* which was the hangout of the sporting element so powerful politically in Magna City. Directly across from, and built at the same time as the new City Hall, it was rumored that city money and city material had gone into its construction and at least indirectly, this was true.

Dora, a small, bright-eyed woman, was reputed to be several times a millionaire, and though this was no doubt exaggerated, she was very wealthy, her association with the City Hall crowd enabling her to pick many juicy plums out of political pies. There was as much city business done at the *Commercial Club* as at the City Hall. Throughout her checkered career she had always kept friendly with the police and free from entanglements with admitted gangsters, knowing that way led to ruin.

Just after dusk, three police cars loaded with uniformed men drove in a roundabout way to a point a block past the club. The men, armed with riot and sub-machine-guns, unloaded, and with the precision that spoke of a well-ordered plan, spread out front and back of the club, forming a cordon. This was done so quietly that not more than a dozen curious passersby were aware of anything out of the way.

A fourth car drove up and stopped in front of the entrance. Prentice and Allen got out, and the driver pulled past the club to the end of the street. The two men hurried awkwardly up the wide steps, each concealing something under his coat. As they reached the door another car drove up in front and waited. Allen rang the bell, stepped to one side, and Prentice, producing a sub-machinegun from under his coat, crowded the door. A man dressed in a white jacket opened the door. Prentice shoved the stubby muzzle of the machine-gun in his belly and forced him back. Allen, motioning to the waiting men in the car outside, followed him in and left the door open.

Prentice asked: "Where's Dora?"

"I'll call her, sir." The man's face was as white as his jacket.

Prentice said: "Oh, don't bother." To one of the uniformed men who by then were inside the house he said: "Keep him here."

A door opened into the reception hall and Dora stepped out, looked with surprise at the knot of uniformed men by the door, recognized Prentice and asked: "Now what's up, Dal?"

"It's a shakedown, Dora. Of course, if you want to tell me where Vitori and his hoods are hanging out—" He left the sentence unfinished.

She motioned him apart from the others. "Dal, I had to keep them here but I didn't want to. I'm glad you'll take 'em off my hands 'cause it'll give me an out. Upstairs and down the hall to the end door on the right. There's a fire-escape past their window, so watch the outside."

"Thanks, Dora. That's being smart."

"Will you try and work it so there'll not be any shooting, Dal? It would burn the place up plenty."

"I'll do my best. Bruner here?"

She looked quickly at him. "Not tonight. You're a smart —— Dal."

He grinned. "*I* think I am." He turned to one of the men in uniform. "Take that mug outside and give him to Hallahan to keep out of the way. Tell cap to watch the fire-escape on the right." He turned to Dora. "If we can get 'em out without a brawl, I can keep you in the clear, Dora. You must have been screwy to keep 'em here."

She said without heat: "That —— —— of a Bruner. It was either keep 'em or have Richards know too much. That black-mailing —— knew everything that happened here the last six months."

"I wish I did." Prentice grinned. "Why don't you be like me and keep your nose clean."

"Bruner told me he'd have you out tomorrow."

"I've got him in tonight." He said to the men: "Well, let's get at it. Upstairs, at the end of the hall to the right. Allen and I'll go first." They filed up the stairs and Prentice rapped on the door.

A voice asked: "What is it?"

Prentice mumbled some words indistinctly. The voice called louder: "What is it? What d'ya want?"

He rapped again louder. He could hear voices quietly talking inside the room. He rapped again, then called loudly: "It's the law. Open up, Vitori."

The voices ceased. Prentice could hear a window being opened.

He called again: "It's the law, Vitori. The back's covered so don't try it."

The voices spoke quietly again.

He tried again. "Open the door or we blast in. Right now. Come out, and come out right." There was no sound and he warned: "We're coming in!"

The voice called back: "Then come in, you ——!" and a bullet split the wall by Prentice's side. He promptly turned the machine-gun loose, first a burst of shots into the lock of the door, then as a hose, back and forth across it until the drum was empty. Dropping it and pulling the heavy .45 from under his arm, he crashed his shoulder into the door. It held under his first assault, but on the second lunge the weakened lock gave way and he crashed through, the force with which he had struck the door, throwing him to the floor.

As the door burst open he had a flashing glimpse of three men crouched in as many corners, and a fourth sagging crazily on the window sill. The two men in the corners across from the door fired through it, and Allen, who was directly behind Prentice as he broke in, went to the floor without a sound.

The man in the corner beside the door, fired directly at Prentice as he sprawled on the floor and Prentice fired back at him three times as fast as he could pull the trigger. Then the room was filled with men and the bedlam seemed miraculously stilled.

Prentice sat up a little drunkenly and felt gingerly of his head. He could feel the blood on his fingers. He saw two men handcuffed, saw neither was Vitori and asked: "Where's Vitori?"

One of the handcuffed men answered sullenly: "You got him through the door and then Pete afterwards."

Prentice's head rang dizzily. He said: "How bad did Allen get it?"

One of the uniformed men, stooping over Allen, answered: "Through the hip. It didn't hit the bone but got the artery." He was already working with a first aid kit.

Prentice said: "That's good. Better get a stretcher."

The uniformed man didn't look up. "There'll be one here and a doctor with it. It's a cinch they heard the brawl."

Prentice got to his feet, reeled, and fell flat on his face, just as Hallahan, followed by the police surgeon, hurried in.

"They creased him and he's got a slight concussion. He'll be all right," that callous soul said. He glanced around, commented: "Looks kind of like a slaughter house," and followed the stretcher bearers out of the room.

THE FOLLOWING DAY, Prentice, still a little shaky, white bandage wrapped rakishly around his head, again went in Hallahan's office, meeting two newspapermen just coming out. He dodged them hastily, and told Hallahan: "That's why I left the hospital. Those guys are a damn' pest. I told them I'd give them an exclusive story if they'd lay a little dough on the line." He laughed. "The first three I sprung it on did. Then they got to comparing notes, the wise ———"

"My hero!" Hallahan reached for the drawer in his desk. "Stand a drink, Dal?"

"That's another reason I left. The nurse wouldn't buy one."

"You'd of died laughing this morning, Dal. Richards had the meeting on his hands and every morning paper had you single-handed cleaning out a gang of outlaws. He hemmed and hawed and finally said that you were perhaps a little zealous but a very efficient officer. I owe you a lot for that one."

"Well—pay me then. Give me Allen for a partner when he gets out."

Hallahan looked at him sharply. "You're too smart and Allen's too smart. You'd own the town in six months and have a sale for it."

"Maybe. The town wouldn't care."

Hallahan said thoughtfully: "If I do, will you guys put the brakes on? Johnny was *too* raw."

Prentice grinned at him. "Anything you say, Cap."

"Maybe I will. I've been thinking about it."

"What about Bruner?"

"I was afraid you'd ask that." Hallahan grimaced. "He's out on bail."

"He'll beat the rap." Prentice told him.

"I suppose so. Oh, well! We had him overnight."

"One thing about him being out on bail—I'll get a cut from Hymie." He added slowly: "Why in —— name did you have that punk go with Al and me when we picked him up?"

Hallahan looked sharply at him. "I was afraid you'd pull a Roth on him. You'd of been sunk for sure."

"Maybe! Two in a day *would* be pretty strong."

Hallahan said slowly: "Too strong. It wouldn't have been any maybe at all." He was silent a moment, then added: "There's other days—and other ways, Dal."

The Case-Hardened Samaritan

Dal Prentice was case-hardened when it came to shooting a man who had it coming to him, but he drew the line on kids

PRENTICE, HEAD LOWERED, stood just inside the door watching the crap game. His hat, snapped well down over his eyes, shielded his features, but the very way he wore it proclaimed what he was—a copper—and a tough copper. The big table—green billiard-cloth covered—side-boarded a foot high around its edges, was crowded by at least thirty men, all gamblers, hustlers, petty bootleggers and others of like ilk, and the majority known to the detective. He studied them a moment, saw the man he wanted, and called out: "Hi— Angelo! C'm'ere a minute."

Angelo, short, dark, swarthy, came out of the crush around the table and to the door. He said: "H'lo, Dal. What's it now?" His voice was pleasant, carrying the slight trace of accent it did.

"Sorry, keed. It's a knockover. I'll keep you out."

"How come? I never got tipped."

"Or no one else. Keep back of me." He raised a whistle to his lips and blew shrilly and the game stopped with every head turned his way. He called out clearly: "Going to move you guys out. Be nice and we will."

The door at his back was filled with uniformed figures as he spoke and the silence that met his announcement was broken by only one plaintive voice: "And I got over for two passes and then this. Oh, hell!"

Prentice grinned at this and told the man in charge of the raiders: "Okey, Dugan. I'll bring Cicotti up with me. Treat 'em nice if you can—they're all good boys."

The burly Dugan nodded and ordered the crowd: "All right, guys. Out five at a time. Come on now," and as no one showed any desire to accept his invitation, reached out and pointed: "You! You! Come on, men. Lots of room. Those in front get a seat."

He grinned cheerfully at the milling crowd and got an answering snicker, and Prentice, a little relieved, said to the dark man: "I was afraid for a minute they might beef. They'll be all right and you only pay a finif apiece to get 'em out. If they squawked they'd have had resisting slapped on 'em."

The little man said fretfully: "Now, Dal! I don't get this. There's been no beef in my place. I've been right. What's the idea? Is it your raid?"

"Hell, no! Dugan's in charge and I just came along to make it easy for you." Prentice looked at him curiously. "Ain't you heard? There was a beef in that joint in the hotel at Seventh and Maple, and the old gal that has the place run out and got the beat man and some guy killed him deader than hell. That's what's hotted it up. Everybody's getting it."

Cicotti looked a little wry. "I didn't know, Dal. Can the guy be picked, d'ya think?"

"Sure. The old gal says she knows him but not by name. That's why the general clean-up. We'll have two thousand in by morning."

"I'd think you might've phoned me. There'll be about forty guys I'll have to pay off for. I got to pay their fines. You know that."

"Can't help it. You know, Angelo, I can't tip when it's a cop killer we're after. I'm sorry." He called out to the man that just came in the door. "C'm'ere, Al. I want you to meet a friend of mine."

Cicotti grinned: "Yeah! Just pals. If you guys aren't in a hurry I'll buy a drink." He led the way to his office and Prentice winked at Allen and followed.

Angelo Cicotti was a fixture in Magna City. He was popularly supposed to be owner of the gambling house he ran, but Prentice knew, as did all others wise in city politics, that he was merely a figurehead and had no more than a working interest in the place he operated. He was scrupulously honest and had a wide knowledge of the peculiar philosophy of the gambler, and was hired on this account as manager of the house by the city crowd, the owners of the place and the real rulers of Magna City. He and Prentice had been friends for years and Prentice felt a real affection for the odd little gambler.

CICOTTI PRODUCED BOTTLE and glasses and after the first ceremonial drink was taken Prentice asked idly: "Who's got Bruner's kid? You know, Angelo?"

Cicotti's tone was questioning. "Why, Dal! How would I know?"

"Damned if I know. I heard you did, is all."

"Who told you that?" Cicotti turned from the bottle and faced Prentice squarely.

"Bruner."

"Honest, Dal?"

"I'm telling you. I'd of been down here even if it hadn't been for the raid."

Angelo's brown eyes looked worried, "How'd he get that idea? How come you're working for that chiseler?"

Prentice's voice was sullen. "I'm not working for that chiseler. I'm working for Dal Prentice. Every minute. I got put on this damn' snatch case because Bruner thinks I'm smart. It's not my idea."

"If you were smart, Dal, you'd know I couldn't tell you a thing. With the class of trade I get here, if I started to stool for the coppers I wouldn't last a week. And besides, I don't know a thing about it."

"I heardja the first time. Okey by me, Angelo. I thought I'd tell you about what Bruner thinks, is all."

"——! Dal! What can I do? I'm on the spot if he thinks that."

"You got the idea at last, hunh? You can tell me what you know about it. If I get the kid back to the —— —— this'll quiet down, won't it?"

"I don't get this. I thought Bruner was your—" He hesitated. "Your enemy. The man that killed your friend." He looked puzzled. "Why do you help him?"

Prentice said patiently: "Now listen, Angelo. I'm not helping him. He killed the man I worked with—that's right. His little boy has been kidnaped and I'm helping *him*, not his old man. Get that! I hate his guts but I like kids. See!"

The little gambler looked at him oddly. "In my country we're not so forgiving. No."

"Now, Angelo. Be nice. You got kids yourself."

Angelo's face lightened. "Six. Yeah, six I got. I'll buy a drink." He tipped the bottle, hesitated. "If I tell you what I heard, will you clear me on this with Bruner? That worries me."

Prentice said slowly: "It should. He's bad. But I tell you something, Angelo. They wrote him a letter and said they were going to start to work on the kid and they never even told him what they wanted. The poor —— cried when he showed me the letter. It's a dirty business."

"I'll tell you then. But you promise to tell no one besides Bruner that I tell. You promise?"

Prentice nodded.

"Abe Cohn's got the little boy."

"You're screwy. He works for Bruner. He's Bruner's pet."

"I'm right. I heard it straight. He and Bruner had trouble over Abe wanting a cut on the big money and Bruner couldn't see it. Bruner's blackmailing the joints around town because he's friends with the commissioner and has a newspaper he could print stuff about people who don't pay off in."

"I know that. That's old."

"Abe Cohn's Bruner's leg man on the collections and he figures he should get a cut instead of just so much a week. Did you know about the trouble?"

"No. When this happen?"

"About a week ago. Now I heard this. Abe grabs the kid and figures he can force Bruner into turning over what he's got on our crowd to get the kid back. That Abe's a smart yid. He's going to work through somebody else and Bruner'll never know he's in it."

"Where'd you hear this?" Prentice was leaning forward, untasted drink in his hand, and Allen was as interested.

"From a dealer I had. He quit me a week ago just before I fired him. He was high and cracked wise about all the dough he had coming pretty soon. I was sore and I told him just how broke he'd be all his life and he got snotty with me and told me how his good friend Abe Cohn was going to cut him in on the racket that Bruner was working when he had it. Abe's got that far with it—he's even getting his boys together."

Prentice's voice sounded thoughtful. He drank reflectively. "The whole thing sounds screwy, but it might just be. The kid has been gone about that long. Who was this dealer?"

"Little Solly. He used to run around with Abe all the time. When I had a joint on Spring ten years ago they used to give me a play. Abe worked up and Solly turned into a cheap hustler." His voice suddenly sounded aggrieved. "He was knocking down on me and didn't think I knew enough to catch him at it."

"A chiseler, hunh?"

"He's no good. He's not tough but he'd like to be. This snatch racket'd be about his speed, but I don't see how he had the nerve to buck Bruner."

"Dope head?"

"He's high on marijuana most of the time. No heavy stuff."

"That hay is heavy stuff if you hit it all the time. It's heavy enough so a hayburner don't use his head."

"Well, he's high all the time."

"Why in hell would Abe cut a mugg like that in?"

"For a fall guy. I figured that when he told me."

Prentice pursed his lips. "Now that's an idea at that. That'd be like Abe. Keep himself in the clear all the time. Where's this prize package live?"

"I don't know. I never pay any attention to that."

"Well, buy a drink then. Has this Solly ever been up to see us about anything?"

"Hell, yes. I bailed him out of a raid on a joint right after he come to work for me. He was mugged and printed on suspicion before he got word to me and he'd never have brains enough to buy his picture out."

"And glad I am. We can trace him from the picture easy. Now listen, Angelo. You just sit tight. I'll clear you on this with Bruner."

"Are you going to tell him what I said about Cohn? He'd tell Cohn and I'd be in just as tough a spot."

"Don't be a sap. I ain't going to tell him. I got no use for that heel, Cohn, anyway. I ain't going to take you up, Angelo. Go up in the morning after the line-up and pay your boys out. The sergeant'll have the list of them from here."

"Thanks, Dal. If I hear anything I'll call you."

"Fine."

"Well, I'll buy a drink."

"And it's time. Well, Al, looks like we get action on the snatch. I appreciate this, Angelo." He grinned. "And the drinks, too. Be seeing you."

THE TWO MEN went back to the station to put into

motion the complex police machinery that would locate missing Solly. This had to be done quietly, as any suspicion that he was wanted might endanger Bruner's kidnaped boy. Selected men made inquiries from equally carefully selected stools; others wandered casually around the known haunts of the suspected man. At noon the next day one of these last telephoned to Prentice at the station.

"This guy lives at 462 Douglas. About three blocks off Temple. I picked him up in a poolroom and tailed him to it."

"What kind of a place is it?"

"A bungalow court with a bunch of Filipinos and taxi dancers in it. I tailed him there and watched for about an hour and I got the beat man watching while I'm phoning."

"Well, go back and let the beat man off. And tell him he's to go about his business just like there's nothing happening. We'll have to case it till we can find out how many's there. Any vacant courts close?"

"One next door and one across."

"The one across'd be the best. Show who runs the place your badge and go in the back way. What's the name of the courts?"

"Elysian."

"Keep out of sight and I'll be up."

He told Allen, listening at his shoulder: "There ain't one chance in ten that they've got him in a court. They could've taken him in at night, all right, and that's when they snatched him, but they'd never take a chance in a joint like that. Noise'd wreck'em and you can depend on having snotty neighbors even in a hot spot like that."

They drove up to Douglas Street in Prentice's little coupé,

and leaving Allen in the coupé with instructions to follow any car that might possibly take the wanted man away in case one came before he returned, Prentice idled up to the manager's apartment. He found a very blonde, very hardboiled woman who looked with disfavor at the identification card he showed her.

She snapped: "And how am I supposed to rent courts to people when I've got a bunch of coppers hiding in them watching decent tenants?"

"Decent!" Prentice raised his eyebrows.

"Yes, decent! Mister Solomon pays his rent every week and has since he moved in, and he and his little wife make no noise or disturbance of any kind. She's a very good housekeeper, too."

"Oh, you've been in their apartment, have you?"

"Certainly I have. I have a right to. We furnish everything, including linen, and I take them clean linen every week."

"You've been there this week, then?"

She confirmed this. "Yesterday."

"Notice anything odd? This is a bum bunch, I'll tell you that. And I can do a lot to have your license taken away. I don't like the kind of talk you're putting out."

She lost some of her aggressiveness. "Why, no." She glanced at the card. "No, Lieutenant. Not exactly. Lots of times there's kind of a funny smell in there."

"D'ya know anything about marijuana?"

"That's it." Her face brightened. "I was trying to think. We had a man in the courts before that somebody said used it and his place smelled like that. Very orderly he was, though."

Prentice said sardonically: "You must run an orderly place."

"Oh, I do. Never a bit of trouble."

"Well, you play ball and I'll not see anything. You don't and you'll have the vice squad up here so fast it'll make your head swim. Get me!" His voice was grim.

"Yes, sir. I'll not say a word to Mister Solomon or his wife. That's what you meant, ain't it?"

"That's the general idea."

"I won't say a word to anybody."

"Fine. We'll get along then. S'pose you let me in the back way then, into this court the other officer is in."

She nodded, and he followed her down the little alley back of the courts.

The other officer proved to be very comfortable. He had pulled a davenport in front of the window facing the suspected Solomon's, and was stretched at full length, peering through a slit in the curtain, when Prentice appeared. He was McCready, another old officer on the Magna City force and a man who had worked with Prentice on the riot squad years before. He grinned at Prentice, said: "I think we're watching a rat all right, but at the wrong hole."

"Has he been out?"

"Naw. His twist come out and come back in a few minutes with a bunch of groceries, is all."

The manager, who had followed Prentice in, volunteered information. "She buys all her stuff during the week down at the corner store, but on Saturday she goes down and picks up stuff at sales."

"Are things that tough with 'em?" Prentice's voice was accusing. "I thought you said they paid their rent on the dot."

"Well, they're paid up now. They were a little behind so I held some of their things so they wouldn't move out some night.

They paid up all right."

"When?"

"Last week. They was behind about thirty dollars."

Prentice drooped an eyelid at McCready. "See, Mac. He was broke and now he's in the money." He asked the manager: "What other lies did you tell me?"

"Why, none. Well, to be honest, I don't think they're married."

McCREADY HELD UP a hand for silence. They could hear voices raised across the street but the words were indistinct. In a moment a man came out and McCready nodded to Prentice, who slipped out the back door and raced down the alley. He was ahead of the man when he reached the sidewalk and he walked, still ahead, down the street and climbed into the coupé with Allen, who asked: "What happened?"

"Nothing yet. McCready's watching the joint and we're going to tail this monkey."

They waited until he had reached the corner, then drove quietly past him and parked in front of a small cigar store. The man came up from behind, glanced incuriously at the coupé, turned in the store and went directly to the phone and Allen slid from under the wheel and followed him in.

As he entered the store, Prentice called out: "Get Camels for me," and Allen nodded and stood next the man at the phone as he told the clerk his wants. He idled a moment, got the number the man called and went back to the waiting Prentice.

He told him: "Michigan 2050," and Prentice nodded and wrote it down in a notebook. The unsuspecting Solly came out of the store and turned back to his apartment and Prentice said: "I don't see any sense in waiting. I don't think the kid is there, but we can send the landlady in first and make sure, and if this Michigan number ain't the kid's hideout I can sweat it out of Solly in ten minutes. What d'ya think?"

Allen answered briefly: "Sure! Why wait?"

They drove the coupé back to the apartment courts and went inside to McCready, finding the manager still with him. Prentice ordered curtly: "You go in and see if just them two are there. And keep your trap shut about us. That plain?"

She nodded, asked: "What'll I say?"

"Oh, anything. Tell 'em you want to look at the meter. That you think the guy made a mistake on the last reading. How's that? Then come back here."

They watched through the window as she rang the bell and was admitted. In a moment she was back and said: "Nobody's there but them. And that smell is there plenty."

"Okey, sister." He told McCready: "You go around to their back door, Mac, and when you hear the front door open come in. Don't fool around knocking."

Giving McCready time to get placed, and followed by Allen, he walked purposely to the front door and rang the bell. He saw the shade at one of the windows quiver, then the door swung open to reveal Solly, yawning widely. There was a crash at the back door and as Solly swung that way Prentice stepped into the doorway, one big shoulder blocking its closing.

Solly took a couple of paces back, said: "Why, you men are officers!" in apparent surprise.

"Just right. You don't mind if we come in, do you?"

"You are in. Of course you have a warrant."

"Hell, no! You're picked on a charge of disturbing the peace. That okey with you?"

"Why, we haven't made a—"

Prentice hit him with the flat of his hand across the face and Solly cried out: "Hey!" and spun across the room to fall sidewise against a davenport. "I'll make it resisting arrest then. You like that better?"

"You can't—"

"Can't what?" Prentice was standing over him, glowering down at him. "Whad'ya mean I can't? Why can't I?"

McCready came in from the kitchen, gripping the shoulder of a slight girl. She was white-faced, plucking at her lips with nervous fingers.

Solly, looking up at Prentice, said hastily: "I didn't mean that. Of course you can charge me if you want to."

"And we can shake down the place and maybe find a bunch of hay. We can do that if we want to, hunh? You don't mind?" Prentice sniffed. "I bet we find it, too. Or we can say we did, at least."

"That's the way with you guys." Solly's voice was a thin whine. "If a guy's getting along all right you try and frame him."

"Whad'ya mean—try and frame him? If I try—he's framed. And you look like a picture to me now, baby."

He reached down, grasped the little man by the hair, and jerked him to his feet. Solly let out an involuntary scream of agony and the expectant Prentice turned to Allen solemnly. "You see! Now he's disturbing the peace. Making outcries and the rest of it. I guess we'll have to take him along. You take a look through the place; he's higher than a kite right now."

Solly felt of his head tenderly. "I ain't done nothing."

"What does Michigan 2050 mean?" Prentice shot at him suddenly. "Answer me! Quick!"

"Why I—I don't know."

Prentice slapped him again, full handed, with his whole weight behind the blow and Solly dropped like a log. The slight girl screamed and McCready shook her roughly. He snapped: "The boy friend'll do the talking, sister. Just you keep quiet."

"This is an outrage. You're two big bullies."

"You're right, sister. Listen, Dal. We've got 'em on a morals charge besides. Let's take 'em down where we can work on 'em right. This Solly needs a going over—I can see that."

Prentice looked at Solly. "I know this little b—— will like that. I bet he tells me a lot of things I didn't know." He snapped at Solly again: "What's that Michigan number? Tell me, you ——"

Solly glared back, kept silent.

Allen came in from the kitchen and handed Prentice an envelope, without comment. Prentice glanced inside, said: "And that'll be another charge."

"Why you wouldn't book me on that, would you?" Solly's voice was desperate. "That's federal—that's the big house."

"It comes under the narcotic act. I'm going to hand you everything in the book, baby." He recited in a monotone. "Disturbing the peace—resisting an officer—possession of narcotics—" He cocked an eye at the girl, "at least a morals charge, and unless she's older than she looks it'll be contributing to the delinquency of a minor—and kidnaping. Hell, baby. If you're lucky you'll get life. You're all fixed up."

"I can bail out."

"Like hell. You got a swell chance of raising the bail they'll ask for on kidnaping."

Solly snarled: "You can't hang a kidnaping rap on me. I can beat that. You can't stick me on that."

"You'll sign a confession and be damn' glad to when I get through with you. Listen, Al, go over to the landlady's and call—no, wait. We'd better take 'em down in the coupé. No sense in taking a chance of Abe getting a rumble. I'll take 'em down and stop back in a fast wagon for you."

Solly whined: "You ain't going to book me on this dope charge, are you, Lieutenant? I ain't selling it, honest."

"Why, you little —— ——! D'ya think I'm coming up here and pick you up for getting high? It's kidnaping—you damn' fool. The other's just thrown in."

Allen volunteered: "Mac and I can ride too. I can ride in the rumble seat with the twist and Mac and the mugg with you in front. How's that?"

"Better. We won't be wasting any time. Let's go."

They loaded the sullen Solly and the girl in, as planned, and drove to the central station. The two were booked on open charges pending the result of the coming raid. Prentice told Hallahan, his captain, of what he had planned, while waiting for the Michigan 2050 number to be traced.

"This is a sure bet," Prentice said, "He wouldn't likely be calling anyone but Cohn now. We'll go up and bust in before they know we're around."

Hallahan objected. "If you crash in like that with a squad, Dal, they're liable to give the kid the works. He wouldn't be able to identify them and a jury wouldn't give 'em any more of a jolt for murder than for kidnaping. It's getting to be safer to kill somebody than it is to rob the corner grocery. If the parole board don't let 'em out the governor does, that is, if they're convicted. Hadn't you ought to stake out the place and get a line on it first?"

"Can't. Abe'd wonder what happened to Solly and take a powder with the kid. If we make it fast enough they won't have time to hurt the kid. And we'll do that. I'll see to it."

"Maybe. It's your case. It seems to me you're taking a lot for granted, though—you don't know that this Michigan number has a thing to do with it."

"I got a hunch. If it ain't I'll beat it out of Solly."

A clerk came in with the information that the Michigan number was that of a house at 422 North High and Prentice got up to go.

Hallahan asked: "How many men are you taking? How many cars?"

"Twenty and four. And Allen and Mac."

"And me! It's your case and you're the big man on it, though. I just got it in for Abe Cohn and this might be my chance to get my Sunday cut at him." The old man reached for his hat.

"Okey, Cap! Glad to have you. You'll see action, I think."

HE DID. 422 North High was an old-fashioned white house set next a tan house and separated from it by a gap of not over three feet. Both houses had flat roofs, the tan house being the lower by about the same distance. Both were sadly in need of repair.

Following orders, two cars stopped at the corner before they reached the suspected house and the other two drove on to the farther corner, dropping two plain-clothesmen in front of the house, who were instructed to collar anyone coming out. The others piled from the cars and formed a wide cordon around the block.

Prentice put Hallahan in charge of these men, told him: "If any shooting starts, don't tighten up. They'll all come dashing out if there's a blast and I don't want anybody out of the whole damn' block to get away. They might be just around in some other house and gone in there to phone." He told McCready: "Pick any four men you want, Mac, and follow Al and me in if there's any trouble. We'll go first."

McCready made a rapid selection, and Prentice and Allen walked back to the house, followed shortly by McCready and his men. As the two neared it, a man came out, took a startled look at the officers stationed at the door and ducked back into the house. The nearest of these men made a grab at him as he disappeared, then followed him through the door.

Prentice was running towards the door, having started the moment the policeman had followed the other man into the house. He jerked his service revolver from under his coat and called harshly to the other of the guards: "Keep out! Come in with Mac." He darted to the side of the door, then dived in the manner of a football tackle through the doorway, his body not over a foot from the floor as he entered.

He heard the roar of a shotgun as he was in the air and twisted like a cat as he landed, ending on his knees and one hand. He was shooting at the dim shape at the far end of the hall, when Allen catapulted through the door in like manner. Both men knew that in a moment of excitement the average man shoots high and were taking advantage of this fact in going through the lighted doorway. The figure at the end of the hall shot once again, and Prentice, through the crash of his own gun, could hear the action of the shotgun as the man pumped in another shell. Allen, behind Prentice, shot once, and the man took a couple of wavering steps towards them, dropped the shotgun and fell on his face.

Prentice's breath was rasping in his throat. Still watching the fallen man, he gasped back to Allen: "Wh—where's the copper?"

"I half fell on him when I landed."

Prentice was still on one hand and his knees. He rocked back on his haunches, looked curiously at the hand he had been balancing himself with on the floor. In the dim light the palm looked black. He smelled of it, said: "——! It's blood!"

Allen said in a sick voice: "This guy's Charley Johnson, and he must of got the whole load in the head." Prentice turned his head and saw Allen's flashlight turned full on what had been a face. He turned back hastily and retched.

McCready came bursting through the door and Prentice got to his feet. He said: "Take the downstairs, Mac, and go through." He retched again.

McCready asked anxiously: "You hit? Dal! You hit?"

Prentice said: "No! Charley Johnson was, though." He waved at the figure on the floor and Allen again turned his light on the body.

McCready whispered: "Oh, my ——!" and Prentice said harshly: "Now be gentle with the prisoners, Mac, *if* you get any. Come on, Al." He led the way up the stairs.

At the top, they peered cautiously down the deserted hall, and saw at the far end a trapdoor open to the roof, and leading up to it, a ladder. Prentice called hastily down to McCready: "Mac! Hurry! Send a couple of men into the house next door and watch the roof. Call in some men from Hallahan. Hurry!" He told Allen: "Stay here and watch the hall," and went down the hall to the ladder.

He climbed this, but as he peered over the roof there was the crash of a shot outside and he ducked hastily back. He came back to Allen and told him: "They're over there trying to raise the door on the other roof. We've got 'em for sure. You watch this trap and I'll find the kid."

He opened the first door at the head of the stairs and confronted a nicely dressed woman holding a small boy in her lap and he snapped out: "You're who?"

"Madge Bruner."

"Who?"

"Why—Mrs. Bruner. Are you an officer?"

He stared at her vacantly a moment, answered: "Yes, ma'am. Prentice. You're all right now."

The little boy raised his head. He had been crying. "Mama said the police would come and get us."

Prentice said vacantly, "Us!" and the woman said gently: "Was anyone hurt in the shooting?"

"Two men killed. How long have you been here?"

"Why, since I was taken out of my car." She seemed puzzled. "Weren't you looking for me?"

"Just for the boy." He turned and went to the door, then turned back. "Will you stay here for a little while, Mrs. Bruner? There's liable to be some more shooting."

"I hope there won't be. They treated us very well."

Prentice looked at her oddly, went out.

McCready was at the top of the steps with Allen. He said: "There was nobody down there and we're going through up here. Al says they're on the roof."

"They saw me stick my head out, and shot. You got the other house covered?"

"Yeah! Got two men with a tommy watching the trap and

they can't get off the roof. How're you going to get 'em down?"

Prentice looked at his hand. "Pack 'em. We can get on the roof of a house across the street and pick 'em with a tommy."

McCready looked at him curiously. "Your hand's all blood. Did you get hit?"

"No. Charley Johnson did."

McCready looked at him in a puzzled way, and Prentice explained: "I had my hand on the floor where Charley was. He bled. Will you send a man for Hallahan? And tell him to come inside." He beckoned to Allen and turned back into the room.

The little boy offered again: "Mama said the police would come and get us and they did. My mama's always right."

The woman smiled slightly and Prentice asked: "Did I get that right, Mrs. Bruner? You were taken at the same time the boy was?"

She nodded, said: "They were very nice. I thought that they were just going to steal the automobile, but they made us go with them and put gags on us." She confessed honestly: "I could have called out through my gag all right, but I was afraid they might hurt John." She patted the little boy's shoulder.

Prentice glanced at Allen. "They didn't gag you tight, then? They weren't rough about it?"

"Oh, no! They were gentle. And very polite."

"And afterward?"

"They brought us here and kept us locked in. They told me there was no one in the house next door and that if I made trouble they would take the baby away."

"Feed you good?"

"Not so very. Everything was canned."

"I see," Prentice said thoughtfully. "Did you know any of the men?"

"No. That is—" She hesitated. "I have felt that I have seen one of the men at my husband's office. I'm not sure, however, and I don't see how that would be possible."

Hallahan came into the room and Prentice took him over in one corner and talked quietly to him. They came back into the middle, and Hallahan asked sharply: "Why didn't your husband report your absence, Mrs. Bruner? Can you tell me?"

She looked at him in genuine astonishment. "Why I supposed he had. He must have."

"He didn't." Hallahan went to the door and beckoned one of the men in the hall. "Take Mrs. Bruner downstairs and keep her and the boy out of danger. I don't want her on the street and we're going to get the men off the roof now. If they come down the trap there'll be shooting in this upper hall, so watch out." The man nodded and went out, taking Mrs. Bruner and the boy with him.

Prentice asked: "Did you get the same slant I did, Cap? She's honest. She wasn't lying about it."

Allen put in: "Did you tell Hallahan about how they treated her?"

Prentice nodded, and Hallahan said: "It looks that way, Dal, but I don't see what you can do about it. How're you going to get these hoods down?"

Prentice grinned. "Shoot 'em off."

Followed by the other two, he went out in the hall and stationed two men, armed with machine-guns, to guard the trapdoor. Sending McCready to see that the same arrangement was made next door, he started across the street carrying another of the ugly weapons. Hallahan said doubtfully: "You're going to give 'em a chance to come down, aren't you?"

Prentice's voice was careless. "Oh, sure! The same chance they gave Charley Johnson."

He knocked on the door of the house across the street, showed his badge to the woman who opened the door, and headed for the stairs. She asked fearfully: "Where are you going?"

"Roof. Is there a trap?"

"Why, yes."

"Please show me." He followed her up the stairs, looked with approval at the stairway leading to the roof and told her: "Now you go down and hide in the cellar. Mind now." He grinned as he watched her flight down the stairs.

Still smiling, he climbed to the roof and crept over to the low parapet that shielded him from the men exposed on the opposite roof.

DAL PRENTICE WAITED impatiently while the jailer unlocked the cell door. Little Solly stood up as he entered and said: "I been thinking it over and that's why I wanted to see you. That's why I wanted to see you before you look up that Michigan 2050 number."

"Yeah! Well, I'm here."

"Listen. That's a plant you're goin' to run into. It's framed so you go out."

"How? How's it framed?"

"You and this wise mugg that sides you will go up and case the joint and they're watching for you all the time. Abe Cohn's sitting there with a slug with your name on it. They'll lam out of there and they got an alibi all fixed. Bruner ain't taking no chances on this one going wrong. If he turns the heat on you on the street he's in a rumble with the rest of the force and the way this is framed he's in the clear. Get it?"

"What are you telling me about it for?"

"I been thinking it over and I'd be the fall guy. I'd be down here on a snatch charge and you'd be bumped on the same case. I'd get beat to death and you know it."

"You would, all right."

"That's why I wanted to see you before you mess around."

"Was Cicotti in on it?"

"No. We knew he was a friend of yours and Bruner figured that you'd make the rounds of the joints to see what you could pick up and that Angelo would crack to you."

"A frame, hunh? What'd you get out of it?"

"A grand when you were knocked off. It'd be no use though—I never could spend it, I figure."

"Who was in it besides you and Abe?"

"Three guys from out of town and Bruckner, the guy that plays with Cohn. They got Mrs. Bruner there to take care of the kid. Bruner himself don't know they're there. He thinks they are somewhere else."

"Is she in on it?"

"Lord, no! She's scared to death about the kid. She don't even know Abe. I'm telling you this straight. You're supposed to run into a slug."

"And you figure you'll be smart and tell me now, so I won't get hurt, hunh?"

"Yeah!" The little man smirked. "If I tip you off like this I figure you'll give me a chance to get out of town. You will, won't you?"

The smirk was wiped off his face as Prentice hit him in the

mouth. "You little rat ———! Why didn't you tell me this at the apartment! We lost a man on this."

Solly got to his knees, horror in his eyes. "It's gone through! Didn't anything happen?"

Prentice hit him again, stood over him. "Happen! Happen, hell! We got a man killed. You'll play smart, will ya?" He went to the door of the cell, called: "Hey, jailer." He fumed up and down the little cell, swearing to himself.

The jailer came and incuriously looked in. "You through, Dal?"

"Yeah. When you get time, work on this little rat for me, will ya? He got Charley Johnson killed."

"How?"

"By playing smart. Let me out." He stalked back to the homicide department, and the waiting Hallahan.

Hallahan looked at him narrowly, said: "Mrs. Bruner wants to go home, Dal. What'd you find out?"

"Plenty!" Prentice turned his somber gaze on Mrs. Bruner and the child. "Mrs. Bruner, we'll send you up to your house and I'll take the boy to his father's office."

"But I just called Mr. Bruner. He's on his way here now."

"He must of changed his mind. He asked me to do this just a moment ago." He spoke to Hallahan, who was watching him closely. "You send Mrs. Bruner up with Pete, will ya? Al and I'll take the boy up to his father. I want to see him anyway."

Hallahan looked puzzled. "Wait a minute, Dal. Will you pardon me a moment, Mrs. Bruner?" He took Prentice by the arm, led him outside the room. "What did you find out?"

Prentice's face was flushed, his eyes hot looking. He said sharply: "And I was right. The whole damn' mess was a frame.

Bruner figured Cohn was getting out of hand and he works this stunt with him on that account. He's bound to win, no matter which way it went. Either Cohn gets me or I get Cohn, and he's ahead either way. That's why he said nothing about his wife. That's why she was treated so nice. That's why the guy with the shotgun was waiting in the hall. That little high-spot told me plenty—don't think he didn't."

"Was Cicotti in on the frame?"

"Hell, no! They knew I'd ask questions. They never figured on a raid—they figured Al and I'd walk around and nose into it." He swore violently, added: "And here's Charley Johnson wiped off."

"All you can do is pick up Cohn."

"And hold him how long? She'll never testify against him when she realizes that'll get her old man in, too."

"No, I suppose not."

"I knew it was a phoney just as soon as she told me up there who she was."

"She picked Cohn's picture as the guy she thought she saw in her husband's office."

"You get her to make an affidavit to that effect. I'll pick him up on the strength of it. It's all we can do—maybe."

"Maybe what?"

"Nothing. I got an idea."

"What in hell's the idea of you and Al taking the boy? I don't get that."

"You will." They went back in the office.

Hallahan said: "Mrs. Bruner, I'll send you home now. Mr. Prentice will take the boy to his father."

"I don't understand why."

"I don't either. It's Mr. Bruner's idea."

Prentice interrupted curtly: "Mrs. Bruner, if I should miss your husband, kindly tell him that I'll be waiting at his office. Come on, young fellow." He held out his hand to the boy, who looked at his mother questioningly.

She nodded, and told him: "Go with the policeman, John." Her eyes looked troubled. "There is nothing wrong, is there, Mr. Prentice?"

"Why ask me? You're out of the jam, ain't ya?"

"You looked rather odd for a moment." Her voice hesitated. "I'm very sorry about the men that were killed. And an officer, also."

Prentice's voice was very grim. "And an officer with a wife and three children."

"Oh, I'm sorry."

"And the man that started it will be sorry, too. Come on, lad." He took the boy by the hand and walked to the door, turned there and repeated: "If I should miss your husband, Mrs. Bruner, ask him to wait for me at his office." He smiled sardonically at Hallahan and left.

Hallahan watched his departure with a puzzled look. "I'll have Lieutenant Peterson drive you home, ma'am. I don't understand this, but as Mr. Bruner asked it, why it's what we'll do. I want to tell you that you were mighty lucky to get out of this scrape as well as you have."

"I realize that. Mr. Bruner will be very grateful."

"No doubt." Hallahan's tone was dry. He called: "Hey, Pete. Take Mrs. Bruner to her home."

"You bet." The stolid Peterson led Mrs. Bruner to her car.

AFTER HE HAD placed the boy in the back of the car, Prentice acquainted Allen in a few words with what Solly had told him.

Allen's face was black. "The ——! We lose a man. Charley Johnson and him with three kids himself. What'll we do?"

"The same thing."

"The same thing! Oh! Hell, Dal, I won't go for that."

"Why not?" Prentice's voice was persuasive. "We can't prove a thing on him. Solly's word wouldn't hold in court for five minutes and Bruner's wife couldn't testify even if she would. It's another rap he'd beat, is all. This way he'll be hurt and the kid'll be okey."

"But where can we take him?"

"Home."

"Ix-nay."

"Why not?"

"That's the first place Bruner'd think of. There might be a beef and the brat'd get hurt. I'll go for it, but you got to think of a better place than that."

Prentice puzzled a moment, then grinned. "Listen." He turned to the boy in back and asked. "Listen, son. How'd you like to ride in a real police car when it makes a lot of noise and goes fast? How'd you like that?"

The little boy answered: "Fine," and Prentice turned to Allen. "You remember that Johnny and I used to have a shack out on the beach road. Up Mariposa Canyon. We'll take him there."

"You can't leave him there, Dal. Not a kid that age. He'd be scared to death, alone."

"Alone hell. You'll stay with him."

"Not me. I'm going with you. If you're going to pull a stunt like this I'm going along."

"Okey, then. We'll get Mac on it."

"Maybe. Maybe he won't go for it."

"He will. He knew Charley Johnson and the kid won't be hurt. You run in and get him."

As Allen went in he met Mrs. Bruner who, escorted by Peterson, was coming out. He passed her silently and beckoned to McCready in the big general room.

McCready lounged over, grumbled: "Well, what is it now?" and Allen grabbed him by the arm.

"Come on, Mac. We want to talk to you." He led the protesting McCready to the car and told Prentice: "I'll sit in the back with Mac and tell him the story. How'd you like to ride in the front seat, son, just like a regular policeman?"

The boy's eyes were shining. He sensed that the big policemen were friendly. "Just fine. Will we go fast?"

Prentice's smile at him was crooked. "Plenty."

He turned the big car's nose towards the trunk road that led past the little canyon, a few miles up the coast. He heard the murmur of Allen's voice in the rear and as they got out of the downtown traffic and on the boulevard leading to the ocean said gruffly to the boy: "Cold, son?"

"A little bit. I'll be all right."

"You bet you will." He called back to Allen. "Put that coat of yours around the kid, Al. I don't want him to catch cold." Allen complied and the ride was finished in silence. As the car pulled up to the rough little shack the boy asked: "Is my papa here?"

Allen answered cheerfully. "You and this man will have to wait for him here. This man will look after you. He's a policeman, too."

Prentice grinned. "There's some doubt about that, ain't there,

Mac?" and the boy said confidingly: "I like policemen." He slid his hand into the uncomfortable McCready's big paw.

McCready said gruffly: "Listen, Dal. I don't think I'll go for this shot. It ain't the tyke's fault his old man's a lousy ——"

"No, and it ain't Charley Johnson's fault, either. The kid'll be okey. If anything happens to us you can phone in the morning. But not before."

"Does Hallahan know?"

"Nobody knows. If this works he'll know it and if it don't he won't. There's coffee inside and some canned stuff. You can get water right on the back porch. You'll be all right. Blankets and everything and there's a lamp on the table. Al and I'll be back." Ignoring the protests of the reluctant McCready, he turned the car and headed back to town and Bruner's office.

THE NIGHT ELEVATOR boy said surlily: "Am I supposed to know everything? Call him and see if he's in," and Prentice cuffed him sharply with one hand, showing him his badge with the other.

"All right, funny. Is he or ain't he? You ain't making so many trips at this time of night that you don't know."

The boy said hastily: "Yeah! He went in about half an hour ago. He and two other guys."

Prentice looked at Allen, who grinned. "Okey, kid. Take us to the floor below and show us the stairs. And keep your trap shut. Get me?"

"Yes, sir." The boy was awed, not so much by the badge as by the warning look Prentice gave him.

They quietly climbed the one flight of stairs to the floor the office was on and watching closely, eased to the doors of

Bruner's suite. The one on the left said "John Bruner—Investments—Walk in," and was dark. The following door said "John Bruner—Private," and there was a light inside and the muffled murmur of voices.

Prentice tried the dark door, found it unlocked, and motioned Allen inside and as he obeyed, walked to the other and knocked.

There was a moment of silence, then the door swung open and John Bruner said cordially: "Come in, Prentice. I was expecting you."

Prentice looked over his shoulder and saw a hard-faced man, hand in coat pocket, sitting on the table. The room was apparently empty except for him and Bruner. Prentice slid warily inside, slid along the wall until his back was away from the open door. Hand under his coat, he watched the man on the table.

Bruner reached past him, closed the door and said heartily: "That sure was a fine piece of work, getting the boy and his mother back like that. I certainly want to thank you. Where is he? Did you take him home?"

Prentice asked, with a motion towards the silent man on the table: "Just you two here?"

Bruner's voice was easy. "Sure. Just who you see." Prentice did not miss the flick of his eye towards the clothes press in the corner of the room.

Hand still inside his coat, Prentice said curtly to the man on the table: "You scram."

Bruner said, his voice reproving: "Now, Prentice. That isn't necessary. He's a friend of mine."

"But not of mine."

Bruner shrugged broad shoulders. His light blue eyes congealed. "Where's the boy?"

Prentice nodded towards the man on the table. "Tell your hood to take a powder, and I'll tell you. Not till then." Again he saw the glance at the corner of the room.

Bruner said: "It's all right, Jerry—I'll be seeing you tomorrow." His voice was unpleasant.

As the man slid from the table, the glass in the door between the two rooms crashed and the man swung his head that way. Prentice in the same instant had drawn the gun under his coat. His voice was harsh. "Up with 'em! You!"

The man stiffened and glanced at Bruner, his hand tightening in his pocket, then slowly raised his hands to shoulder height. Prentice stepped back until the muzzle of his gun covered both men and ordered: "Come on in, Al. Shake this mugg down."

Allen reached through the broken glass of the door and unlatched it, wary eye on the sullen Jerry. He took the gun from his coat pocket and searched Bruner, finding no gun, and Prentice jeered at this last. "What's the matter, keed? You hiring all your shooting done these days?"

Bruner smiled back. "I don't get you, Dal. You come in here and get rough with a guy that ain't bothering you a bit. Of course, it's all right with me after today. You know how you stand with me after getting the boy back."

Prentice took two steps, to the side and slightly back of the man Bruner called Jerry. His arm, weighted with the gun, fell heavily and Jerry sagged to the floor with the crunch of the blow. Bruner cried out angrily: "Prentice! Are you crazy! That broke his jaw."

Prentice looked blank. "Well, what of it? I don't care." He

glanced at Allen, then at the clothes press, and Allen nodded slightly. "I wanted to talk to you without a bunch of hoods listening in. That plain enough?"

Bruner controlled his anger with an evident effort. "I don't get this, Dal. I thought we buried the hatchet."

"I dug it up. Where can I get hold of Abe Cohn?"

Allen was seated on the table, half facing the clothes press. He held his gun carelessly on his lap. He joined in. "You know that Abe was the guy back of this, don't you?"

Bruner appeared surprised. "You're crazy. Abe and I are good friends."

Prentice jeered: "You must be. You got it fixed so Abe's just the same as sunk. Just pals, hunh?"

Allen saw the closet door spring open slightly, and with the gun still on his lap, eased the hammer back with his thumb, holding pressure on the trigger so the lock would not click as the gun came to full cock. Bruner said: "What do you mean?" and hazarded a quick glance at the closet.

"This snatch of yours. What the hell did you think I meant?"

"Of mine? Oh, I see. Of course it was my boy that was kidnaped."

"Oh, hell! Don't play dumb. The whole thing stunk but I didn't get it till it was all over and I got your tip about Abe."

"Tip!" Bruner's eyes seemed to glaze. "Tip!"

"Yeah! —— sake, talk out man! It's just Al and me here and we know the score. If I didn't want Abe so bad myself I'd be —— damned if I went for it. Of course I can stick him on it with you turning him loose." He added admiringly: "You know, you're pretty smart at that—you get rid of Abe and his bunch of boys'll never blame you for a minute."

"Are you crazy?"

"—— no. Abe was the crazy one ever to go for a stunt like that. He was the fall guy. Solly told me the whole works—just how you and him fixed the frame for Abe."

Bruner risked another swift glance at the clothes press, cried out: "No! No, Abe! Don't!" and Prentice turned with apparent surprise. "Why I thought you wasn't here, Abe. This'll save me a trip."

Abe was half out of the closet, a heavy automatic lined on the greenish Bruner's stomach. His face was livid. He snarled: "Like hell it will, copper. I'm going to bust this rat —— in the belly and you're going to watch me do it." His hand tightened on the gun and Allen shot from his lap, the bullet catching him in the throat. He dropped the gun, put both hands blindly in front of him and fell and Bruner said huskily: "Oh! my ——!"

Allen said cheerfully: "Now this is just like old home week. Who else you got hiding around?"

Bruner groped for a chair, sat down heavily. He repeated: "My ——!"

Prentice's voice was bland. "Well, let's be going, Al. We got the whole bunch that was in the snatch now. Abe and the guy in the hall and the three guys on the roof and Solly. It was quite a crowd."

Bruner cleared his throat weakly. The greenish look was fading from his face but he seemed unable to tear his eyes away from Cohn's body. He asked: "You got the boy in the car downstairs?"

Prentice stopped at the door. "I have not. It was the funniest thing. A bunch of big rough men stopped us and took the kid away from us. They said in time the kid might get to like it."

Bruner jerked his eyes away from Cohn's body. "What's that? What's that, Prentice?"

"You heard me."

"But, Prentice! I don't get this?"

Prentice said unpleasantly: "There was a guy named Charley Johnson killed in that raid. He's got a wife and three kids and I'll bet they thought as much of their dad as you do about that brat of yours. And the pension and insurance money ain't going to go so damn' far. What do you think?"

Bruner choked out: "You wouldn't take it out on the boy? I didn't have anything to do with this Johnson.

"You used this same kid as a decoy to spot us, didn't you? You knew that Abe Cohn was getting out of line and that one way or the other you was bound to win, didn't ya? Johnson got his in the raid, you know that."

"I didn't know the boy was there—or his mother. That's why I had Cohn up here—to have him tell me about that. It isn't the boy's fault."

"It ain't Johnson's kids' fault either."

"What do you want? Prentice! The boy's all right, isn't he?"

"So far," Prentice said brutally. "Of course I don't know how long he's going to like it where he's at."

"How much do you want?"

Prentice glanced at Allen, considered. "Listen. If you'll establish a trust fund—or better yet, give it to Hallahan to fix, for Mrs. Johnson that'll give her the same income that Charley got we might think it over." He held up a hand warningly. "Wait!" They heard the sound of footsteps in the hall—the sound of a siren outside the building.

"I'll do that, Dal."

"It won't hurt you. You'll just squeeze down a little harder. That ain't all, though. I think the police milk fund for the poor kids ought to be fattened up about ten grand, too."

He went to the door and opened it, to see the elevator boy and a uniformed man. He said cheerfully to the last: "Come in and take a look and then call the wagon. But make your call from downstairs."

As they left, Bruner raised his head with a faint sneer. "Is this right? I'm to put up enough dough so that it'll bring this woman as much as her husband made. And ten grand for the police fund. I can raise it tonight and give it to Hallahan. Is that right?"

"Just right."

"And then I get the boy?"

"You do. He'll be waiting for you and the money. I'll call Hallahan and when you put up the dough the kid'll be home in an hour."

The sneer was plainer.

"But what about you and Allen? Where are you heroes going to get your cut?"

Prentice slapped him across the mouth and Bruner raised his hand to his lips and looked curiously at the blood on his fingers.

Prentice said slowly: "Listen, louse! You're such a dirty —— —— you won't believe me, but I like kids, and if I didn't, you wouldn't be left around where you could do even this much. So, swallow it, —— and like it."

Robbery—with Violence

Dal Prentice acts on the principle
that a crook can't take it

THE TRAIN PULLED into Magna City and Prentice stood to his feet, automatically pulling the man with him erect. Seated, the handcuffs linking the two were not apparent, but Prentice had given his seatmate no warning of his intention and the prisoner uttered a muffled exclamation as the links bit into his wrist.

The seat across the aisle was occupied by an elderly woman and she cried out indignantly: "Was that necessary! It's brutality like that—" and stopped, embarrassed by the detective's steady stare. She ended weakly: "Why, he's hardly more than a boy."

Prentice said, his voice sardonic: "That's right, lady. Only a boy and already he's indicted by the Grand Jury for murder and has got a couple of priors." He laughed. "Quite a boy."

The prisoner grinned sheepishly at the woman, then at Prentice. "Let's get out, copper. One thing about the jail is that you got a little privacy."

Prentice grunted assent and, ignoring the woman's outraged sniff, the two men went to the end of the Pullman, waited for the door to be opened. The prisoner looked over his shoulder and seeing the lady was out of earshot, commented: "I bet she's off a farm. Or did she look for you to kiss me?" His voice was pleasant and he seemed to bear no ill-will towards the burly officer.

Prentice grinned. "Last stop. You were a mugg to get caught, kid. We ain't got a thing against you but a murder rap and you know about these narrow-minded juries. You've been mugged and printed often enough to know you ought to 've laid low."

As he stepped off the stand the porter held there was a click of cameras, and the boy hastily covered his face with his free arm. The detective told him kindly: "You can't dodge 'em, kid. And you'd be a fool to try. You're only a kid and if you get that mug often enough in the papers, they'll put out petitions for you. You'll get a lighter rap at least and maybe beat it."

Prentice shouldered through the newspaper men and to the police car waiting in the space marked *Reserved,* climbed in the back with the prisoner, blew a sigh of relief and spoke to the driver. "How's tricks, Al? It's a wonder to me the hoods ain't took the town. I been gone two weeks."

Allen, his partner, lean, dark, sardonic, grinned back over his shoulder. "They got part of it—the part we don't want."

"What's new? Does Johnny here go to jail or to the D.A.'s office for questioning? Or shall we turn him loose?" He poked the prisoner's arm.

"D.A.'s office." Allen hunched his shoulders and settled to his task of driving the police Buick through the heavy traffic. A truck blocked the way and he opened the siren, said irritably: "Damn these drivers. Think they own the streets."

At the District Attorney's office, Prentice delivered his prisoner to one of the guards there to receive him and told him kindly: "You're in a spot, lad. I'd keep shut until I got a lawyer. Good luck to ya." He handed the boy a package of cigarettes, slapped him on the shoulder and turned back to the car and Allen.

Allen seemed preoccupied. He answered Prentice's query about their joint apartment with a laconic, "Yeah! I paid it," seemed uninterested in Prentice's glowing description of New

York's night life, and paid attention only when Prentice asked bluntly: "What in hell's wrong? Can't you talk?"

He answered uneasily: "Hallahan'll tell you. We're going there now," and swung the car to the curb in front of the central station.

They got out and went through the main room, Prentice waving and shouting salutations to friends scattered among the men off duty. Followed by Allen he entered the room devoted to the use of the homicide department, said: "H'lo, Cap!" and blinked his eyes in surprise at the woman seated across the desk from Hallahan. She was the proprietress of the famous *Commercial Club*, where the big political bosses of the town, and other prominent citizenry as well, could always be found.

She smiled at him and his "Hello, Dora," and sat quiet. Hallahan said gruffly: "Sit down, Dal. Have a good trip?"

The grin had left Prentice's face. He sensed the tension hanging over the room. "Yeah! Those New York coppers don't ever sleep and there's a speake every other door. They showed me the town."

"Any trouble?"

"Naw! The kid waived extradition and acted fine all the way back."

"Well, that'll make it easier for him."

"Hope so. He should get a medal. The town's better off without the rat he shot. Just because the killer's a kid he gets a lot of notoriety. He's only about twenty-three and I feel sorry for him even if he did damn' near talk a leg off me." He scowled. "What's the rumble?"

Hallahan cleared his throat, glanced at Dora Madison, then at Prentice. His voice was apologetic. "Look for yourself, Dal. Of course I know it's all right." He threw Prentice the newspaper spread across his desk, got up and walked to the wall and stared unseeingly at one of the reward posters that lined it.

THE PAPER WAS the Magna City *Record*—and the glaring head-lines were *Veteran Police Officer Discloses Inside Work of Graft Ring*. There was a smudged picture bearing a faint resemblance to Prentice and a sub-title *Detective Prentice Tells of City Steal.*

Prentice purpled and read an article supposedly written by himself "in collaboration with a *Record* reporter," and as he read, tugged at his collar and swore under his breath, Allen and Dora Madison watched in silence.

He looked up, snarled: "This is the first I've seen this thing. You ought to know that. I've been on vacation an' got it cut short to bring the kid back."

Hallahan swung around from the poster. "Sure! I know that. You started it when you shook Bruner down the time he faked the kidnaping of his own son to make a plant for his hoods to get you. If it was just you it wouldn't be so bad, but it gets Dora in bad. It gives names and dates and the whole damn' works, and the hell of it is he's got the stuff to prove it. You know he owns the paper."

Dora spoke for the first time. Both her voice and appearance were that of a lady, but the words she used would have fitted a stevedore much better. She ended her cursing with: "Don't be dumb, Dal. It's what he's been promising to do and he takes a cut at you at the same time. Some people'll believe you've turned rat and that's what he wants. Because I own the *Commercial Club* and the gang meets there I'm in it. He's out in the open at last."

Prentice shrugged heavy shoulders. "—— sake! Why choose me!"

His voice was sullen and she added quickly: "I don't mean it's your fault. You and Bruner got a mad on and it's your own affair, but a lot of people are going to believe this and I'm the monkey."

"Oh, *you're* the monkey! The hell you are! He killed my partner—damn' near killed me—pretty near lost me my job—and you're the monkey. —— sake! He's blackmailing half the town and starting every beef in the rackets. And you're the monkey! Talk sense."

"I know you've got plenty against him, Dal," Dora said

placatingly, "on your own account. He's a hard man to beat. You've tried to pin a couple of raps on him and they wouldn't stick. You've got to handle him differently—diplomatically—outwise him."

"Diplomatically hell!" Prentice exploded. "There's only one way to make him stay off me—get him where I can beat hell out of him; pound him to a jelly, hurt him so he won't ever dare to look cross-wise at me again."

Prentice stood up, paced back and forth. Hallahan cleared his throat, and Dora spoke again: "I've got an idea about an angle that might work."

"And so've I. Go up to his office and get in the room alone with him and claim I thought he was reaching for a gun."

"Don't be a fool! A gun'll hang you instead of a rope one of these days." Her voice was sharp. "He's got the dope in this stuff he's starting to spring in his damn' paper and if he's killed the whole mess will show up. He's smart. Will you quit walking up and down like a parade? I've got nerves and I can't talk to you on the run."

Prentice glared at her, started to speak, and sat down.

She made her voice persuasive. "Now listen, Dal. He's got that stuff planted some place and if we can find out where and get hold of it we can stop this. And that's the only way. What do you think? Don't that make sense?"

"Hell, no! He'd have it in a safe deposit box."

"You damn' fool! Would he have it where a court order could get it for proof of blackmail? Don't be such a chump. He's got it where he can get it and where nobody else can. That's my guess."

"Maybe! What about it?"

"That's up to you. Or should I write it out?"

Prentice spread his hands, palms out. "Why pick on me? I've got my own beef with him."

"You started this when you shook him down. That cost him about sixty grand. He's sore and pulled this to get even."

"Al and I didn't get any part of the dough." He turned to Hallahan for confirmation. "Did we, Cap?"

Hallahan shook his head, started to speak but Dora interrupted with: "What difference does that make? He paid it."

"And I'm the fall guy now."

Hallahan pointed out dryly: "But, Dal! You could keep Bruner's stuff and make him pay well."

"Like hell! This is the thanks I get. I get his kid back when he gets crossed and we kill a hood that's got a gun on him. That's grati—"

Dora stopped the outburst. "That's old. He's a rat. What about this?"

Prentice sparred for time. "What do I get? And what if I get in a jam?"

"What if you do? Aren't you in one now?"

Prentice swung to Hallahan, asked: "What do you think?" and Hallahan answered slowly:

"Lessee just what you got to gain or lose, Dal, if you just go and take that stuff away from him. Bruner was a pretty big guy in this man's town when he was working the political reform racket and doing his dirty work under cover. He had lots of pull and lots of friends.

"When he had your partner killed, you went after him bullheaded and drove him into the open—graft and all. He's lost his pull and his friends. The only protection he has is what he can buy and that don't amount to anything.

"Everyone knows now he is a crook, and this thing is just between you and him. If you don't get his proofs on that story he's printed, you're sunk. You'll get a rap you can't beat. But you can't go for it as a regular business of the Force. You got to do it some other way. You're covered if you don't make it too rough and don't get caught. It ain't orders, though."

"How'll I work it?"

"That's up to you. You can have McCready. He worked with you and Al last time."

Prentice scowled at him, said bitterly to Allen: "No wonder you didn't talk. —— sake! Let's get out of here." Followed by Allen he strode from the room. Hallahan looked at Dora, slowly nodded his head.

MULVANEY LOOKED APPREHENSIVELY at the two detectives. His voice was plaintive and his eyes circled the shabby room. "I ain't done a thing. You can ask the guy I work for if I ain't on the job every day—and the room's clean as a whistle."

Prentice kept silent, glowering at the ex-convict, and Allen said smoothly: "We just want you to help us out a bit, Pat. You used to be a pretty good man."

"I'm shooting straight now."

Allen's voice was soothing. "Sure. Of course you are. And so are we. That is, we want to."

"Whadya want?"

"Maybe we got a little job for you. Maybe not."

Mulvaney's eyes flared, showing bloodshot whites. "What you mean by that?"

"Well, I'll tell you. We got a box we want opened."

"Get a safe expert."

Prentice broke in irritably. "For —— sake, Al. Why fool with the ——!"

He snapped at Mulvaney: "We have. You're him. Shut up and come on." He reached over and jerked the reluctant Mulvaney to his feet. "Play ball, guy. If I wanted to I could tie you up on enough to hang you. And believe me, I will."

Mulvaney gulped and reached for his coat and the three men went out to the car parked in front of the cheap hotel.

Prentice said briefly to the man in the driver's seat: "Got him. He'll do—if he's smart," and Mulvaney complained querulously: "Hell, copper! I can't open one with fingernails."

Allen said: "We got the tools. Shut up," and Mulvaney subsided, muttering to himself.

The car pulled silently into the semidarkness of a tree-lined street, stopped, and the four men got out, the man in front carrying a small handbag. They walked with no pretense of concealment to a large house set well back from the street, but when Prentice rang the bell, the other three were in shadow that concealed their features. A butler came to the door, said formally: "Yes, sir. What is it?"

"Mr. Bruner in?" Prentice's hat was well down over his eyes and his head was bent, giving the man at the door only the barest glimpse of his chin. The butler hesitated before answering, "Yes, sir. Who shall I tell him—"

Prentice's hand came out of his pocket and the blackjack it held swished towards the head of the startled servant, who sensed rather than saw the blow and dodged too late. He slumped and Prentice caught him in his arms as he fell and lifted him clear of the doorway into the hall. One of the three who had followed him in, grunted, and Prentice whispered: "He ain't hurt. Mac, you stay here and watch the door. Al and I'll start from the back."

Leaving McCready, Mulvaney, and the unconscious butler in the shadow, and followed by Allen, he went cautiously down the long hall—gun out and in his hand. Both men wore rubber-soled shoes—had put silk masks over their faces. The third door down the hall showed a film of light under it and Prentice jerked his head at Allen as they passed it carefully.

They went clear to the back of the house, and in the kitchen, found the cook, two maids, and the chauffeur, all playing bridge. The cook, facing the door, was dummy, and Prentice stopped in the doorway, the mask concealing the grin on his face. She looked up from her task of spreading her cards on the table, saw the masked man in the doorway and opened her mouth in astonishment, and Prentice snapped: "On your feet! All of you!" The surprised quartette obeyed.

The cook opened her mouth still farther, and forestalling her scream, he told her, "Shut up," and moved the muzzle of the gun threateningly. She gulped and remained silent. Allen crowded past him and Prentice asked: "Who else is there in the house? Tell the truth or—" He waited a moment, snarled: "Come on! Speak up!"

The woman blurted out: "Mr. Symmes and Mr. Bruner."

"Mr. Symmes?"

"He's the butler."

Prentice nodded, and she stammered: "Mr. Bruner, he—he's in the library.

"I know where he is. Where's Mrs. Bruner?"

"She took the little boy out of town."

Prentice nodded at Allen. "That checks. I'll get Mac and pack the butler in here and we'll let Mac watch 'em."

Allen nodded and Prentice started back through the hall but as he neared the door that had shown the light it opened and a voice said irritably: "Who's there? Symmes! What's all this noise about?"

Prentice had moved with swift steps to the door and as Bruner stepped into the hall, he slammed his gun into the man's stomach with sickening force. Bruner cried out and doubled up involuntarily and Prentice snapped: "Shut up, Bruner. We'll talk after a while."

He called back over his shoulder to McCready: "You and Mulvaney take the mugg into the kitchen, Mac, and watch 'em all. Let Al and Mulvaney come back here." He jabbed the muzzle of the gun deeper into Bruner's belly, snapped: "Back up—and shut up." The door closed behind them.

ALLEN, FOLLOWED BY Mulvaney, came in just in time to hear Bruner's, "I know damn' well who you are. What are you trying to tell me," and Prentice's, "What da'ya mean? We're robbers." He made no attempt to disguise his voice nor did Allen, who said cheerfully: "Sure! We got gloves on and everything. You can't prove a thing."

Bruner grunted, said: "I thought you were on a vacation, Prentice?"

"What makes you think I'm Prentice?"

Bruner's laugh was scornful but he was careful to keep his hands at shoulder height. "Hell! Your clothes. Your voice. The way you walk and talk."

"You sure?"

"Of course."

Prentice took a step forward and smashed the gun barrel rakingly across Bruner's face. He said unpleasantly: "Still sure, are you?" The hand with the gun was raised in readiness again, and Bruner stepped back until he half sat in a chair. He felt his face, blurted out shakily: "No! No! I'm not sure."

"That's good. Where do you keep your safe?"

"You can't get away with this!"

"No!" Prentice moved ahead and Bruner sat back in the chair, covered his face with his forearms. Prentice tapped delicately at these with the muzzle of the gun and Bruner's voice was muffled as he cried out: "On the wall! Behind the books!"

Prentice looked at him in disgust, said to Allen: "The yellow ——! Before he's even hurt. Quits like a dirty pup." He jerked his head at the plush tie that held the portieres at the French window. "Bring me that cord that holds the curtains."

Allen tore this loose and went to Bruner's side. Prentice lifted the muzzle of the gun, waved it significantly, and Bruner held his hands out in obedience. His face was a pasty yellow and his extended hands were shaking so badly that Allen was forced to steady them as he threw the first loop of the improvised bonds around them. With Mulvaney watching in astonishment, they bound Bruner up like a trussed chicken, finally gagging him with his own handkerchief.

This done, they went to the section of the wall Bruner had indicated, tore down books until a small safe set in the wall was revealed. They called Mulvaney over and while he was examining it, Allen went out into the hall, got the handbag and opened it, dumping the contents on the floor. Mulvaney grunted in professional interest, reached down for an electric drill and looked up at the light fixture. Allen nodded understandings and without speaking, screwed the plug in while the ex-convict set the drill in working order.

Prentice called out suddenly: "What in the hell! We brought the mugg along in case Mr. b—— wasn't here and he is. He'll tell us what the combination is and be glad to do it."

The gagged Bruner shook his head violently, but as Prentice approached, swinging the heavy gun, changed the motion to a nod of decision. The gag taken from his mouth, he said sullenly: "Spin it two or three times then ten—back to the left to thirty—twice around to the right and to seventy four."

Prentice said regretfully, "I was hoping you wouldn't want to tell us. I get a bang out of this."

Bruner shuddered and his face changed color as Prentice shoved the gag back into place. Allen was twirling the dial on the safe and on the second try the door swung open.

The two men looked through the contents of the safe, glanced meaningly at each other, then walked to Bruner. Prentice yanked the gag out: "All right, ——! Where's the stuff?"

"What stuff?" Bruner looked weakly defiant.

Prentice exploded: "I'm sick of this!" He seized the wretched Bruner by the hair and struck first one side of his face, then the other. He was breathing heavily, when Allen succeeded in dragging him away, and his eyes looked glassy.

Mulvaney looked on in horror and Allen blurted: "——! Dal! Don't go screwy! Get hold of yourself. You'll kill him."

Bruner was slumped in unconsciousness on the floor. Allen took a glass of water from a carafe on a stand nearby and dashed it in his face. He stirred, said weakly: "You asked how to open the safe and I told you. The stuff you're after is in the corner. Pull back the rug." His eyes watched Prentice with hate in their light blue depths.

The rug when pulled back disclosed a trap set flush with the floor, and this opened, revealed a boxlike hole possibly two feet square and almost completely filled with papers—manila envelopes, names written neatly on them. They opened some of these, looked at the contents, and loaded the tool bag as full as possible which didn't account for more than a third of the loot. Prentice looked perplexed and Allen suggested: "He'll have something upstairs in one of the bedrooms that we can use. I'll see."

He was back in a moment with a Gladstone which took the rest of the papers with ease, and this loaded, Prentice went back, replaced the gag and stood over the cowering Bruner.

He spoke, his voice deliberate. "This is the blow-off, Bruner. I'm telling ya. You'll stop the paper because you've lost the proof of what you've started to print and the people you've been blackmailing are in the clear. If you think you've got enough hoods working for you to buck the crowd and just take the town over you've got the police to figure on and you can't make the grade.

"I'm telling you, you're through. I'd knock you over myself right now and like it but I won't take a chance on you having anything else hid around. You lay off. You got a partner of mine killed and I'll kill you like a rat if ever I get an excuse. We got your kid out of a jam for you while you were trying to spot me and Al, kept another rat from killing you and still you ain't had brains enough to quit when you could. You're in too deep to get out now and I'll walk on your grave."

His voice had not risen but his eyes had taken on a glaze as he talked. He stepped ahead and began methodically to kick Bruner in the side until Allen stepped in between.

"Quit it, Dal! This ain't fool proof. There's too many in it." He nodded back at Mulvaney who quavered: "That guy goes off his nut."

At the sound of his voice, Prentice swung towards him and he shrank back with his arm shielding his face. Prentice grunted in disgust, said: "——! Let's get out of here." Bruner made muffled sounds in his gag and Allen told him: "No, you'll stay there. One of these bums that works for you will get out and turn you loose."

Prentice snarled: "To hell with the ——!" Allen followed him out the door, saying: "C'mon, Mulvaney. We'll go to the car and the others'll come."

Prentice went to the kitchen and told McCready: "Okey! Let's lock 'em in." Obeying the frightened cook's instructions they found the keys for one of the maid's rooms and locked the servants inside. Prentice told them sardonically: "Have fun, folks. If you're lucky somebody'll come and let you out."

They locked the door and followed Allen and Mulvaney to the car parked down the street. They drove rapidly back to Mulvaney's hotel and Prentice and Allen followed him inside.

Allen said shortly: "You get out of town, Mulvancy. All the way out and we don't care where as long as it's a long way away from here. If you talk, nobody'll believe you and we'll drag you back here on a fake charge and you'll leave in a coffin. Be smart. Is that plain?"

Mulvaney cast a furtive glance at Prentice and nodded. Allen asked: "Got any dough," and at Mulvaney's, "Thirteen dollars and a half is all," he counted out five hundred in crisp new twenties. "This is all. And go that far away. Get me?"

They swung out and left Mulvaney frantically throwing clothes into a handbag.

Driving to the station, Allen said: "I don't like the way Bruner acted. Like he had something up his sleeve. Notice his face when we left?"

"Don't be an old woman. He was sick and looked it. You're too nervous. You have any trouble, Mac?"

McCready, driving the car, called back: "Not a bit. They never made a peep."

Prentice told Allen tolerantly: "See, Al? Everything went fine. There'll be no kickback."

AT THE STATION, Hallahan and Dora were waiting as they had asked them to do.

Prentice said: "Come in, Mac. You're in it and you might as well be all the way in." He tossed the bags to the top of Hallahan's big desk and sighed in relief. "There's the stuff."

Dora asked eagerly: "What happened?"

"Not a thing. It couldn't have gone smoother."

She nodded at the handbags. "Did he tell you where the stuff was," and Prentice grinned at her. "Yeah! I cut him up a little and he cracked plenty quick—the yellow tramp."

Hallahan grumbled to himself and Prentice turned to him. "What's that, Cap?"

"I said damn the Indian stuff. If he ever gets you it'll be too bad."

"I didn't hurt him—much."

"He's lost some teeth and he's got some broken ribs," Allen pointed out.

Hallahan said gloomily: "God help you boys if ever you slip."

Prentice's voice was reasonable. "How did we slip? We wore gloves and he can't prove it was us. We were masked all the time and besides that—we never left this room. You've got to back us on that if there's a rumble."

"That part's all right but you might've slipped up some place else. What did you do exactly. What caused the rough stuff?"

Prentice detailed the night's happenings and when told about Mulvaney being ordered out of town, Hallahan looked up sharply. "There's your catch. That guy'll talk. And where'll you be? Whose idea was it getting him anyway?"

Prentice said sullenly: "Mine. If Bruner wasn't there we had to have somebody that could open the crib."

"You could have gone back. Just going to the house wouldn't have tipped it."

"We're no worse off than we were before. What should I've done? Killed the poor ——? He didn't seem to be such a bad guy and he played ball with us. He won't talk. Al put the fear of God in him."

Hallahan said wearily: "I'm talking about why you took him along at all but I won't argue. If Al can scare him so can Bruner. Or didn't you think of that? And Bruner can pay him more dough than he thinks there is in the world."

"Bruner don't know him. We were all masked all the time."

"You didn't call him by name or anything like that?"

"I don't think so."

Allen interrupted: "You did, Dal, and so'd I. Just as we left," and Dora snapped: "It's the old gag. The papers or the child and God knows, Dal, you must have the brain of one to take along anybody like this cheap yegg and then tell Bruner who he is. That beats me."

Prentice lost his temper completely and turned viciously towards her. "Shut up, ——! It seemed like a good idea and I did it and it's done. If it was a bum idea it's too late now. Cry your damned eyes out and see if that'll change it. We got the stuff and that's what you wanted, ain't it?"

She spoke soothingly. "All right, Dal. Don't get hot. You did fine and it's just that I'm worried."

The phone rang and Hallahan picked up the receiver, said: "Yeah, he's here. All right." He held his hand over the phone, told Prentice: "It's for you. Sounds like your boy friend."

Prentice took the phone gingerly, as if he were afraid of it. His voice was cautious. "Yeah! Prentice talking. Why sure— been here all evening. Oh it's you, Bruner."

Hallahan, at Prentice's side could hear Bruner's voice, thin, tinny. "Of course you've been there all evening. I know that."

"You would. Why?"

The tinny voice was unpleasant. "I'm going to give you a break. Get that stuff back here and I'll call it off. And five grand and a way out of town."

"And if not?"

"If it's going to be war you'll be the first one hurt. You've got till six in the morning."

"And then what?"

"You can't watch all the time. It'll be just a little while." The phone clicked and Prentice still held the receiver, looking at it stupidly.

Dora asked sharply: "What was it? What did he say?"

"Nothing. He says I got a chance to bring the stuff back before he turns loose his wolf."

"Hooey!"

"And five grand and a way out of town."

"More hooey! It's worth more than five grand to us, Dal. I told you I'd see you were taken care of."

McCready spoke from the side. "Why didn't he tell us that at the house instead of phoning," and Hallahan broke in impatiently: "He was alone at the house and scared to death. Use your head. You guys were just lucky you didn't catch him with a couple of red-hots. He always goes around with at least one side man and sometimes two. He's covered now."

"I don't see any difference. We'd have been rubbed out any time he got a break before." Allen's voice was easy.

"I guess you don't get it. Before the lid blew off he had to take it easy with you because if he worked too rough, the rest of the Force would have butted in, protection or no protection. He's lost his drag and his protection along with it and the Force will lay it on him whether he leaves you alone or not. He'll be just like a mad dog now—his only chance will be to fight it out." Hallahan's voice carried conviction, but Dora said weakly: "You're crazy. He'll quit now."

"All right. We'll see. I don't want this stuff here. I'll send you back to the *Club* with it, Dora, and I'll have a car in front and in back of you. You'd better phone you're coming so you'll be taken care of at that end. What do you think?"

She nodded, picked up the phone and talked briefly, leaned back with a sigh. "It'll be safe there now. I'll have to camp out with a bunch of yeggs to take care of me until what's there can be checked out to whoever owns it."

Hallahan rang a buzzer for his clerk, told him: "I want three cars and a crew for each. Get 'em out in front," and the man saluted, said: "Yes, sir."

"I'll buy a drink before you go, Dora. Watch your step and I hope you spread it so it'll be good that the boys came through on this. Dal may have started it but he got the stuff back for you."

She nodded. "All right, Captain," and turned to Prentice. "The best thing to do, Dal, is for you to make a statement and swear to it, that the article in the *Record* was false and was printed without your knowledge or consent, and we'll have that published in everything but the *Record*. With the libel suits that we can make stick, now that we've got the proof, it'll blow over. But be careful. Hallahan may be right." She lifted her glass, ended: "To a good night's work. Here's luck," and drank.

As she left, Hallahan commented: "She talked sense on that be careful stuff. You watch out. I'm going home so you guys better call it a day too."

McCready, Allen, and Prentice left the office together and Prentice said hopefully: "Maybe the old boy's just thinking up a lot of stuff that *might* happen. Maybe Bruner'll take himself away somewhere."

Allen disagreed. "You're wrong and he's right. There'll be more. You'll see plenty yet."

FULLY A WEEK passed by, unrelieved by any event, then, though both Allen and Prentice were as careful as two men in deadly danger could be—the crash.

Prentice was in their apartment shaving, and as he watched his reflection in the glass the cabinet that held it seemed to fall towards him. He put up his hands to protect his face and dimly felt a blow on the head. He regained consciousness in the emergency hospital with Hallahan at the side of his cot.

Still dazed, he mumbled: "What happened?" and Hallahan told him: "You were bombed. Somebody tossed a pineapple through the door. Didja leave it open?"

Prentice thought for a moment and came a little farther out of the fog that still gripped him. "Don't know. How's Al? Killed?"

"Hell, no! Bruised up and got a partial concussion. He's all right now but he was goofy for a little while."

"How long was I out?"

"That was at ten this morning. It's five now."

Prentice put a hand up to his head, felt it gingerly. "——! That's sore."

"Should be. You had seven stitches taken. You got a break when you were in the bathroom and Al happened to be in the kitchen. That's all that saved either one of you."

"Any line on who done it?"

"Well, of course Bruner's back of it." Hallahan looked nervous and tried to make his voice casual. "Your friend's back in town—he didn't go far away."

"Who?"

"Mulvaney."

Prentice tried to sit up but subsided back on the pillow when the room started to whirl.

Hallahan said anxiously: "Take it easy, Dal. Doc says you got a shock and you'll have to stay here for a couple of days."

"Did you see Mulvaney?"

"No, but I heard about him. Don't worry about that though—there's nothing been started as yet and a Grand Jury'd never return an indictment on that kind of evidence I don't think."

"Is it up before the Grand Jury?"

"Well, Bruner's trying to take it there. He's been to the D.A. and if he makes enough of a fuss the D.A.'ll have to do something. You know that. It won't stick, though."

"Why kid me? What did he say we took? He's got a lot of guts squawking when we took the stuff we did."

"He don't say anything about that of course and he knows you can't. He says you took money and papers. Leases and things. And roughed him up. Mulvaney was with him and told his story. You'll get clear on it, Dal; the D.A.'s trying to play with us."

"Why kid me? I'll be the fall guy sure as hell."

"Now, Dal! You know I wouldn't kid you." Hallahan's voice sounded hearty but Prentice could hear the worried note in it.

The nurse came bustling in, said: "Now, Captain! You know the doctor said Lieutenant Prentice mustn't be bothered."

Prentice complained: "Bothered hell! It's past that," and Hallahan told him: "I called Dora and told her about the blast and she told me about Mulvaney. She told me to tell you not to worry about it though."

"Of course not. I shouldn't worry." Prentice's voice was fretful and he plucked with nervous fingers at the bandage on his head. "I'll be the sap because they'll figure if it comes to a beef they'll have to have a fall guy. I'm the monkey."

"Now, Dal! Don't be like that. Dora won't cross you. I'll tell her to come up and see you."

He left with the nurse, and Prentice tried to sleep, was just dozing when Dora came. He asked abruptly: "Well, am I it?"

She didn't pretend to misunderstand. "Not yet, Dal, and I don't think you will be. I went to the bat for you and they're going to try to call the D.A. off on it."

"What if they can't! Bruner owns that damn' paper and the D.A.'s got to put up a show if Bruner rides him hard enough."

She shrugged. "Time enough to worry about that. I had a hunch about this Mulvaney business all the time. If it wasn't for him you'd be in the clear."

"Yeah! If! Now I'm the patsy."

"Now, Dal! Don't worry! Hallahan said the kid you brought back from New York wants to see you and sent word to the station."

"What about?"

"He wouldn't tell Hallahan. He's out on bail and that's a funny business because it was set high."

"It would be. This state sets bail on a murder rap up in the air so that a guy with dough can get out and buy up a jury in his spare time. They figure if a guy's got money he can afford it and if he ain't got the dough it wouldn't do him any good to be outside. Didja see Al?"

"I'm going to. He's all right though. Just shook up." They chatted about inconsequential things for a few minutes before she left.

Released the following evening and being met by Allen, they idled over to the station, where Hallahan, after inspecting the court plaster decorating Prentice's forehead, handed him a note. "It's from that kid. He's called up a dozen times and finally sent this around by a messenger boy."

Prentice said in some curiosity: "Wonder what he wants? The way he talked he was broke and now he's out on bail."

The note was short. *"Call Thornzoall 9142,"* and was signed *"Johnny Anders."*

Prentice picked up the phone, called the number, and with

his hand over the mouthpiece asked: "Anything more about the Grand Jury?"

"The D.A.'s stalling as much as he can. There's nothing yet."

Prentice said into the phone: "Could I speak to Johnny Anders? All right—call him please." To Hallahan: "Maybe I ought to buy a ticket and use it."

"Don't be a fool, Dal."

A voice said: "This is Johnny Anders," and Prentice asked: "What's the rumble, kid? What about? Why can't you come up here? You sure it's important? Well, all right."

He put the phone down, said fretfully to Hallahan: "This may be a plant I'm running into, I don't know." He tossed Hallahan the note, added: "If it is, look him up. Come on, Al," and sauntered out to the street and called a cab.

He told the driver: "Out North Main to Sichel Street," and climbed inside. His head ached and he said savagely to Allen: "If that little mugg has got me out here to tell me the story of his life again I'll break his damn' neck."

Allen asked curiously: "What's it all about?" and Prentice said: "He wants to see me—says it's something about me and won't meet me at the station or where he lives. We're to go out to a beer joint and meet him there."

"We or you?"

"We." Prentice laughed. "He ain't fool enough to think I'm going around by myself. It's a cinch he's heard about the heat." They sat silent during the rest of the ride.

Leaving the taxi at the corner they started up the dark street, both men watching nervously.

Halfway up the block they came to a decent looking white house, a little detached from its neighbors. Prentice volunteered: "This must be it. He said the first white house."

He knocked at the door and when it was opened, shoved roughly past the man peering out at them. Prentice said gruffly: "We're law but we just want to buy a drink. Be nice and we will." The man nodded, answered: "Fine. We're squared but I didn't know you."

At the little bar they both ordered beer and the barman after serving them looked questioning. "One of you boys named Prentice?"

"Yeah! Me."

The bartender said softly: "There's a back room. First door to the left of the bar. Guy that wants to see you is there." His eyes flicked around the room. "Make it look good though."

Prentice nodded, and followed by Allen, carried his beer over to a table. After a few minutes they idled to the end of the bar and into the back room.

ANDERS WAS WAITING, palpably nervous. He said without preamble: "You're on the spot." Both detectives laughed, and he insisted: "It's no joke."

Prentice sobered. "We know it. I just got out of the hospital when I phoned you."

"Now listen. You know I'm out on bail. You know who put it up and why?"

"Hell, no. How would I know?"

"Well, I was there in the gow and the jailer came up and said my lawyer wanted to see me and I hadn't sent for any lawyer. I goes out and there was a guy named Fielding there. Here's his card."

"I know him. Or of him. He's a shyster ———!"

"Well, he asks me all about it and I didn't tell him much. You said to me to keep quiet until I saw a lawyer and I figured this was a phoney, see. He wants to know about the two raps I had to take, and I told him about one of those. You know I used to be a guard on one of Angie Rocco's beer trucks." His voice held pride and Prentice interrupted hurriedly: "I know. You told me about that on the train." Under his breath he added: "Fifty times."

"Well, I told him about that and how I shot a guy that tried to stick us up and got pulled in by a state man too far up the route for Rocco to spring me. I got five for concealed weapons because we had a tommy."

"Yeah. Then what?"

"Fielding says am I a good shot and I said I was and then comes the stinger. He says 'How bad do you want to get out?' and I say plenty. He says 'Bad enough to do some shooting?' and I says 'Yeah if I'm covered.'"

Prentice grinned, commented: "This is good. You're in the can for one shooting and you're willing to go for another one. You must be a hound for punishment."

The boy smiled back a little uncertainly. "Well, the next thing the jailer comes and says bail was made for me and here's Fielding waiting for me again. We get in a car and go—" He paused dramatically—"to a guy named Bruner's house."

Prentice stiffened. "What!"

"That's right. Bruner's house."

"Go on." Both Prentice and Allen had lost their air of half amusement, were listening intently. Allen got up and went to the door and snapped the lock.

"Well, Bruner says do I remember the copper that brought me back from New York, and I says yes. He asks me if you were a friend of mine and I stalled and said that being in the can for a murder rap looked like I was pals with all the coppers. Then he tells me that he's the guy that made bail for me and if I'd do a job for him he'll clear me on the charge I'm in on. He says he knows where the guy is that really bumped the mugg I'm supposed to've killed and that he'll turn him in. I told you it was a bum rap, you remember that."

"Yeah, I remember."

"Well, I says what have I got to do and he tells me that he hates your guts and that's the job. He says that nobody'd think of me doing it because I'd be out on bail at the time and they'd think I'd be too shaky to pull a job. Get it?"

"I'll say I do. Did you hoist the pineapple at our joint?"

"No, but I know who did. A guy named Jerry Hogan."

"I know him too. One of Bruner's guards."

"That's him. He told me you bounced him on the jaw with a gun once."

"I did. Wish I'd hit the —— harder."

"We were both supposed to camp outside your place and sand you out some night when you came home. The pineapple was Jerry's idea and Bruner was sore as hell about it. He's afraid you'd get scared and not give us a break."

"What are you telling me for? What if the mugg at the bar here talks about you talking to me and it gets back to Bruner?"

"He won't talk. My stepfather runs the bucket but he's off shift now. I figured if I played with you you might dig up this guy I'm framed for. You treated me decent on the train and I want to give you a break and besides—" He hesitated, blurted out: "The way they talk and the way this Jerry acts it looks like a phoney."

"Does, does it? Who's the guy you're framed for?"

"He's named Salvatore Rocco. He's the brother of the guy I worked for. He's in San Francisco."

"How do you know that?"

"Well, Bruner told me this so that I'd know he knew enough to get me out. He said he knew all about it."

"Salvatore Rocco, huh. I know him. Listen kid, go out and give us a chance to talk this over. Come back in a minute and bring us a couple of glasses of beer when you do."

He left, and Prentice asked: "What do you think, Al? Does it sound like a stall?"

"It's phoney all right, but maybe Bruner just figures the kid is dumb. He's right at that—did you hear the damn' fool brag about how good a hood he is? He acts like it takes brains to make the can."

"Shall we give it a play? I remember the punk kept saying it was a phoney rap he was dragged back on and that he didn't have no dough so that part about bail checks. San Francisco 'll pick up Rocco for us and we can keep that quiet until the blow-off."

"How d'ya suppose Bruner picked the kid?"

"Probably just happened. The kid was in for a shooting and probably bragged all over the jail-house about how good a gunman he is. He's just made to order for Bruner."

The boy came back and Prentice told him honestly: "Listen, Kid. How's this? I'll get this Rocco pulled in San Francisco and if your story checks that'll clear you. Will you play ball with us if I do that?"

"What do you want me to do?"

"We'll give you and this Jerry a break but I want you to tip us when the play's supposed to come up and keep out of it when it does. Act just like you're going through with it but duck when the action starts. If we can nail this Jerry right, we might be able to tie Bruner in with this frame."

"Yeah, and then I'll have to appear as a witness." The boy's voice showed evident fear, and Prentice said soothingly: "Now, Johnny, not unless we had him nailed to the cross. The chances are we won't be that lucky. I won't ask you to do a thing there'd be a kick-back on. As far as Bruner'll know, the San Francisco police just picked Rocco up on suspicion and he confessed and that cleared you."

"What if he don't confess?"

"Don't let that worry you. If he's guilty he'll talk. San Francisco's a mick town and those coppers are old fashioned. They hate secrets. He'll talk." He looked suspiciously at the boy. "You ain't kidding me about this Rocco, are you? Sure he's guilty?"

"—— yes! Don't you remember I told you on the train I was framed and Bruner told me just how I was."

"This'll clear you, then, if it goes through. You just leave a message saying when and whereabouts we're on the spot, and when the shooting starts keep out. We've got an even break that way. That plain?"

"Uh-huh."

The two detectives started for the door but Anders called them back. "I just remembered. They're going to have some guy named Mulvaney up before the Grand Jury in a couple of days and try to get an indictment against you for something. I heard Fielding and Bruner talk about it. Didja know about that? They already seen the D.A."

Prentice laughed. "We heard something about it. We'll stick

close to the station and wait for something to happen. You can get us there."

"Well, I might have to get you in a hurry."

"Station's only place you can reach us."

"I'll let you know some way. I'm supposed to go to Jerry's hotel tonight and get the dope. He's staying at the *St. Regis*—some class, huh?"

THEY LEFT THE beer joint and Allen commented thoughtfully: "Bruner sticks by his boys, at that. Jerry's supposed to do work and they'll have the kid there to take the rap. And with him being out on bail he'd be a cinch to take it."

"I figured that. I remember Rocco was a pal of Bruner's. Chances are, Bruner framed the kid on this trouble—at least helped on it. Here's a kid not over twenty-three at the most and in the racket and proud of it. If we get him clear on this Rocco deal it'll be our boy scout act—our good deed."

At the station they drafted a wire to the San Francisco police, giving them a full description of the wanted Salvatore Rocco, and asking them to keep the arrest secret when it was made. Prentice also sent a private wire to a Sergeant Donovan of his acquaintance there, telling him some of the details of the case to insure Rocco's confession after he was picked up. He smiled wickedly at Allen as the messenger boy took the blanks, said: "And poor Rocco'd wish we had him instead of Donovan. That Donovan's a ——! I think we'd better sit pretty close around here and keep off the street. We ain't got an apartment to go to."

Allen said sadly: "And there was damn' near a full case of good whiskey in the kitchen," and they mourned their loss.

There was no message and about twelve they went to a nearby

hotel for the night. About three the following afternoon the tele-phone rang for Prentice, and Anders' voice said hurriedly: "You're to be tailed out of the station to wherever you stay at nights now and we're to give you the works in the lobby in the morning."

The phone clicked before Prentice could ask for more details. Both men stalled about the station and made plans until five, when Hallahan came in. He looked worried, snapped out: "Glad you're here. The Grand Jury returned an indictment against you that's supposed to be secret. The D.A.'s supposed to try to dig up more against you, but he tipped me ten minutes after. They had Mulvaney and Bruner up. I saw Mac on the way in and he's worried stiff—talking about getting out of town."

Prentice asked bluntly: "Should we?"

"Hell, no! Sit tight. That's what I told him. Maybe somebody can get to Mulvaney with more dough than Bruner's paying him, and the trial won't be for at least a month, and lots can happen in that time. Maybe Mulvaney'll change his mind, and without him there isn't a thing against you. The bail'll be set low—the D.A.'ll see to that."

"We got a fat chance." Prentice's voice was bitter. "We get the stuff for the big boys that gets them out of a jam but they won't lay any important dough on the line to get us out of one. Hell, no!"

Without telling the worried Hallahan anything about Johnny Anders' message, they left, going to a different hotel, one with a lobby they had selected as being best for the coming events. They registered and had dinner sent to their room, debated whether they should call Hallahan for help in the morning and finally deciding against this on the grounds of possibly arousing suspicion in the mind of Jerry.

They had figured out that the only possible way of procuring evidence—evidence strong enough to use as a club to force Jerry Hogan to turn against Bruner—would be to let the shooting actually start, then trust to luck to see them through it. And also trust to luck that Jerry wouldn't be too badly hurt to talk.

They left a call for eight o'clock and went to sleep with little discussion of what the morning might bring—both men having a tremendous confidence in themselves, a confidence perhaps justified by what they had already survived.

After breakfast in the morning, they went cautiously out of their room, and disdaining the elevator, walked down the stairs. Instead of going clear to the lobby, they stopped at the mezzanine floor, and from its little balcony could see Jerry and the nervous Anders, seated facing the door of the elevator, adjoining the foot of the stairs.

Prentice whispered: "Probably got a car outside for a getaway. How'll we work it?"

"You stay here and I'll crash the stairs. When he sees me he'll start it and you cover him from here. We got a two-way shot at him that way. How about it?"

Prentice grinned. "Fine. Except that I'll crash the stairs."

Without further words and without giving Allen a chance to protest, he stepped to the stairs and started down, but met two women when a few feet from the bottom. The women were still in Jerry's sight when they looked up and saw Prentice, gun out and tiptoeing towards them. They promptly screamed and scuttled back into the lobby.

The alert Jerry didn't know what had happened to cause their fright, but his movement was instinctive. He was on his feet and partially protected by a pillar before Allen could say a word, and when Prentice, seeing there was no chance for surprise, ran down the last few steps to the lobby, Jerry fired twice.

Prentice cried out, and half fell, half slid to the floor, dropping his gun as he did so. Allen shot once from the balcony, then turned and raced for the stairs. Jerry came out from the shelter of the pillar and shot once again at Prentice; then Johnny Anders stepped to Jerry's side and, with the muzzle of his gun not over a foot away, shot him three times as fast as he could pull the trigger.

Allen reached the foot of the stairs as Jerry fell, and seeing Anders' smoking gun and thinking he had shot at Prentice, raised his own. Prentice cried out again and jerked him by the foot and Allen fell on top of him, his gun crashing as he went down, the bullet missing Anders and breaking the front window.

The lobby was in pandemonium. The two women had retreated to the clerk's desk and were both screaming; the door was jammed with a frantic mob trying to get out; the clerk was shouting "Police!" Anders was walking from the body of Jerry to Prentice and so excited that he paid not the least attention to Allen, who was trying to untangle himself from the prostrate Prentice and shouting, "Drop that gun!"

A traffic officer shouldered his way through the crowd at the door and seeing both Anders and Allen with guns in their hands, shouted: "You're under arrest!"

Allen dropped his gun at this and tried to lift Prentice to his feet and Prentice promptly passed out and slumped in Allen's arms. The traffic man jammed his own gun in Anders' back and jerking him around wrested from him the gun he unknowingly held and cried out: "Who started this mess?"

The only cool person there, was a very blonde and vacuous looking telephone girl, calmly watching the fracas and plugging in an emergency call for the police. The traffic policeman, after a quick glance at the body of Jerry, called to her: "Send for an ambulance," and she answered easily: "I did that when the shooting first started. It should be here by now, Mister."

Hallahan arrived at the same time as the ambulance, the call having gone through to the homicide department, and with his help the riot was finally straightened out, Prentice, with a slug through his shoulder and another through the fleshy part of his leg, again going to the emergency hospital, and Jerry, who had died on his feet, being taken to the morgue.

In order to protect Anders from any suspicion on Bruner's part of having double-crossed him, he was taken by Allen and Hallahan to the station and booked for attempted murder, though Allen explained to him that the charge was only for appearances' sake.

WITH ANDERS OUT of the way, Hallahan scored Allen bitterly. He walked up and down his office, head down and cursing. "You ——— damn' fools! Deliberately let a play like that come up and work it yourselves. You're crazy!" He stopped in front of Allen, glowered at him. "And you leaving the balcony and running down the stairs. And going screwy when you got down. It's a wonder Dal wasn't killed. You made a fine botch of covering him, didn't you? What was the idea?"

Allen answered defensively: "Well, I couldn't see this hood from the balcony. He was behind a post and I took a crack at his arm and missed and figured I'd have to rush him."

"And get yourself shot along with Dal! You were taking a chance with the kid, too. If it hadn't been for him— What made you go off your nut when you got there?"

"Well, the whole damn' thing had gone sour and I got rattled. We thought—"

"Thought hell! You can't! And here's Dal in the hospital with an indictment staring him in the face."

"Me, too."

"Oh, damn you! You can take a powder if it gets too tough and Dal can't."

Allen rose with dignity. "I'm not going to stand—" but Halla-han waved him back in his chair, said fretfully: "Oh, shut up and sit down. Can't a man even talk to you without—"

He reached for the phone and called the emergency hospital, told the clerk: "Ask the doctor attending Lieutenant Prentice to call me when he gets through with his examination." He whirled on Allen again. "If you guys get out of this will you remember for —— sake that you're not the whole police force?" Allen looked sullen and he ended a little kindlier: "Dal and I've worked together for a good many years and he's hit bad."

The phone jangled and he answered: "Yeah, this is Halla-han. How is he?" The worried look gradually faded from his face as he listened and his voice was almost pleasant when he turned back to Allen. "Doc says his shoulder is broken but he don't look for any trouble. They're going to move him to the Sacred Heart hospital and he can't have company for a couple of days." His voice again resumed its fretful note. "You'd better see Hymie and get it fixed for bail for him. This'll break quick now."

PRENTICE'S FIRST VISITOR was Allen, and with him, Hymie Lefkowitz, bail broker. Allen came in smiling widely and told the wan Prentice: "Well, it's started. Five grand for bail and Hymie puts it up for only two-fifty apiece for us."

Prentice scowled at the natty little Jew. "Of course you're losing money."

"I give you my word, Dal, I—"

"Oh, nerts! Save it! What's new, Al? Something's happened, I can tell."

"San Francisco picked up Rocco and he cracked about the kid getting framed. How's that? The kid's out and the way he acts you'd think that you're the king."

Prentice kept his scowl. "Nice for him. It don't help us."

Hymie broke in volubly. "They treat you good here, Dal?"

"Lousy! Nothing to eat and less to drink. What are we charged with?"

Allen said easily: "Robbery with violence is all. We're suspended until it comes up. Hallahan had to. They give us a break."

They left after promising to stop the next day and the next visitors were Hallahan and Anders. The boy was jubilant. "I got out of that all right, Mr. Prentice. The charge has been dropped and the bail given back."

Prentice cut in with a curt: "Heard about it." To Hallahan: "Looks bad."

Hallahan said gloomily: "Does at that, Dal. I called Dora last night and she promised to do something." His voice sounded embarrassed. "You know, Dal, I had to suspend you for a while till this is over. Commissioner made a fuss."

"Oh, sure— A lot Dora'll do. I guess I slipped at last." He

failed to cheer up any during the rest of the short visit and was still downhearted when Dora was announced.

He said harshly to her: "Looks like I'm it."

She shook her head and handed him a copy of the afternoon paper, folded back to a small notice on the second page. It was brief—*Gangster's Body Found*—and informed Prentice that one Pat Mulvaney had been found shot to death along a side road leading out of Magna City and that robbery was apparently the motive as Mulvaney's pockets were inside out and empty.

Prentice read it through twice and looked up, his eyes questioning, and Dora shook her head. "You're wrong, Dal. We paid him off last night and he signed an affidavit that what he had testified was false. He was going to sneak out of town but Bruner must've got wise and spotted him." Her voice was serious. "He's crazy, Dal. A killing like this don't help him. He's off his nut, just can't take a beating."

Prentice shook his head. "You're wrong, Dora. He's taking one—and that's the trouble. The kid's out and his friend Rocco's in and Al and I are in the clear and your crowd has got the stuff back he's been blackmailing them with, so he's lost his protection. He'll be out in the open now—and no way to cover up." He thought, and his frown gradually changed to a smile—then to a whole-hearted laugh.

Dora asked sharply: "What's the joke," and he answered, grinning widely, "I just thought what Hymie's going to say when he finds out he don't get a chance to chisel two and a half off me. And of Al when he gets thinking about already having given Hymie his."

Hospital Case

Dal Prentice couldn't figure himself a
hospital case when action was going on

DAL PRENTICE STOOD at the top of wide hospital steps, an interne half supporting him. He stared down at the police car and growled at the man in the white coat beside him: "I'm all right! Go back and peddle your papers, butcher."

The interne grinned widely. "Now, Lieutenant, is that nice? If you fell on these steps, I'd have to listen to you cry for another month. That leg isn't so strong yet." He helped the burly detective down to the car and said: "Be seeing you."

Prentice shook hands.

"Like hell you will. I'll have you down to the station for killing a patient before you get me up here as one. Be good." He turned to the dark, lean-faced man driving the car: " 'Lo, Al. Get a good look at Doc here. There'll be a general alarm out for him any time."

The dark man grinned: "Sure! Get in the car an' shut up." He raced the motor with a heavy foot.

The surgeon leaned in the front seat.

"You remember that case of Scotch you promised, Lieutenant. I can use it all right."

Prentice nodded, waved his hand as the police Buick pulled away from the curb with a soft clash of gears. Allen, the driver, jeered: "You're free with Scotch whiskey, I'll say that. Why not buy a case for me?"

"Now, Al! He's a good guy. He used t' come in the room and talk to me a lot. —— knows you didn't break your neck coming up."

Allen had averaged a call a day at the hospital during the time his partner had been there with a bullet in his leg, but he let the slur pass. Making conversation, he said idly: "There was a new one today. Some mugg caught his wife with another guy and the damn' fool killed him. I'd have made him a gift."

"You would!" Prentice waved a big hand. "How's my boy friend—Bruner, the b——? Quite a comedown for a guy that was riding the city a short while ago; now just a common mugg in a racket, working it like everyone else."

"Well, you pulled him out in the open, showed him up and he had to quit being the political shot, the big-hearted citizen that was taking his under cover."

"He shouldn't 'a had my side kick killed," Prentice growled. "He could 've been payin' us our graft and ridin' nice himself. Well, what's he doing?"

"Hasn't done a thing. Layin' low. Say—What th' hell!"

The Buick was doing a smooth forty in the outside lane of travel, but a van, Magna City Furniture Co. painted on its looming side, was pulling even with the squad car and of necessity was well out past the middle of the road. Allen snarled: "Th' damn' fool! Trying t' pass a police car like that—" and stuck his head and one hand out the side, motioning the truck-driver back.

He snapped out of the corner of his mouth to Prentice: "Kick on that siren, Dal. I'll take this —— down if—" He drew his head and arm back suddenly and weaved the Buick's snout towards the curb as the truck pulled ahead half a length and crowded them.

Prentice cried out: "Hey!" The Buick hit the curb on two wheels and tipped on its side and threw him half across the sidewalk. The truck stopped, turned a little sidewise.

Prentice saw the muzzle of a tommy gun stick out from the truck cab and jerked at the gun under his arm. As the gun came clear he shouted to Allen who was caught under the wheel: "Stay there, Al!" and started to crawl towards the shelter of an entry way leading into a store. Half-way he knew he couldn't make it and as he saw the machine-gun tilt towards him he stopped creeping and fired at the head of the man holding it.

On his third shot he saw the head drop back, and the tommy gun just beginning its stutter, dropped to the street. Prentice resumed his crawl and gained the protection of the entry. The truck pulled away and Prentice emptied his gun at the back tires and the truck rear end, aided by Allen, who had managed to extricate himself. The tires weren't the puncturable sort and the truck careened around the corner. Allen ran to Prentice, who was cursing viciously. He asked: "How bad, Dal?"

Prentice stopped swearing long enough to say "The bum leg," and then went on cursing.

Allen ran into the street, commandeered a car that had stopped at sight of the wrecked Buick, helped Prentice into the car and ordered: "French Hospital! Back six blocks." He asked anxiously: "Hurt pretty bad, Dal?"

The driver swung the car in the middle of the block. Allen flashed his badge at the driver and told him: "Open it up. You're all right on traffic."

They made the six long blocks in half that many minutes. Helped by Allen and the commandeered driver, Prentice went up the steps—and met the interne who had seen him out. He said weakly: "You win," and slumped in a faint.

FROM THE SAME room he had left, he welcomed Allen

the next day. Propped up on pillows, he grinned sourly at his: "How's it, Dal?" and grunted: "So Bruner ain't doing nothing, huh? I'm back here for another bit. And that damned grinning ape of an interne I-told-you-soing me all over the place."

Allen attempted to cheer him. "The Doc says you ain't hurt, Dal. It just opened up the leg a little and you bled some."

"Oh I suppose I'll get over it. And get smacked down again." He returned to his complaint. "I thought you said Bruner was laying low. If he is, I'd hate like hell to see him get action. No one I know of but him is out for me, or would pull it that quick."

"We thought he was, Dal." Allen's voice sounded worried. "I don't get this last. I knew he was out for us but I didn't think he'd have guts enough to try a blast out on a main street. We

found the truck five blocks away. That ought to make you feel better."

"Why should it? Fix this damn' pillow under my back, will you?"

"Well, there was a guy in the cab with his left eye shot out. And the back of his head. The mugg that had the ta-ta gun."

"What about the driver?"

"The finger's out for him." Allen pulled the pillow straight behind Prentice's heavy shoulders—shoulders covered with the cotton hospital dress. "We got a description from five or six witnesses that saw him lam out of the truck and we know who it is."

"Who?"

"Carlo Russo. You know him."

"Yeah! The hood they call Blackie. Sometimes they call him Wop."

"That's him. He's a hoppy. We'll get him easy."

The nurse came in, said: "Lieutenant, there's a Miss Madison to see you. I told her you had a visitor but she said you'd see her just the same."

"Sure!" He told Allen: "Dora's been up pretty often. Sent me stuff, too. She's nice peoples." He said to the woman who came in the door: "H'lo, Dora. Looks like here's where I spend the rest of my life."

"Squawk! Better here than on a slab."

Dora was small, dark, quick. She ran the *Commercial Club*, the unofficial seat of the Magna City government—and did her share of the governing. Her voice was worried as she said: "I didn't come up here to pat you on the back, you damn' fool. I came up to do you some good. And me."

Allen said sardonically: "What'll it cost, Dora?"

Prentice grinned. "Now, Al. Dora wouldn't pick up a dollar if it cried and asked her to." He asked Dora: "Is this a rib? Or did you sneak a pint in or what? I'd go for that. Or is it a secret?"

Dora looked at Allen sharply, then back to Prentice. "If I tell you smart coppers something, something the whole force hasn't found out, will you work it out my way?"

Prentice said: "Sure!" He bent shrewd eyes on Dora, shook his head at Allen who started to speak. "Go ahead with the filth."

"Hold your breath then. I know where the greaseball you're looking for is. The mugg that drove the truck that put you to bed again."

Allen stood up, growled: "Nice work, keed. I'll get a squad and—"

"You'll raise hell." Dora faced him, her eyes snapping." You told me that—"

"Sure! But, Dora. We get the mugg and we can—"

"You can go to hell." She turned her back on him, said to Prentice: "How bad was it this time, Dal?"

"I just landed crooked on the game leg when I fell and it opened up a bit. I could use it now if the Doc'd say so. As long as I was easy on it."

"That's fine." Still ignoring Allen, she sat on the bed. "When you get out come and see me." She flashed an ugly glance at Allen. "Leave the ape in the zoo."

Allen said apologetically: "Now Dora. Don't be that way. Play it out the way you want to. I'll be good."

"You sure?" She stared at him. "I don't want to get a friend of mine a funeral. Or if that don't mean anything, I don't want to star in one myself."

"Okey, keed! I'll say and do nothing. How's that?"

"Well, then, listen. Is that door closed?"

Allen went to the door, threw it open and peered down the hall. "Okey!"

"Well, you know I used to—" She hesitated a moment and Prentice said helpfully: "Sure! We know."

"Well, then—I had a girl working for me and she took over the place when I quit the racket. She phoned me at the Club a while ago and I met her and she told me one of her girls had been getting a big play from this fellow Russo you're looking for. And that the girl goes out last night after she got a call and don't come back."

Prentice whistled softly. His eyes had a far-away look. "If we could spot the gal—"

"Will you shut that big Irish mouth? I know where the gal is. Peggy said that she saw a rent receipt from the *Miramar* apartments. Now does that make sense?"

"All we'll have to do is dynamite in and take him out."

"And have to kill him doing it."

"What of it? We ain't friendly. I wouldn't fret."

"I would. Wait a minute before you crack wise. He ties in with something else. Bruner rowed with his secretary but before this guy left town he cleaned up a few little odds and ends for himself. Along with Bruner's safe. He come to me with a bunch of stuff that'll fry his boss. He wanted ten grand but it was all clear profit and he took five C's after I pointed out that if he didn't get out of town quick, money wouldn't do him no good. Bruner missed the stuff and thought the secretary come to you instead of me and that was why the blow-off. This only happened yesterday morning. Does it make sense?"

"You high! You mean you really got the nuts on Bruner? It's no rib?"

"If you keep smart I have. But Russo's got to be taken alive or we ain't got a thing. Wait'll you hear this."

"Go on."

"You remember when Graves, the contractor that used to do all the main street work, was found in his car?"

"Yeah! He had three holes in his belly, if I remember right."

"Well, Bruner killed him."

"Don't guess, Dora. This is important." Prentice was sitting straighter in bed, his eyes flaring in interest, and Allen was watching as closely. "There was a hell of a rumble on that and we never could turn up a thing."

"I'm not guessing. I know. It was all there—if you could read it. If you could figure it out."

"But proof! That's what it takes."

"There was a big manila envelope labeled Graves. Inside was

a lot of letters he had written Bruner. There was a receipt for five grand from this same Russo you're looking for and another from a man named Bruckner for the same amount."

"I killed Bruckner when he shot a cop."

"I know. Bruner started that mess too. Well, besides the receipts there was a statement that they witnessed Graves' death. There was one from Bruner's butler too, but no receipt for dough. It was all written out pretty and sworn to, that Graves drew a gun on Bruner during an argument, that Bruner tried to take it away from him, and that in the struggle for the gun it had gone off and killed Graves."

"Why would he keep that stuff?"

"My gawd, Dal, use your head! It's a phoney, can't you see. During the struggle the gun wouldn't go off *three* times and shoot him, would it? I can see it as plain as if I was there. Graves and Bruner were alone, probably in Bruner's house, and Bruner went screwy and killed him. Instead of waiting and hiring it done he must have lost his head."

"I can see that. Go on."

"These two hoods probably walked in right after it. I can't figure he'd be fool enough to send for them. They were smart enough to get some dough out of it. Probably they took the body out and drove it away in Graves' car."

"What about the butler?"

"He's still working for Bruner."

"And Bruckner's dead. I still can't see. What good's this stuff?"

"What if you pick up Russo with an attempted murder over him? What if you get the butler and sweat him? Would they stick with Bruner or save themselves? With you holding this stuff, Bruner hasn't a thing to back up his story. Now do you see why Russo can't be killed?"

"Yeah!" He thought a moment. "What's the angle you got figured?"

"I'd give him the stuff back. I know you won't."

Prentice's face darkened. His lower lip clamped over the upper. His voice sounded nasty. "You're right there, baby. I won't." He looked down at his body, under the clothes. "You're—right—I—won't."

"You'd be better off. You've got to get to this Russo before he does. A dead man can't do it. If Bruner finds him first he'll be a stiff and a stiff can't talk."

"I can't figure why he hasn't got 'em out of the way already."

"I can. He's figured you'd be out of the picture. He's that sure."

"I can get out tomorrow all right. Doc says that I—"

"That might be too late. I've got a better stunt. Allen and some other copper could do it as well as you and Al, if it works out."

PRENTICE, ON THE bed, was facing the door. Dora, sitting on the side of the bed, was facing him, and Allen was standing by the window, turned partly towards Prentice and partly towards the door. Dora started: "I could get hold of—" and stopped, staring curiously at Prentice's face.

She turned her head slowly towards the door, following Prentice's gaze, saw the knob move slightly, and asked: "What is it?" Allen gripped her shoulder, whispered: "Go ahead and talk. But don't say anything." She nodded, continued: "What is this guy that killed his wife going to get, Dal? Life or fried?

I suppose you heard about it?" Her voice was still easy but her face was paling.

Allen slid a gun from under his arm as she spoke and took two noiseless strides to the side of the door. He stood there waiting, nodding encouragement to the frightened woman.

Prentice answered casually: "I read it. Life probably instead of the medal he's got coming. She was throwing a few curves and he caught one."

"But he had no business to go ahead and shoot," Dora argued. "It might not have been the man's fault at all."

"If it was some places he'd get by on this unwritten law stuff. But I don't know here. These Magna City juries are so damned narrow-minded. If I was on the jury I'd—"

The door swung open with a rush and two men stepped inside, past Allen, who was covered by the door when it opened. The last man in closed the door without looking behind him. Both men carried stubby automatics, the one held by the first swinging from Prentice to Dora while the second man replaced his in a coat pocket. The first snapped: "No noise or I blast. The window's on a fire-escape and a car's waiting below, so figure it out."

Dora shrank away from the bed and Prentice, her hand pressing her dress against her heart, and the second man snarled: "You, too, twist! Be smart! You're all right if you behave."

Prentice, staring into the gun muzzle, said calmly enough: "What is it then, you heel? You can't get away with this."

The second man stepped even with his partner, reached in his hip pocket and produced a blackjack. He balanced it tentatively, started to say: "This—"

Allen stepped behind the two and crashed his gun against

the head of the man covering Prentice. The blow was struck with all his strength—the man slumped back against him as he fell instead of forward—and in the second it took him to get untangled the man with the blackjack took a running dive through the window and out.

Prentice was trying to free himself from the bed covering—Dora screamed shrilly once—and Allen pushed the unconscious gunman clear and plunged towards the window. He leaned out and shot once, there were two answering shots from outside, and the window splintered into fragments around him. He jerked back hastily and Prentice said: "Nice, Al, nice! There *was* a car."

Allen holstered the gun he held in his hand and bent over the man on the floor, but as he did the door opened and the interne dashed in followed by a nurse. He stared at Prentice, half out of bed, at Dora standing against the wall, white-faced, then at Allen and the man on the floor. He stammered: "I heard—heard—" then shoved Allen away and knelt by the man on the floor.

While he made his examination they heard more feet pound in the hall and a uniformed policeman pulled up short in the open door. He too stared at the man on the floor, gasped: "I heard shots and—"

"Got here in time to phone for me. I'm Prentice, Homicide Squad," Prentice interjected. "Call Homicide, get Captain Hallahan and tell him I said to send up a car. Tell him two men besides the driver. Got it?" He watched the uniformed man's salute, asked the doctor: "Is he dead?"

The doctor shook his head. "Can't tell yet. His skull is fractured for sure and I'll have to lift a piece of bone. He may not come out of it."

Allen said: "Don't waste your time, Doc. He'd hang anyway. I busted him as hard as I could. If he comes to I'll buy you that case of Scotch instead of Dal."

The nurse came to her feet from beside the doctor and without a word walked to Allen and slapped him in the face. There was a moment's silence, with the doctor staring up from the floor. Then Prentice said: "Brute!" and laughed, and the nurse said stormily: "The man is seriously hurt. Have you no decency?"

Allen said: "Sorry!" and felt his cheek. "You see, Miss, the man was planning on killing Lieutenant Prentice in cold blood and I didn't feel much sympathy at the time. Of course now—" He bowed.

Dora said: "Quit clowning. D'ya suppose that man who got away heard anything? If he did, I got to get back to the *Club* before Bruner does. He hasn't a thing to lose no matter what he does. He can fry only once."

Prentice said with decision: "Doc, let somebody else take care of that mugg and fix me up so's I can get out o' here."

"Lieutenant, you're in no shape to leave."

"No shape to stay here now."

The doctor pursed his lips. "It's your responsibility. If you're careful, I don't suppose it will kill you."

"I'm always careful." He winked at Dora. "Ain't I keed? Who saw the door open?"

The man on the floor was taken away on a stretcher and Prentice's leg was rebandaged in such a way he could yet use it. The doctor warned: "Watch that leg. Another stunt like that of yesterday won't help."

"That's why I'm going now. To stop all this and that."

CAPTAIN HALLAHAN CAME with the squad car. Short, stocky, white-haired, he combined thirty years of police experience with a certain knowledge of every crook, every racket and racketeer, in Magna City. He scorned politics and politicians and while forced to use them he did so grudgingly—so grudgingly that the Commissioner's job, his by all rights, was given to a man notoriously inefficient and incompetent. He had protected Prentice and Allen a score of times in the past and they had full confidence in his co-operation.

Prentice told him as he came in the door: "Hell to pay! You bring the car yourself?"

"Uh-huh! What's up?"

"Plenty!" He turned to Dora. "Any reason for not going to your bucket?"

"None that I know."

Hallahan asked again: "What's it all about?"

Prentice slid the crutch under his shoulder, took a pair of shaky steps. "Tell you at the *Club*. We want to get down there and quick."

He hobbled to the police car with the doctor's help. Allen and Hallahan keeping a watchful eye out for possible interference. They drove to Dora's *Commercial Club*, dropping Allen at the central station on the way.

Once inside the apartment Dora reserved for her own use, Prentice told her: "You get the dope and bring it here. I'll tell the Cap what the score is while you dig it up. Then you tell us what you got figured out."

He explained to Hallahan what Dora had discovered and Hallahan swore softly. "We had a shakeup in the department over that murder," he said. "Graves was big. And to think we might have had Bruner on the big charge all the time he was making us this grief."

"Might have had is right. You couldn't have proved it."

"If we could only prove it now. He's caused more sin, sorrow, and suffering than any ten men in town." Hallahan's tone was fiercely hopeful.

Dora came into the room with the envelope labeled "Graves," and they studied the statements and the receipts together.

Hallahan said heavily: "By ——! Dora, I think you're right. I'll be eternally damned if I don't think a jury would too."

He reached for the papers to replace them in the envelope, but Prentice held them, said: "And then what?" He stared up at Dora's intent face. "I think I'd better call him up and tell him I've got them. That hood that got away at the hospital has got to him by now, that's a cinch, and told him you were up there with me. He might put two and two together and work on you next. I'd better keep 'em and tell him about it. That'll clear you. What do you think?"

She said doubtfully, "I don't know," but Hallahan broke in: "It's the only thing to do, Dora. If he thinks you got 'em he'll lay off Dal and you'll be it. Why should you take the rumble? I can keep 'em at the station till we need them—I got a box in the property safe that's okey."

"The only thing is, will he stick around or take a powder after he knows his number's up?" she questioned uncertainly.

Hallahan told her: "He'll probably stick until he finds out who gets to Russo first. He isn't just going to quit."

Prentice reached for the phone, paused undecidedly. "If we didn't do anything about it until we picked up Russo it'd be better. We could put a guard on Dora. He wouldn't really be sure she was in it. This gal you talked to wouldn't be advertising around that she tipped you, would she, Dora?"

"Not hardly."

He asked Hallahan: "What do you think? It'll be short and sweet. If we don't get Russo, Bruner will."

Hallahan shrugged, looked at Dora. He said slowly: "Leave it up to you, Dora. You can play it safe or take a chance. I'd never ask you to."

Dora hesitated a moment before answering. The memory of the two men breaking in the hospital room still whitened her face. "I'll take a chance once. It can't be more than a couple of days, one way or the other."

Prentice nodded and smiled at her, called Headquarters on the phone. He asked for the Homicide Department, then with his hand over the mouthpiece suggested: "What about picking up the butler now? They could go right up and get him and call us back here. What do you think?" He said into the phone: "Wait a minute."

Hallahan considered. "We could hold him as a material witness and see he don't get out on bail. It's a protection for him and we've got to have him and a chance to work on him anyway. Tell 'em to go ahead."

Prentice gave brief orders over the phone, hung up and turned back to them. "They'll go up right away. I sent Peterson because he knows the butler. McCready and Blair'll be down here inside of ten minutes. McCready's a good head and Blair's the best of the rest." He added modestly: "Except Al and myself, of course."

Hallahan snorted. "That's understood! What about yourself? You need a guard yourself, it seems to me. I'll have half the force playing guard to the other half if this keeps up."

Dora suggested: "He could stay here. He wouldn't be any good for the stunt that I thought out for Russo anyway."

"*You* thought out for Russo! Since when did you join the force?" Hallahan looked curious and Prentice explained: "We promised Dora that we'd make the pinch the way she wanted it. That is, if we can."

"You can all right." Her voice sounded confident. "It's a cinch."

"Sure! They all are," Hallahan growled.

"See if it isn't. The girl that's got my old spot will do anything I tell her to do. You get that part of it clear in your mind and you'll see why the stunt'll work. Take a couple of men and slide 'em into the *Miramar* without a lot of fuss. Then just have 'em keep out of sight but where they can watch Russo's apartment."

"That ought to be easy."

"Then Peggy'll go in and up to the apartment and knock on the door. Russo or the twist will ask who it is and she'll tell them and they'll let her in. The gal will know her voice so they won't think it's a bum play. The chances are though that either Russo will open the door with a gun in his hand or that the gal will with Russo covering her. If your men try to crash then they'd have to kill him. If Peggy goes in and makes a stall about wanting the kid to go back to the bucket why he won't think anything about it. Then when she gets a chance to, or gets ready to go, she'll open the door and your men will be waiting right outside and they can grab him cold before he's got a chance or time to make a play. How's that for a stunt?"

"It might work. What if he goes to the door with a gun when she leaves?"

"It'll be a rumble. You wouldn't be any worse off than if you tried to crash it. We've got to take that chance. If I've got that bird figured right, it's the only chance there is to take him alive. He'll know he'd get the works for trying to kill a copper and fight if he gets any break at all."

Hallahan asked thoughtfully: "Are you sure this friend of yours will go for the shot? She'll be all wet with the rest of the hustlers from there on."

"She'll do it for me," Dora said confidently. "She owes me more than that and besides, I got her out when she jammed once and she knows I could help her back into another one. I can still pull a little weight."

"We might be able to fix it so neither Russo or his girl friend would know she was in the play. McCready and Al here, could do the stunt and fix up an act for her to put on when they take the hood. Neither of them would talk and she could squawk a bit and they could take her along and then you could bail her out or something like that. I could have the case killed and your bail returned in a couple of days after that. We could make it look pretty good—book her in and everything."

"She'll go through with it one way or the other. If she could be squared I'd like it but she's got it made if it don't work. She could leave town now and not have to walk."

Prentice complained fretfully: "I wanted to be the one to get Bruner. Damn this leg of mine. I'm out of it just when we get action."

"What's the difference, Dal, as long as he's got?" Hallahan soothed him. "As soon as this hood's taken we'll run him in and try to keep it under cover until we get enough out of him to warrant picking Bruner up. It won't be any trouble to have him bound over if those two muggs talk." He added thoughtfully:

"They'll talk when they see they have to. McCready can go with Al just as well as not if you stay here. You can still shoot if there's trouble and you and Dora can tell dirty stories while you wait for somebody to shoot at."

The phone jangled and Dora picked it up, said: "Miss Madison speaking. Yes, just a minute." She handed the phone to Prentice, heard him say: "That's fine, Pete. Just wait." He muffled the mouthpiece, told Hallahan: "They got him all right. No beef at all. Pete says that when he rang the bell the bozo opened the door himself and they just reached out and took him. It was a cinch."

"That's a break." Hallahan's voice showed relief. "I was afraid Bruner might have got an idea and wrecked him."

"What about having him brought here? He's just a witness and we could talk to him here as well as not."

Hallahan vetoed this instantly. "Hell, no! What if he don't want to talk and we got to get rough. Tell Pete to sink him."

"That's right too." Prentice spoke into the phone. "Listen, Pete! Book him as a material witness and put him in the hole. There'll be no bail so don't worry about a beef. Hallahan will be up pretty soon." He looked sadly at Hallahan, asked: "If he's stubborn, d'ya think you can make him talk, Cap? I know I could."

"Think you could?" Hallahan grinned.

Prentice stared down at his fist, absently closed it. "Oh, I could, all right. There's ways."

Hallahan told him: "And I know most of 'em. Those I don't, Al does." He stood up as an attendant knocked and told Dora two officers were waiting in the hall. "Al and I might as well get at it. Dora, you get this friend of yours here right away and frame it. I'd be careful where I went though and keep the boys with you."

"She can come down here as well as not. If she comes in the back, nobody'll see her."

"Fine! As soon as we get something out of the butler we'll be back. I'll leave Mac and Blair here but I'll bring somebody back to take Mac's place when he goes with Al. You'd better have this twist here so we can go over the stunt with her and make it as fool-proof as possible. She can wait."

"I will. She'll do what she's told, don't worry about that."

Hallahan smiled mirthlessly. "She's the only woman in the world that will, if she does." He grinned at Prentice. "I'll get the dope all right. Don't worry."

Prentice sighed. "I always found out a man would talk if he was damn' sure he'd be beat to death if he didn't. Don't miss, for —— sake."

"I won't and I won't leave any marks on the mugg. But he'll talk." He swung out, and Prentice commented to Dora: "And you know I got a hunch he *will* talk." He sighed again. "Just when there's action I'm on the shelf. Always a break."

HALLAHAN AND ALLEN went through the jail proper, clear to the last tier in the back cell-block. The cell itself was bright—light flashing from the ceiling to glaring white-washed walls, scantily furnished, an iron bunk fastened to the wall, with no mattress for covering. Hallahan, followed by Allen, stepped inside, said to the jailer who had admitted them: "That's all, Sam. I'll sing when I want out. Close the corridor doors though and don't mind a little racket." He frowned at the prisoner, a dark, suave, slight man, snapped: "Your name's Collins, is it?"

"I've told your men it was." The man's voice was steady. "There's going to be trouble about this when Mr. Bruner finds out what has happened." He seemed entirely unafraid.

Hallahan jeered: "He's going to have more to find out than what's already happened. Did they print you?"

"No, of course not. They said I was to be held as a witness. They refused to say what I was supposed to have witnessed, however." He fumbled in his pockets, asked: "Have either of you men a cigarette? They took mine and put them in an envelope."

"Don't worry about that. You'll get 'em back. Were you ever in jail before?"

"Never."

"You sure?"

"I've told you. Why are you questioning me?"

Hallahan watched him narrowly as he said: "We picked up a man named Russo and he told us a lot of things."

"What has that to do with me?"

"Plenty. He talked about Graves."

"What about him?" Collins' voice was still steady, but Hallahan caught a flicker in his eyes.

"How was he killed?"

"Why ask me?"

"Because you know." Hallahan turned and nodded at Allen who stepped ahead.

Allen snarled: "Listen, wise guy! Graves was killed and you're in the soup because of it."

"Am I charged with murder? If I am, I'm entitled to an attorney and don't have to answer questions."

"You're not charged, but this boss of yours is going to be. If you're charged it'll be for aiding and abetting."

"He's done nothing wrong and neither have I. You're making a mistake."

"You're sure of that?" Allen's voice was ugly. He was opening and closing his hands and his thin, dark face was murderous.

"Quite sure. I've worked for Mr. Bruner, who is an attorney, for five years and I know something about my rights."

"You're not in court, mugg, you're in jail. You thought of that?" He stepped ahead and gripped Collins by the coat, shook him slightly. "And the funny part of that is that this smart boss of yours is facing a murder rap. He won't rate if he does go to the bat for you but he won't. He'll pass the buck to you. You thought of that?" He glared into Collins' face.

Collins stared back at him. "I've done nothing."

"Then, talk. What about Graves? How was he killed?"

"I'll tell that on the stand."

"You'll tell it now." Allen picked him up with both hands and threw him on the iron cot. "You'll start now. I don't like this lip."

"This is third degree." Collins stared doggedly up from the bunk.

"It is now. It's going to be the thirty-second in about a minute. Did you see this —— you work for kill Graves?"

Collins pursed his lips stubbornly, then thought a moment and admitted: "No harm in telling you that. Mr. Bruner killed Graves when he was attacked by him. There were two other witnesses."

"There aren't now. Bruckner's dead and Russo's told the truth. Listen, mugg, you're going up for an accomplice if this keeps up. We know that story's a phoney—know what happened."

"Then why ask me, if you know. I'll tell my story on the stand."

"If you're able," Allen gritted. He jerked the man up from the couch and spun him until he faced away, jerked one arm up behind his back and caught him by the other elbow with his free hand. He sent skilful fingers probing into the hinge and Collins shrieked in sudden agony.

Allen nodded at Hallahan over his shoulder, faced Collins that way, and pressed again. He snarled: "Talk mugg, or I'll kill you with my bare hands. Tell the Captain what you *did* see." He pressed again into the elbow-joint and Collins screamed: "Stop it!" Allen released his grip and he sank to the floor moaning.

Hallahan said casually: "New one on me, Al. What is it?"

"It's a Jap stunt." Allen's voice was grim. "Don't leave a mark except maybe a little bruise. It's the nuts for a wise mugg like this that's so wise." He said to the man on the floor: "Might as well spit it out. I know a lot of stuff that's worse than that."

"I won't." Collins shuddered as Allen's big hands reached for him.

SOME TIME LATER Hallahan joined Prentice and Dora at the *Club*.

Hallahan said: "He was good, I'll say that. I damned near believed him. We printed him before we left and sent a wire to New York to verify what he said, but there's no doubt. Bruner's baby-faced butler is damn' near as bad an egg as Bruner is. No wonder Bruner didn't have to give him dough for a statement. He had enough on this Collins to hang him three times over."

Dora commented: "We live and learn. And you say he acted innocent?"

"Innocent as hell! Never even been in jail, he said. And him a three time loser in New York State alone." Hallahan grinned at Prentice. "This partner of yours could make a mummy talk. We got the whole thing down with a stenographer and he signed it. Dora caught it on the first bounce. Then Al started to work on him again. We figured Bruner was holding something over him and sure enough, he gives us a lead on this personal dirt. He'll fry along with Bruner."

Dora asked: "Has anyone called the hospital and asked about the fellow up there?"

"I sent a man up to print him is all. Why, what difference?"

"Just curious!" She gave a number into the phone and stared over it at Prentice. "This butler of Bruner's had two grand bounty on him. Who'll get that?"

Prentice looked sour. "We should, but no chance. It'll go to the department fund."

"Tough, ain't it," Hallahan jeered. "I suppose you and Al picked the mugg as a bad one. If anybody's entitled to it, Dora is."

"Well, see that she gets it then."

"And have her cut back with you and Al. No chance."

Dora made silencing motions, spoke into the phone. She hung up, said: "He never came out of the ether. Doc said that somebody from the station printed him and then took him to the morgue."

Hallahan said thoughtfully: "Seems damn' funny that neither you or Al knew neither one of those two hoods."

"We didn't. Never saw either one before. Bruner probably imported them for the job."

"You'll know 'em next time."

"We will. —— I'm worried about this Russo. Al said he'd phone?"

"The minute it was over. I'll go up to the station and meet 'em when it's over." He asked Dora: "Sure the gal won't do a cross-up?"

"Positive."

Prentice fretted: "We should have heard by now," and Hallahan soothed him with: "Give them time. If the gal got inside all right—"

"Sure! If! You know Al. He's likely to go screwy and crash in if something went wrong and get a bullet in the gut."

"Oh hell! We'll hear. Don't be an old woman."

"Dora, why in hell don't you buy a drink while we wait?"

"Why don't you, ape? We sell it." She rang the service bell.

ALLEN, CROUCHING BY the closed door of Russo's apartment, McCready at his back, held up his hand warningly as they both heard voices nearing the door. He tensed his lean body and as the door opened slightly threw his full weight against it, forcing it wide. Peggy was standing by the side as arranged, but Russo, instead of being in the clear and under Allen's swinging gun, was caught by the door and forced behind it as it opened.

Allen caught this instantly, dropped his gun, pulled the door back and grappled with Russo who had a gun half out of his pocket. He caught Russo's wrist with both hands and shouted to McCready, but in the second it took the slower man to get in the room the gun discharged and Russo went limp, slumped to the floor.

Allen, according to plan, called out: "Watch the twists, Mac!"

and bent over Russo in a quick examination to rise in relief. He said: "Caught him slanting down the leg and broke it. He may die but it won't be from that." He snapped at the girl standing at the back of the room and screaming: "Stop that, twist! He ain't hurt bad," then took off his belt and knelt by the moaning Russo.

Peggy flickered an eyelid at McCready, complained: "What you guys trying to pull? Come in here where nobody's bothering and start shooting. I'm going to call the cops."

McCready growled: "You're talking to 'em, sister. What in hell d'ya think we are? Boy scouts?"

"What's the idea of this then? You didn't show any warrant."

McCready grinned: "Shut up! If you're nice you can sit next to me in the wagon. You're pinched," He said to the other girl. "You too, sister."

Peggy said: "What for? I ain't done anything. I just came up to see my friend."

"Make me believe it. This guy is wanted for attempted murder."

Allen said from the floor. "That'll hold you until the ambulance gets here. The belt will stop the bleeding." He asked the girl in back: "Where's your phone, sister?"

"No phone." She had stopped screaming at his order, stood looking sullenly ahead with tears streaming down her cheeks.

"What do you do? Lean out the window and shout?"

"There's one in the hall, heel."

"Thanks! Mac, you watch 'em. We'll take 'em both."

"Sure! I told 'em that."

Allen grinned widely at Peggy as he turned his back on the other girl, said under his breath: "Like shooting fish."

He strode through the crowd already collected outside the apartment door, recognized the manager and said cheerfully: "All okey! The wagon'll be here in ten minutes and you'll lose a couple of tenants," then called Hallahan at the *Commercial Club* and changed the meeting from the station to the hospital. When McCready started for the station with the two women, he rode up with Russo to the hospital in the ambulance.

GETTING A CONFESSION from the wounded Russo proved easy. Facing a charge of attempted murder, knowing he could expect no sympathy from a court or prosecutor who had been blackmailed in the past by the man who had hired him for the killing, he broke completely and backed up the butler's story and Dora's deductions in every detail.

By the time his leg had been set and patched, and his story told it was after midnight, however, and Hallahan, confident that Bruner did not know of Russo's arrest and subsequent confession, decided to delay Bruner's arrest until the following morning. He returned to the station and released Peggy and Russo's companion, gave the last an order to leave town immediately and, after calling Dora and Prentice at the *Club* and telling them of the latest developments, gave Allen orders to arrest Bruner as soon as a warrant could be procured in the morning. He then went to bed, happy in the thought of a good day's work well done.

Allen, on his part, was as little expectant of trouble. With the morning half over, when the warrant was in his hand, accompanied by McCready, he went to the office of the Magna City *Record*, the yellow newspaper Bruner controlled, certain that Bruner would be in his office as usual. He was somewhat surprised, yet not perturbed, when told the wanted man had not as yet appeared. He then went immediately to his residence.

Even then, on being told that Mr. Bruner had left for his office, he had thought he had passed him on the way. A return call to the *Record* disabused his mind of that notion and for the first time he began to worry. A rapid check on all of Bruner's known haunts followed and when this failed, he resorted to the full power of the police, sent out a general alarm, closed all roads out of town and wired surrounding cities giving a full description of the wanted man.

This done, no action could be taken until one of the agencies set in motion reported progress, and he was forced to listen to the irate Prentice who blamed him equally with Hallahan.

Prentice, still guarded with Dora at the *Club* from possible attack, was furious. He failed to understand why Hallahan had waited until morning for the arrest and when that badgered man explained patiently that, due to Bruner's undoubted influence, he wanted a warrant so there would be no question as to the legality of the arrest, he flew off the handle completely.

He raged: "We had him cold and you lose him. If I'd been on it we'd have him sunk. Oh, damn this leg. You ought to go before the board for retirement. You're getting childish. Warrant! Warrant, hell!"

Hallahan tried to calm him with: "But neither Al or I thought he'd—"

"That's the beef. You didn't think. And here I am stuck. I might have known you'd fumble it. You and your —— damned warrants."

The outraged Hallahan left after more of this, and Prentice started in to drink—sullenly—alone. Allen tried in turn to make peace but after one attempt stayed away, and Dora, half afraid of him in this mood, left him entirely alone.

The situation did not change for three days. Prentice, red-rimmed eyes staring at his crippled leg, was drinking steadily in spite of the doctor ordering him to stop—Hallahan was worried over possible demotion for losing his man—and Allen, now in charge of the case, was constantly in the station in contact with the search. The break came suddenly—almost pure luck—and entirely police routine, routine unaffected by the ponderous police machinery searching for the fugitive.

At ten the fourth morning, Prentice, already half-drunk, was called to the phone and the excited Allen told him: "We're set, Dal, ol' boy, ol' boy! We got the dope."

Prentice, nerves on edge from liquor, answered bitterly: "Another rib! He's out of the state by this time."

"No, I tell you. He's at the *Silver Slipper*. Jack Roth's old place. He's there with about a dozen hoods."

"Sure he is. I suppose he wrote you a letter."

"—— Dal, don't be that way. I tell you he's there."

"Did you dream this hooey?"

"Listen, Dal! I went to the line-up this morning. First time in a month. Who do you think I saw?"

"Why, Bruner, of course. I know all the answers, screw-ball."

"Stop it, Dal! Listen! The hood that made it out the window at the hospital. Big as life."

"Huh!"

"I'm telling you. I picked him out and worked him over with Mac, and we got the dope."

"Go on." Prentice had lost his jeering tone, was gripping the phone so hard his knuckles showed white.

"He was hiding out at the *Silver Slipper*. We thought it was closed, but Bruner's been using it all the time as a hideout for his red-hots. The other morning about five, the big shot showed up himself."

"Sounds screwy. How'd this mugg get picked up? Walk into the station?"

"He was a stranger and Bruner figured he could come in town and get the news. He figured that outside of you and me and Dora, nobody knew him. He happened to be in a clip joint down on Tenth and one of the boys didn't like his looks and picked him up. What a break!"

"You're not ribbing me." Prentice's usually quick brain was still clouded.

"Hell, no! It's straight. We'll get him tonight."

"Why not now? He'll get away again."

"The hell he will! I've got fifty men around the place now. If we tried to crash it in daylight we'd lose half the force. This hood says they got six tommy guns and all that goes with 'em. All same army."

"How'd Bruner get wise that the finger was out for him?"

"Hallahan, and don't think I didn't tell him. He let this twist that was with Russo go and tells her to scram, and she calls up Bruner on her way out of town and tries to put the bite on him for some dough. Bruner met her and just to be sure Russo hadn't told her about the hideout he took her along. She's there with Bruner and nine others if the heel's telling the truth and I think he is."

Prentice tittered: "What a break for a hustlin' gal. Alone with a dozen men."

"Sober up, Dal!"

"I'm sober, you lug. Sober enough. When you going to go on it?"

"At dark. About nine. I've got it bottled and we can stop traffic."

"Come on down."

"Maybe an hour. I'll be busy that long." The phone clicked.

Prentice stared at it a moment, said: "Nailed, by ——!" in a curious tone. He stared down at his crutch for a moment, mumbled: "To the cross!" and shouted: "Dora! Hey, Dora!"

She came into the room, looked at him, said: "No more now, Dal."

His face was white, his hands were shaking, but his eyes had lost the dull look they carried and were glowing like hot coals. He said: "They got him, kid! He's sewed up and sacked."

She said: "Bruner!" but not hopefully.

"Just that!" He hobbled towards her on the crutch, held out his hand solemnly. "Shook me by the hand."

She evaded his lumbering advance, asked doubtfully: "Snakes?"

"Snakes, hell! He's holed up, I tell you. Al's got him cornered."

"Well, thank the Lord! I've been afraid to even take a bath with these coppers of yours watching me so close."

"Buy a drink then."

"Dal, you've had plenty. You're on the edge."

He insisted: "Buy a drink," then explained: "I kept tight so I wouldn't think about that —— getting away but now I've got a right to celebrate."

She assented doubtfully, rang the service bell, and they drank to the success of the raiding squad.

THE *SILVER SLIPPER* was set in a grove of trees some four miles from the limits of Magna City, its overgrown two-story bulk crouching over a circular gravel driveway like a dog over a bone. The trees surrounding it made an ideal protection for the raiders until they were a few feet from the house, but unfortunately were just too far away to permit effective use of tear bombs or grenades from their shelter.

Allen, in charge of arrangements, had formed four squads of ten men each and planned to rush all sides of the house at the same time, but knowing that they would be exposed to fire during the rush across the open strip, hesitated to give the order that would mean certain loss of life. Outside of a covering fire from the trees they would be entirely unprotected until they reached the shelter of the house itself. He went back to where Hallahan was talking to the worried police commissioner, said: "As near right as we can make it. Shall we go?"

Hallahan's voice was ugly, strained. "Might as well, I guess. Won't make a damn' thing by waiting. ——! I hate to send men into that."

Commissioner Richards said doubtfully: "Couldn't a man sneak up and throw a grenade through the windows? It's very dark."

"But not dark enough. We tried that, and they spotted him before he got ten feet from cover. He got four bullets from a ta-ta gun in the legs and the man that got him back got one in the shoulder. You must have passed the ambulance on your way in."

"Maybe if we gave them a little more time to make up their minds they might give up. The place is like a fort."

Hallahan shrugged. "You're the boss."

"No harm in trying," Richards argued. "Give me that megaphone." He walked nearer to the house, bawled into the cone: "Bruner! Hey, Bruner! Jack Bruner!"

The house remained grim—silent.

"We'll give you half an hour to come out. Think it over!"

A machine-gun stuttered from inside the house, searching the wood in the direction of his voice, and he ducked hastily.

Hallahan said: "Hell, man! There ain't a hood in there that ain't got a price on his head for murder. You're wasting breath."

Richards, from the shelter of a tree trunk bawled out: "Send the girl out then. Give her a chance." An answering shout from the house said: "Come and get her," and the tommy gun loosed another burst.

Richards said hopelessly: "Give 'em the half hour!" and they settled down to wait, watching the dark house.

PRENTICE FOCUSED BLOODSHOT eyes upon his watch with difficulty, glared across at Dora. "It's five after nine. D'ya suppose the brawl's started yet?"

She said: "How would I know? My ——! you're drunk, Dal."

"Am I?" He stared at her owlishly. "What d'ya think?"

She shrugged. "Al said nine, didn't he? It's after that now."

"It is y' know." He reached for his crutch, stood to his feet with difficulty. "I'm goin' t' see."

"You are like hell. You stay here."

He said stubbornly: "I'm goin' t' see." His eyes were glassy and he swayed on the crutch, almost fell.

"Sit down, Dal! Don't act up! I thought you could carry your liquor better than that."

"You did, huh!" He spoke with difficulty, his tongue thick, but maintained his wobbling progress towards the door.

She slid in front of him and his erratic temper flared. "Get outta my way, ——!" He reached her where she stood barring the exit.

"Now, Dal! You gone screwy?"

"Screwy hell!" Bracing himself against the side of the wall by the door he reached out and gripped her by the shoulder and, aided by the purchase his back against the wall gave him, threw her out in the room, half across it. He jerked open the door, mumbled thickly: "No damn' woman—" staggered out in the corridor and towards the front entrance.

She came to the door and stood watching him, smiling thinly and without humor and nursing her bruised shoulder. She said half to herself: "He can't do any harm—" shrugged and turned back in the room, heard the front door slam and after a moment went there, half-opened it and peered out in time to see Prentice flag down a wandering cab.

She hurried out, said to the driver who had pulled into the curb: "Listen, Jack! This man's drunk. Don't take him." She reached for Prentice's shoulder as he half fell in the cab but he shook her off, muttering to himself.

She pleaded: "Listen, Dal, come back with me."

"Like hell." She could barely hear the mumbled words.

She told the driver again: "He's drunk. Let him out. He's no fare," and the driver half-turned on his seat, said to Prentice: "Get out, sport! The lady's right."

Prentice seemed to sober a little. He snarled: "Drive, mugg!" fished in his pocket and with difficulty brought out his badge. He flashed this, said: "I'm law! Get this hack outta here."

The driver flashed a glance at Dora. "Listen, copper, you're pretty tight. Why not go with the lady and—"

Prentice slipped the badge into his vest pocket and his

hand came out from his coat with a gun in it. He said: "Jack Roth's old place on the Market road. Th' *Silver Slipper*. You movin'?" The lock clicked as he eased the hammer back.

The hack-man stammered; "——! y-yes." White-faced, he turned back to the wheel and the cab lurched away from the curb. Dora watched it go, said: "The drunken ——!" slowly. She went back to the *Club,* still nursing her shoulder.

HALLAHAN LOOKED AT his watch, muttered: "Time's up!" but as he got to his feet, Prentice, helped by a uniformed policeman came up behind him. The man saluted, said: "Lieutenant Prentice came in a taxi, sir. We stopped him at the deadline but he said he had to see you." His teeth flashed in the dusk as he grinned: "He wants action."

Richards sniffed the whiskey odor that clung to Prentice, blurted out: "He's been drinking."

"He's not on duty, Commissioner," Allen volunteered. "He's still a hospital case."

The ride had practically sobered Prentice but had not improved his temper in the slightest. If any, it was more vicious. He glared at Richards, shook himself free of the policeman. "What's the matter? I thought it was nine o'clock."

Allen told him, more with the idea of distracting Richards than with any hope Prentice could help: "It's the space around the house, Dal. It's open as hell and they got it covered plenty. We been trying to figure some way to crack it." He explained the plan of attack they had decided to use.

Prentice hobbled to where he could see the house, studied it a moment and came back. He said: "I know a way. It'll beat that all to hell."

Richards snapped: "Why waste time? I tell you the man's been drinking."

"Yeah!" Prentice turned, stared him up and down. "Yeah! Well listen! I *still* know a better way."

Richards shrugged disgustedly and walked away and Prentice said: "Heel!" loud enough for him to hear. He told Allen rapidly: "Send a car and get one of the big fire trucks. One with the high sides that carry ladders."

Allen stared and Hallahan looked bewildered. Allen asked: "Why?"

"I'll drive it into the bucket, that's why. You can put some men in back with riot guns. The high sides'll protect them from the smash."

"You're drunk, Dal!"

"Like hell! Well, maybe a little. It'll still work."

Allen said slowly: "By ——! it would. I can drive it and if we open it up she'll crash clear in. It's a wooden building and flimsy as hell, with no foundation at all." He turned to Hallahan and asked: "Why not?"

Hallahan objected: "But it won't—" and Prentice interrupted him. "You can start the boys from the sides just like you figured and at the worst it won't do any harm. It'll give 'em something to think about. Why the hell not?"

Allen leaned over suddenly and clapped Prentice on the back. "And you half tight. What a man you'd be if you'd go on the wagon." He dashed off and hurried to the men waiting to attack, changing orders.

Hallahan said: "Oh hell! God hates a coward," told the uniformed man with Prentice: "Hustle to a phone and call Cap. Mills at fire station 24. Tell him I said for him to get here with the big ladder truck as soon as ———'ll let him."

He sighed resignedly, told Prentice: "If this fool stunt don't click, you're off the force, baby."

Prentice, still staring at the roadhouse, said: "And you lugs were going in without me." He grinned mirthlessly, patted the bulge under his armpit.

THE DRIVER PATTED the shining red hood, said: " 'Bye, baby," regretfully. He called back: "All set?" and Prentice, in the back, told him: "Let 'er go!" The man grunted, tested the lashed wheel, raced the motor, then, crouched on the running-board, shoved in the clutch pedal with one hand and threw the gear shift lever in second.

He shouted: "Hold tight!" let the pedal come up easy, and as it reached full engagement and the truck picked up speed, rolled off the side and scuttled back into the shelter of the trees. The truck roared ahead, motor full on, smashed into the roadhouse within ten feet of the side entrance at which it was aimed and finally came to rest with more than half its body inside the main dining-room—a broken clutch allowing the motor to race unhindered with the cutout open.

There were four men with Prentice in the back of the truck. As he came to his feet, pulling himself up by the side of the truck, he saw two of the defenders, one crouched low and running towards the stairs leading to the upper story and the other swinging the ugly muzzle of a tommy gun towards the stalled truck. He shouted and fired once with the gun in his free hand at this last man, but as he did he heard the blast of a riot gun at his side and the man pitched headlong. He shouted: "One down!" saw the running man reach the foot of the stairs and crumple there.

The four men with him were out of the truck, one running towards the front door to open it according to plan, the other three searching through the rooms opening from the dining-room like a pack of hunting terriers. One man was brought screaming from the back, handcuffed and shoved out the side door after a warning shout.

The four men momentarily grouped by the side door and Prentice, still in the truck, screamed above the din of the motor: "Help me down!" This done, he leaned against the side of the truck, braced by his crutch, and ordered: "Kill that engine."

The motor silenced, they could hear the mad chatter of gunfire from the upper floor, and he said: "They'll be jumping off anytime. We got to get up there and the stairs'll be covered. See if you can heave an egg up there."

Disregarding his warning shout, one man ran three or four steps up, drew his arm back in the beginning of the over-arm throw that would lob the bomb up, but wilted, rolled back down, and Prentice screamed: "He pulled the pin! Low bridge!" He let go the supporting crutch and fell to the floor just as the grenade in the dead man's hand exploded.

A voice at the head of the stairs was screaming curses faintly heard through the din. Leaving his crutch and dragging his crippled leg behind him, Prentice crawled to the machine-gun the dead gangster had dropped, got it and crept back towards the steps. He said: "I'll spray the top and keep them back and you guys try it again."

He sat back, wounded leg in front of him. The tommy rattled viciously as he swept the top of the stairs. The men with him started, but before they reached the foot, the front door opened and the burly man in the lead of the four or five that crowded through dashed ahead of them and tossed a bomb to the top of the stairs apparently as easy as if it were a baseball.

Prentice shouted: "Good boy, Mac!" had the last of this blotted out by the crash of the grenade, lowered the machine-gun and watched the pack surge up the steps.

The shooting above increased in intensity, if that were possible, during the ten seconds that followed, then there was a sudden lull and he sighed, said to himself: "All over!" and started to creep back to the truck and his crutch. He saw a shadow move in the cloak-room—saw the shadow resolve itself into a man—turned the Thompson gun he had, luckily held on to that way and said: "Hold it!"

He felt a blow in his bad leg as a flare of light blossomed towards him. He loosed a short burst from the tommy; then passed out—hazily feeling the hot gun barrel against his face—hazily hearing men coming through the side door.

THE INTERNE SAT on the bed and smiled cheerfully. "All's wrong with you, Lieutenant, is a hell of a hangover as near as I can see. What's another hole in a bum leg between friends?"

"You go to hell!"

"Naughty, naughty!" The white-coated man shook his finger. "I'll not show you the paper with the nice writeup if you keep that up."

Prentice grinned weakly in spite of his pain.

"No kidding, Lieutenant, that was a nice piece of work. I've got this friend of yours, McCready, here."

"Mac hurt bad?"

"Plenty, but he'll come through all right we think. Bullet

through his right lung. If he don't get pneumonia he's a cinch."

"Give me the paper. How many got it?"

The smile faded from the doctor's face. "Five all told. Two besides McCready hurt seriously."

Without the ceremony of knocking, Allen and Hallahan came in. Allen was decorated with a bandage around his head but Hallahan was uninjured. Prentice said: "Well?" and Hallahan shrugged: "Not as bad as it might have been. You're a hero again according to the reporters."

"I thought I'd get fired. Trying to pick a beef with the commissioner."

"Me too. The write-up saved you. Richards admitted that if it hadn't been for the truck act we'd have come out worse."

"Bruner killed?"

"City hospital with three holes in him and two guards in the room. He'll live to fry. Didn't you know?"

"Know what?"

"He was hiding in the cloak-room, and when Mac made it up the stairs he came out." He nodded at Prentice's leg. "He gave you that and you gave him three back for change. I thought you knew at the time."

Prentice said piously: "Thank God for small favors. I broke even with the —— this time."

Allen said: "He'll fry. Even if he could've beat the rap on the other, he's done on this."

Prentice looked thoughtful. "You know I wish—" He stopped, grinning at his partner.

"Wish what, Dal?"

"Nothing much. I'd like to throw the switch—when they burn him."

Murder in Jail

*Dal Prentice, hard as they come, figures
on the wrong end of a work-over*

FIVE MEN WALKED down the steps of the County Jail and forced their way through the crowd of curious onlookers. Five men—first, two uniformed policemen; then John Bruner, prisoner, handcuffed to Prentice on one side and Allen on the other.

There was a clatter of talk from the mob; mumbles of, "That's him in the middle," "That's Bruner there,"—and three camera-men were frantically shooting pictures from as many angles, and fighting off exhibitionists who were spoiling the bulk of them. One enterprising reporter, daring the two guards who were officiously waving the crowd back, stepped close to Bruner as he reached the sidewalk and said hurriedly: "Mr. Bruner, are—"

Bruner's hat was pulled well down in an effort to shield his face, and a cigarette dangled from his thin lips. He said: "Let's get out!" but they did not seem to move. He blew smoke from under the hat brim and watched the street with pale, expres-sionless eyes. One of the uniformed men caught the news-hawk by the shoulder, said: "Keep back, bud! He won't talk."

The reporter said in an injured voice: "Well, ——!" and they argued.

Bruner's eyes flickered to them a moment, then through the crowd and back to the street. He shook his head as if to clear his eyes of smoke.

A ramp at the left led down to the basement of the jail build-ing and as the five waited for the police wagon that would take them to the Court House for Bruner's arraignment on a murder charge, a truck, coming towards them on the same side of the street and some fifty feet above the ramp, weaved erratically for a moment and then, apparently out of control, smashed across the sidewalk and blocked this entrance. Its bulk extended out in the street and following cars were forced well out in the center lane to pass.

A rattle-trap Ford, following the wrecked truck, crashed into the back of it and flames shot from the hood. The driver got out, waved his arms excitedly, shouted for help. The fire leaped to the back of the car with suspicious suddenness, a dense cloud of smoke rolled up from the wreck, and the driver of the truck dashed to the back with his helper and made frantic attempts to clear the Ford away from his endangered truck. The crowd surged away from the prisoner and his guards and turned their attention to the new excitement. The truck-driver shouted hoarsely for help. The uniformed man engaged in the altercation with the reporter started towards the burning car, but Prentice said sharply: "Hey! Let it go!"

Almost as he spoke, even as the man turned back to him, a car slid out from the curb a few feet below where they stood and, taking advantage of the eddy the truck and burning Ford caused in the traffic, backed and stopped in front of them. Four men drifted back from the crowd, fifty feet away, Bruner spat the cigarette out and as if this were a signal one of the four pressed close to Prentice and said evenly: "Get in that car!"

Prentice jerked out: "What!" and glanced sidewise, startled, and the same even voice said: "Don't move wrong, copper. You're covered plenty." Prentice felt a gun jammed in his side and looking past the grin on Bruner's face saw his partner,

Allen, in similar shape, saw the two guards standing motionless.

The newsman, entirely unconscious of anything wrong, pressed in again and the man standing by Prentice reached out his free hand and pushed him away and at the same time growled to Prentice: "In the car, I said! Quick!" He jammed the gun harder in the detective's side.

Prentice gave a desperate glance around and the man insisted: "Quick!" Allen, speaking across Bruner, said: "Might as well, Dal!" and, with the gun pressing harder into his side, Prentice said sullenly: "Oke!" His face showed sudden beads of sweat.

The driver of the car reached back and shoved the back door open, and the man guarding Allen stepped in and sat in the far jump seat. He said harshly: "Come in, muggs," and to Allen: "You first." He pulled the gun from his coat pocket and held it on his lap and while Allen, handicapped by being linked to Bruner, and followed by Bruner and Prentice, clumsily clambered in, watched him narrowly.

The man guarding Prentice had never eased the pressure of the gun against his ribs and followed him in and sat on the other jump seat. The car pulled smoothly away from the curb, and the first man in leaned across and jerked the gun from the spring-holster under Allen's arm and slid it into his side pocket. Prentice's guard did the same for him, but poised it, said: ".45," in a reflective voice. He balanced it tentatively in his hand as the big car hit a green light at the intersection, rolled on and made a left turn at the next block. He seemed puzzled by the weight of the heavy revolver.

As they straightened from the turn, Bruner spoke for the first time, and to the man across from Prentice. He said: "Unlock these damn' cuffs!" jerked his elbow in Prentice's side and added: "He's got the keys."

The man shoved his own gun under his arm, took off his hat, pushed blond scant hair back from his forehead. He was smiling but broke this off to yawn. He asked indifferently: "Why?" Bruner stared at him as if he didn't understand and the blond man offered: "They're easier to watch this way. A one-armed man can't do half what a guy on the loose can."

The strain of his escape suddenly took hold of Bruner, made his voice shake and change key oddly. He quavered: "Damn it, let me loose! Now! You got a gun, haven't you?"

"Yeah! Two of them, now." The smile returned to the towhead. He threw out the cylinder of the gun he had taken from Prentice, picked out a cartridge and looked at it curiously. He said: "That's sure a slug. The damn' gun's too hard to cover up, though." He ignored Bruner, said to Prentice: "Me, I use a .38 automatic. Always did. Don't make no bulge under your coat. See what I mean?"

Bruner choked out: "Take—these—damn'—things—off!" and the blond man swung on him. "You keep harping on that, mugg, and I'll tie 'em around your ——— damned neck. See!" He glared at Bruner and Bruner dropped his eyes. He turned back to Prentice, said: "All lip and no guts. The cheap ———!"

Prentice asked curiously: "Don't you work for him? How come?" But Allen broke in. He asked: "You're Harry, Happy Schultz, ain't ya?" and the blond man said: "Yeah!" and grinned.

Allen told Prentice: "St. Looey, he comes from. This is his racket. He snatched Bald Jake Kranter and got a hundred grand for him." He asked Schultz: "Ain't that right?" and Schultz said: "Hell, no! Thirty-five. The papers made it big."

His grin was wide and he seemed proud to be recognized as he queried: "How'd ja know? I never been West before."

"Saw your picture once and remembered it. You gotta face easy to place."

Schultz fingered his nose, said: "Huh! I shoulda got the beak fixed up. I ain't made ail-jay in five years. Even for investigation. How's that?"

Prentice said: "You got a lot o' guts to snatch two coppers, fella, I'll say that. Lots of guts and no brains."

Schultz corrected him. "Four coppers and some nosy punk that got wise there was something wrong. I seen him stick his head in the other car that's got the harness bulls, and the boys reached right out and took him. I seen it through the back window. That screw that started to ask questions."

"What you going to do with 'em?"

"Not one damn' thing. Turn 'em loose. They'll be yapping about the mean things that got fresh with 'em inside of ten minutes. I didn't want 'em or no part of 'em. Or, for that matter, no part of you."

"That was smart work." Prentice's voice was admiring.

"You know it, bud! The truck was rented under a phoney name and we paid twenty-five bucks for the flivver. It cost us another five to fix it up so she'd burn when she smashed and with a couple of smoke bombs in the back the trick was done. They can't get any cars to follow us because the truck's blocked 'em off. I'll say it was smart. That closing up that runway was good."

"What about the truck-driver? And the mugg that run the fliv?"

"Cinch! I got another car behind to stop and pick 'em up. What in hell d'ya think they was doing out at the back of the truck the way they was? They're in one car and the two boys that was with you and the egg that wanted to know so much is in another. I don't miss."

A SIREN ON the car wailed as they came to a boulevard stop with the red light against them and Prentice said: "For —— sake!"

Schultz grinned: "This heap belongs to the Police Commissioner. Some mugg named Richards. I bet he raises hell when he finds out we borrowed it off him. I bet he just raises hell and—"

Bruner broke in with: "Listen, Schultz! In the first place, you talk too much. Unlock me and I'll—"

Schultz leaned over and slapped him across the face. "You'll shut that trap. See! I got paid to break you out and I'll do it my way. See!" Prentice laughed as Bruner shrank back in his seat and Schultz said complainingly: "I know my business. This is my dish. Once this heel gets to where I'm paid to bring him, he can order his punks around all he damn' well wants to, but not me. See! I get my ough-day for the crash-out but I don't take no talk off any o' these small-time chiselers. See what I mean?"

Prentice caught Allen's swift glance and grinned admiringly back at Schultz. As long as he wanted to talk, it seemed policy to let him. He said: "You know your business all right. That was sure neat."

"I always work neat. That's how come I got this job. I gotta reputation."

"Did this —— hire you?"

"What d'ya think?"

"That he did."

"You lose. He didn't."

Prentice looked puzzled, then across at Allen. He said complainingly: "I don't get this. What in hell's—"

The man supposedly watching Allen was short and dark and ugly faced. He had turned his head away from Allen in listening to Schultz and Prentice and his hand holding the gun in his lap had relaxed slightly. Allen suddenly kicked up at him and grabbed with his free hand at the gun but this failed and the sour-faced man slammed the gun against the side of his jaw. Allen slumped back in the seat and Schultz said regretfully: "That's the way. Never satisfied."

The ugly man reached across and felt Allen's jaw, said harshly: "Hell! It ain't broke none. He ain't hurt one damn' bit." Schultz looked relieved and Bruner broke in again. "When are we going to change cars? The squawk's out for this one by this time and the radio cars'll be on the watch."

Schultz said: "Shut up and leave it to me, will ya!" He seemed to have had an active dislike for Bruner from the first. "If it wasn't that I only got part of the dough that's coming to me, damned if I wouldn't dump you out on the street. You blat all the time. For —— sake, you make me nervous."

Prentice said slowly, feeling his way: "Don't make him sore, fella. He might not pay off."

"No? I'd hate like hell to have to put him together if he don't. I should fool with a cheap heel like him."

"Cheap?"

"Hell, yes. Cheap. I was to get twenty grand for this job—it's no set-up to bust a guy loose like that—and half of it was to be before I turned the trick. Well—they try to pay me off in Liberty Bonds. What in hell do I want bonds for? Them things can be traced if they're hot. The next thing'll be cigar coupons." He looked his disgust at Bruner and his voice got even harder. "If you think you or that shyster of yours ain't going to pay off in iron money inside of five minutes after you're delivered, you're screwy as hell. See! Hell of a big-time hustler you are. Can't raise a lousy ten grand." He turned to Prentice. "Just a cheap punk. —— sake! I got that much dough on me all the time and more too."

The siren wailed again as he reached in his pocket and produced a wallet, showing its bulging contents with pride. "See! For bail. Though I could stay in this town forever and never need it. I cased that gow for three days—even asked directions from some opper-copper, and me with my rep."

Allen stirred weakly and Prentice asked: "What you going to do with me and my partner?"

"Turn you loose after Mr. b—— pays off. I ain't lost anything you guys got, but I don't want to take no chances on you making trouble before I get mine."

Prentice said approvingly: "That's smart."

"Sure! If the hustlers weren't all starving, believe you me I wouldn't be messing around on a deal like this. I pick guys in the racket so there'll be no beef."

Bruner said: "Another five grand if you leave 'em with me."

"Not any. And have something happen to 'em. I ain't nuts."

"Now listen, Schultz. If—"

"Save your wind. This racket is tough enough without getting hotted up over a copper getting knocked off. I'm in dutch enough now."

"That's it. What the hell difference would it make now?"

"Plenty. The difference between five years and the hot squat. Not that I'm any cop lover but I use my head."

Bruner snapped: "You seem chummy with this heel." He jabbed Prentice viciously with his elbow and Prentice reached over with his free hand and slugged at his jaw. Schultz said reprovingly: "Ix-nay!" and Prentice leaned back on the seat and growled: "He started it."

"Sure. But you guys fight your private battles some other time. See!"

Bruner's voice was shaken by the hate in it. He snarled: "Ten, then. And that's all."

"Real dough? None of this bond hooey?"

"Real dough."

Allen sat up and looked blearily at the man across from him.

He said: "You cheap heel! I'll remember that."

The sour-faced man looked back and laughed.

Prentice nodded at him, asked Schultz:

"St. Looey, too?"

Schultz grinned wider. He said: "I wouldn't know," and to the man at his side: "Where you from, kid?"

Sour Face glowered at him, said sullenly: "That mouth o' yours'll fry us yet. You see!"

Bruner said again: "Ten grand. Real dough." His voice had steadied but his pale eyes glowed oddly.

"What you want 'em for?"

"I've reasons."

"I guess you have. You want to knock these muggs over. I know."

"It's not that."

"Then what?"

"They've got some stuff I want. Or rather, they can get it."

"Sounds screwy to me."

Bruner leaned ahead. The cuff that linked him with Prentice bit into his wrist and he jerked irritably to clear it, and Prentice, taking the cuff that encircled his own wrist with his free hand, jerked with all his strength. Bruner gave a half-muffled scream and Schultz said curiously: "Can't take 'em, huh! What a man!" His eyes showed disgust as he watched Bruner nurse his bruised arm.

Prentice said: "Take it easy, —— I'm still tied to you." He spoke earnestly to Schultz. "Don't get sold on this, Happy. It'd be curtains for me and my partner and you'd take the rap. You can be identified on the snatch and they'll stick you for a cop killing, you know that."

Schultz's distinguishing feature was an oversize nose, humped in the middle with an old break. He held his forefinger against one side and breathed noisily through the other nostril, said: "Yeah! But ten grand! That's a lot o' dough," in an undecided voice.

"It won't do you any good on the hot seat. You can't spend it there."

Bruner said: "Now listen! These fellows got enough on me to make it plenty tough. All the way tough, if it comes right down to it. I was taken up on a warrant and during it there was a shooting and I got mine. You know that."

"Sure! Go on." Schultz sounded bored. He tested the other nostril, added: "It was the copper right here that popped you, if I'm right on it."

"That's right. I used to have this town sewed up pretty, but this damned copper wrecked me. He's the one that put me in this spot, him and his partner."

"He's got you up on the big rap, huh?"

"That's right. I was indicted but if I got a couple of confessions these two heels are holding up their sleeves and could get to two men that are held in jail as witnesses, I could beat the case like a damn. Get the angle now?"

"How could you get the confessions?"

Bruner smiled palely. "Don't worry about that. If I had these two where I could work on them—give them some of their own third degree—they'd send after them plenty quick."

Schultz displayed an entire lack of interest. "Sure. And after that, the two eggs they got in the gow would go right ahead and swear you into the chair. Sure! I knew damn' well you were screwy as well as a —— heel."

"Now listen, Schultz! Heineman talked to you, didn't he?"

"You know damn' well he did. He sent for me when you told him to and then tried to pay off in wooden money. He said you were a cinch to fry and that your only chance was to take a powder and that I was the only guy smart enough to get you clear. He didn't say anything about you beating any rap. He said you could go some place where they couldn't extradite you and that was your only out."

"He doesn't know all I know, Schultz. Listen close. I was a lawyer until I was disbarred. Heineman worked for me. I know what I'm talking about. I tell you I can beat this if I get a break."

"Yeah! And it's only worth ten grand to you, is it screwball, to beat it? I'm half smart. If you had a chance to beat the big rap you'd lay plenty dough on the line. Not a lousy ten grand."

Bruner's voice cracked. He pleaded: "I'm damn' near broke. It's the best I can do."

"And you'll turn these guys loose if they come coco? It's no rib?"

The car pulled into a public garage, clear through to the back, and Schultz said: "Out! Change cars!" He clambered out of the car and stood with his hand in his pocket as the prisoners climbed out and transferred to another car, equally as big and well kept. He told an oil-soaked man that came up: " 'Key, keed! Take the hearse out an' lose it. It's hotter'n hell."

The man nodded and they pulled out of the garage and doubled back on the highway. Schultz asked: "It's no rib? Real dough and the coppers get loose when they crack it?"

"Keep 'em until you see the money if you want to. And I'll turn 'em loose afterwards."

Schultz leaned over and tapped Bruner on the knee with the gun he had again taken from his pocket. He said: "As if I wouldn't. Listen then. It's a deal if you put up the dough right away. I'm leaving an hour after we get to the hideout and if the jack ain't there, the coppers go with me. I'll spot 'em someplace and call somebody that don't know me and tell them to tell the law where they're at. See!" He paused and flashed a vicious glance at Bruner's thoughtful face. "And if you think you can connive around and do better than that—if you think up some screwy notion about how some of these dopey punks on your payroll can help you out on this—just take your Sunday cut. Me and Benny here, 'll be right at the party. See!"

"Don't be a fool. I won't cross you."

"You're telling me."

Prentice, knowing in his heart that speech was useless, said: "Don't be a fool, Happy."

"Ten G's is a lot o' ough-day. If you're nice and give the mugg what he wants he won't hurt you."

"Don't stall. You know damn' well it's curtains for us if you go for this."

Schultz looked troubled but his indecision had left him. He scratched the hump on his nose, argued: "But he says—" His voice trailed.

"I can do a lot of talking too. You believe me or him?"

"Well, you. But ten G's is—"

Allen broke in quietly. "Save your breath, Dal. It's no dice. If Happy wants to have all the law in the world looking for him on a murder rap, you can't stop him."

Bruner asked: "Where we going?" He saw Schultz was not looking at him and winked at Prentice.

"You'll see. That mouthpiece of yours is there waiting for you."

"Why not let me loose? This is damned uncomfortable."

Schultz said shortly: "When we get there. Not before. Now save your breath," and they finished the ride in silence.

THE CAR TURNED off the highway on to a dirt road, a full five miles back from where the commissioner's stolen car had been left and not more than that from Magna City. It bounced in and out of ruts for a half mile, turned into the yard of a shabby farmhouse. Chickens scratched dispiritedly in the littered yard and an overalled man opened the door and watched the car empty.

Schultz said: "Okey, keed?" and he answered: "Yeah!" Schultz motioned with the gun he held towards the house, and Prentice, in a last attempt, said earnestly: "Listen, Schultz! Give us a break!"

Schultz waved the gun in silence and they strung into the house, into a filthy hall, where the overalled man searched Prentice roughly and found the handcuff keys. He freed Bruner, left the unfastened cuffs dangling from the two detectives' wrists, and Schultz, watching them narrowly, waved the gun at the stairs leading to the second story and ordered: "Up you go. And don't make no breaks. See!"

With the sour-faced man from the car preceding them and Schultz following, they silently climbed stairs and saw a long corridor, doors opening from it, three on each side. As they passed the first of these it opened and Prentice got a glimpse of a short swart man and heard a girl's voice in a giggle. He snapped out: "'Lo, Heineman!" and the short man slammed the door shut with a curse.

Schultz chuckled behind them and motioned them into the

middle room on the right-hand side, followed them in, made them sit on the floor with their backs to the iron bed that was the only furniture. The sour man clamped the free ends of the cuffs to the side rail, making sure they were locked tightly enough to preclude any chance of being slipped over the lumpy ends of the rail. Schultz motioned him out when this was done and said loudly: "I'd put a guard in the hall and turn you loose in here but you'd try to make a break and hurt yourselves. He gave a quick glance at the door, whispered: "I'd give in quick if I was you. It'll save you a lotta grief."

The door opened and Sour Face said: "That guy's calling you. What's the matter?" He looked at the two men on the floor with distaste.

Schultz winked meaningly at them and strolled out with the other man. They could hear Heineman come out of the front room as the two went down the corridor, could hear the low murmur of voices as the trio went down the stairs. After a few minutes, they heard someone open the door of the front room, heard the girl they had heard in the hall say: "Well, just a minute, Honey." In a little while this door slammed and high heels tapped down the stairs, then silence.

Prentice said slowly: "Looks like the deep end, Al." His voice seemed unworried and of normal loudness but his face was wet and his eyes looked sick.

Allen said: "Sing low, Dal! There might be a guard at that. It ain't the deep end yet and we might get a break."

Prentice said bitterly: "Might! What gets me is this —— getting away after we had him. I can take it, it ain't that. We been looking for it."

"I never figured Schultz for a play like this. His dish has

always been to work on some hustler that couldn't cry. He's been taken up and mugged but I don't believe he ever took a rap."

"He's just like any other heel. Sell his mother out for enough dough."

"Looks that way. What'll we do?"

"Nothing. We get ours anyway so we might just as well take it right at the start. There's a chance that Bruner'll be picked up some time afterwards that way."

"I guess." Allen shifted position in an attempt to ease the drag on his handcuffed arm.

The door opened and Schultz came in, quietly, on his toes. He held his finger warningly to his lips, whispered: "S-s-s-h! Listen, guys."

Prentice gave him an ugly look, snapped out: "All right, heel! We are."

"Don't be like that. Be quiet. The mugg paid off just like a slot machine. He says he'll give you an out if you come coco but I don't believe him."

"I told you that."

"All right, then. You want to listen to a proposition?"

"Not from you—"

Allen said swiftly: "Shut up, Dal." He said to Schultz: "Speak up. I do."

Schultz winked broadly. "You know my racket. If I stick around and get you out do I go clear on this other? I can do it."

"When?"

"Well, not now. I only got Benny with me and the heel downstairs has got him four boys already. If you stall and give me a break, it's a cinch."

Prentice said: "I get it, Al. We're supposed to stall by giving Bruner his damned confessions and this is part of the build-up."

Schultz said earnestly: "You're screwy. I don't like the heel. Can't you see that this is an out for me if it works?"

Allen said: "We'll do it. We'll stall the best we can. When can you get action?"

Schultz shrugged and fingered his nose. "I can't crash in with just Benny so I'll have to wait a chance. He figures I'm going to take a powder but I'll duck right back and turn the trick when I can. I can't say when that'll be."

"What in hell did you turn us over like this for?"

"Ten G's is one reason." He shrugged again and grinned. "Besides, I'm half smart. If I'd turned you loose I'd have had you on my tail for breaking him out and this way I don't. That is, if you don't cross me."

"We won't. We want out too bad."

"I know you won't, but what about your partner? Him and me's been getting along all right but it ain't lasting, looks like."

Allen looked earnestly at Prentice. He said: "Listen, Dal! This might be the break we're looking for. Why not play along?" and Prentice nodded sullenly. Allen asked Schultz: "If we stick it out and don't give the —— what he wants, is that any skin off your neck?"

"Not one damn' bit. I'm paid for what I'm supposed to have did and that lets me out. If I knew what he was like I'm damned if I'd done it. He'd take it off me only he knows damn' well that Benny and I'd go for him first and he's got no guts."

"It's a bet then."

Schultz beamed, turned his head as he heard footsteps in the hall, and as he heard the door open, snarled: "I don't give a damn. I ain't no bull lover." He turned, said: "Hey, Bruner! These wise boys say that the finger'll be out and I'll never make it clear. What about it?"

Bruner looked at him suspiciously, said: "Don't fret about getting away. That's all ready now. I'm going to send you and Benny with one of my boys in another car and he'll take you a few miles up the line where you can get a train." He paused a moment, glanced from Schultz to Allen and Prentice and asked: "What—"

Allen said swiftly to Schultz: "And I hope you burn, you rat." Schultz saw his eyelid flicker, and laughed. "Plenty tough boy, huh!" He leaned over and slapped at Allen's face, and Allen fended the blow with his free hand and struck back.

Bruner grinned: "I'll start you out. The car's ready now— that's why I was looking for you." He put his hand on Schultz's shoulder, steered him out, but turned at the door, said: "I'll be seeing you." His smile was nasty and both captives glowered back at him.

In a few moments they heard the grind of a starter, then a roar as the motor caught. This dimmed as the car went down the road, and shortly Bruner, followed by Heineman, came back in the room. Bruner said: "You going to come through with what I want or must I get dirty?"

Prentice glared at him. "We'd get rubbed out either way. Heineman, you'll be disbarred for this, same as this —— you're working for. See if you're not."

Heineman pulled his hat over his eyes. He was palpably nervous. He said: "Maybe so—maybe not," in an undecided voice.

Bruner leaned over without warning and hit Prentice fair in

the mouth, and Prentice tried to roll with the punch. Handicapped by his bonds, the attempt was a miserable failure and he
spat out a tooth. Bruner said: "No lip! ——!" Prentice, locked to
the bed frame, jerked a foot up and kicked as hard as he could
at Bruner, who stepped out of range and jeered: "Not even
close." He evaded another frantic effort, knocked Prentice's
guarding hand aside, stepped in and struck again.

Prentice wiped blood from his face with his free hand,
snarled: "I'll remember that."

"Think about where the stuff I want is planted. That'll do you
a damn' sight more good." He struck again, and Allen broke
in: "Wait a minute! This ain't going to buy you a thing." His
eyes were hot. He was shaking so the cuff rattled where it was
fastened to the bed.

Bruner hit out again and Prentice ducked and took the blow
high on his head. Bruner cursed and stepped back nursing his
knuckles and Prentice choked out: "Like that, ——?" His voice
was thick and uncertain with rage, Bruner drew a blackjack
from his pocket and Allen said hurriedly: "Now wait! Give me
and Dal a chance to talk this over."

Bruner balanced the blackjack, rapped out: "Talk now."

"Like hell! We'll figure it out. What's the matter?" Allen
added persuasively: "We can't run away, can we?"

Heineman looked sick. His face a dirty yellow, he nudged
Bruner, offered: "Hell, Jack! Let 'em talk." Prentice, at the side,
could see the feeble wink he attempted. "They'll see reason if
they get a chance to talk it over."

Bruner said shortly: "Five minutes, then. That's all." He
looked at the blackjack regretfully and slid it back in his pocket
and, followed by Heineman, left the room.

Allen, listening intently, could not hear them go down the hall and he called out: "Hey! I want to talk to Dal without you listening in." Bruner shouted back: "Whisper, then," and Allen grimaced, said under his breath: "Dal! We can never stall with it going this way. You get slugged a few times and you'll go screwy—you know that."

Prentice said stubbornly: "No. I can take all that —— can put out."

"And be slug-nutty the rest of your life. I tell you he's figuring on beating you to death. I could see it. We'll have to stall."

"Stall, hell!"

"Dal, I never asked many favors of you, have I? I've done my part."

"Well?"

"Do it my way. Just this once."

Prentice had blood streaming slowly from a cut cheekbone, running down over his collar. His lips were already puffing and one eyelid was drooping. He stared at Allen, said disgustedly: "Yellow! By ——!"

"Now, Dal! You know better."

Prentice dropped his glance. He said: "Oh, hell, Al! Do it your way." He lifted his head. "I can take all he can give."

"I know it. But I can't watch you take it."

He called out: "All right, Bruner!" and to Prentice: "Let me do the talking, then. It'll save trouble."

Prentice shrugged assent, and when Bruner and Heineman came in Allen said: "See if I got this right. If we get this stuff for you we go out first class?"

Bruner hesitated a moment, said: "That's right. First class."

Allen said sharply: "I don't mean the wrong way."

Bruner's eyes showed a pale glint of triumph, but his voice

was calm. "I'm glad you got a little brains, Allen, even if this partner of yours never had. You're playing smart and I'll give you a break."

"I'll give you a note and Heineman can go down and get the stuff."

"Like hell! He'd get grabbed and I'd have to trade you for him or some play like that."

Heineman rattled in his throat.

"Well how, then? Your dice. And you might make these cuffs a little easier."

"I might." Bruner's voice was jeering but Heineman nudged him warningly and he said with an effort: "Okey! I'll ease 'em." He held a gun while Heineman slackened Allen's cuffs and then Prentice's. This done, he said: "Now we get to business. I want you to write a note."

"To who?"

"Hymie Lefkowitz."

"Why him?"

"Because that's the way we want to work it. That plain?" Bruner slid the sap from his pocket and Allen said hastily: "Okey! Have it your way. It's your dice."

Bruner smiled nastily, asked: "You want to write the note to who I want? And what I want?"

"——! yes!"

"All right, Heine, turn him loose and he can go downstairs and do it." He slid a gun from his pocket, added: "Make a break if you want to. This is too easy."

"I'm not crazy."

"Just yellow. That's one thing for him——" He motioned to Prentice. "He's at least got guts."

Allen flushed redly, started to speak but stopped. Heineman released him and stepped quickly back out of line as Bruner sneered: "All right, guy." Allen turned obediently towards the door but Prentice caught his wink as he did and felt better.

Some few minutes later Allen was returned and again cuffed to the bed. After the captors had gone he told Prentice that the note to Hymie was merely a request to follow the bearer and that the overalled man had taken it to deliver. The note had nothing in it regarding their situation but contained a two-hour time limit.

Prentice said: "Sorry about the other, Al! I was sore."

"Sure! Forget it!"

"Think Schultz'll come through?"

"If he don't, we are."

"Are what?"

"Through."

They waited for Hymie.

HYMIE LEFKOWITZ WAS the Magna City manager for a national bail bond company, and as he was willing to pay a commission on business brought him, he was a good friend of both Prentice and Allen who had no scruples about accepting this same commission. He was short, fat, far too well dressed—and carried the known loyalty of the Jew when dealing with his own race into his relations with the two officers. They laughed at him and with him—and trusted him. Neither man had any doubts about his not following the request in the note and they waited in patience for his arrival, which was inside the two hours Bruner had allotted him.

Bruner brought him up to the prison room and told Allen:

"Lefkowitz knows the score. You talk it over with him," and left. As he did, Lefkowitz said cautiously: "Watch it! I saw the door of—" he motioned towards the adjoining room—"close as I hit the hall."

Allen whispered: "That'd be Heineman."

Lefkowitz blinked nearsighted eyes. "Heineman, the lawyer?"

"The shyster, rather."

The bond man took off horn-rimmed glasses and polished them, said in a worried voice: "That's bad. Plenty bad. Bruner told me he was going to turn you loose if there's no beef but—" He shrugged. "With Heineman in it and you knowing it, I don't know. I'd think he'd've stayed clear."

"We run into him. I think he was going to."

"I see." He blew his glasses misty, rubbed thoughtfully.

"What the hell's the odds! We both knew he worked for Bruner."

Hymie said thoughtfully: "That's right, at that. They may figure you knew he was in the mud all the time." He brightened. "You know, at that, this ——'s smart. Plenty smart. I'm supposed to go and get these confessions he's worried about and do it any way I can."

"And then?"

"That's the smart part of it. And then nothing."

"What d'ya mean? Nothing!"

"Well, first he says he'll turn you boys loose right then and there and when I tell him not to lie right in my face, of course in a nice way, he says he figures to keep you here until he can see what he can do with these guys in jail."

"He told us he'd turn us loose."

"Did you believe him?"

"Not any."

"I don't see how he can. You'd just make it tough for him or anybody else to get to Russo and the other guy, the butler that worked for him. Heineman can get the butler out any time he wants to, Bruner says. He's got a writ signed by Judge Clark."

"Tough for the butler."

"I figure that, too. They'll shut him up the big way, I think. Though Bruner just told me he had it figured to slide the guy out. He knew I knew what it was all about and told me plenty." He added severely: "That's your fault. You booked him as a material witness and if you'd hung a bum murder rap on him like you did on Russo, Clark could turn the bail down."

Allen said: "When you go back, Hymie, tell Hallahan that."

Hymie held one pudgy hand out in protest. The nails shone glassily and a yellow diamond winked on one finger. His voice shook slightly. "Not me. Bruner told me in these same words: 'You play ball or I'll pitch.' He meant it, too. I tell you boys, that man's fighting for his life and I don't want in. If he can get these hoods of his out and those papers back he's safe. If he don't he's an escaped murderer. I won't want in."

Prentice said reasonably: "You are in, Hymie. Up to your neck, right now."

"Yes and no. I'm here because of you, but I'm not taking sides. It wouldn't do no good to tip Hallahan." He shrugged.

"Why not? If Hallahan foxed up about the butler and you tipped him to keep Russo in the hole where he couldn't be got to by anybody, why not?"

Hymie shrugged again, spread both hands wide. "Just this. I'd be on the spot. You and Dal would be deader than two dried herring and what the hell. Bruner wouldn't be one damn' bit worse off than he is now. He figures you can burn only once for murder. Ix-nay, I wouldn't say a word."

Allen said: "You're probably right. What you figure now?"

"Easy enough. You give me the dope on how to get the stuff he wants and I'll dig it up. He's going to send the same fella that brought me here back with me and I'm to give the stuff to him or come back with it, one or the other. I was blindfolded from the time we left Ash Boulevard and had to sit on the floor of the car. He knows I can't tip off where the place is."

"I know. I can tell you."

Hymie said hastily: *"Don't* tell me. I might not lie good if he asks me do I know where it is myself. *Don't* tell me." His face was sweating and he mopped it, wiped his glasses again with the same gaudy cloth. His eyes, when his glasses were off, showed a soft appealing brown.

Prentice asked: "How long does he figure it'll take for this play of his to go through? Did he say how long it'd be before he'd turn us loose? Which he won't."

"Not over three days. He promised me."

Prentice said: "Promised!"

Hymie Lefkowitz shrugged, answered: "He said."

Prentice shut up, staring at the floor. One eye was now entirely closed, the other nearly so, and his words came with difficulty through his swollen lips. The blood had dried on his cheekbones and collar—dried a rusty brown.

Hymie looked at him in sympathy, ventured: "Looks like you talked out o' turn," but Allen shook his head at him warningly and he subsided. Prentice, starting to change his position, pulled against his wrist where it was cuffed to the bed and cursed to himself, almost silently.

Allen said: "Hallahan's got the dope, Hymie, but I don't know whether he'll give it up or not."

"He will." Hymie's voice was confident. "He may figure like Dal does, that it won't do any good, but he'll do it. He'll figure it might."

"Well, I hope so."

Hymie got up, shrugged his checkered coat into shape on his shoulders. "And then you'll just have to wait, I guess. I sure hope it comes out all right. I'll even pray."

Allen smiled slightly and Prentice grunted. The little Jew turned to the door, stopped and came back. His voice broke with earnestness. "If it's a cross, he'll get his. I'll see to it." He tapped his pouter breast. "Me, Hymie."

Allen said softly: "I know, Hymie, Good luck."

Hymie went to the door and out.

Prentice shrugged, said: "A white man at that. And some people knock the Jews." He shook his head and Allen asked: "What's the matter?"

Prentice shook harder. "I don't hear so good out of this ear. I guess maybe when I ducked into that one the —— —— hurt his hand on, I ducked too far to the right. Or maybe the left."

Allen made a clucking noise of sympathy and they resumed their wait.

LATE THAT EVENING the tramp of feet in the hall was again heard and Bruner, followed by Hymie, came in. Hymie looked tired and worn but there was a broad grin on Bruner's face, He said: "I got 'em. That's the first step."

Allen said: "How's chances for some water?" and Hymie said indignantly: "Haven't they given you any?" He turned on Bruner. "I thought you said they'd be treated right?"

"Let it go, Hymie. You might have known," Allen told him, and Bruner turned back, said: "I'll send some water up. Hymie, you got about ten minutes before you go back." He slammed the door.

Hymie made warning motions towards the room next door and came closer. "Heineman got the butler out this afternoon on that writ. That's action."

Allen said: "Yeah! What about Russo?"

"Heineman tried to bail him out and Clark refused to accept bail. He said he was booked for murder and was a witness in Bruner's case besides and he wouldn't go for the shot."

"I figured he wouldn't." Allen's voice was grim. "When we put that mugg in, we put him in to stay."

"Bruner don't seem worried about him one damn' bit. There's something screwy about that."

"What could happen to him?" Prentice argued. "He's in and he's safe in jail if he ever was any place."

Hymie shrugged. "You may be right." He mopped his fore-head. "——! I had a time. Bruner sent another guy in with me, some young hood that acted like he could chew nails and eat spikes. He was that hard. Hallahan went straight up when I told him, and here was this yegg standing there, grinning at him. He went right around with me, just like Bruner told him to do. Hallahan wanted to take him down and give him the business and the only thing this yegg says was: 'Go ahead and see what it gets your two coppers.'

"There was just the three of us there in the office and I bet it took me ten minutes to get the captain down to where I could talk sense to him. I finally got him to understand I didn't know where the hideout was and that if I did know I wouldn't tell him. This finally makes sense and he goes out and digs up the stuff, and while he's gone McCready comes in and sits at his desk and I thought sure as hell that Mac was going to pick the hood. He must have had a hunch that this guy was mixed up in your snatch, 'cause he just sat there and stared at him and the damned torpedo had one gun under his coat and another one in his pocket and was just set for action. He acted like he wanted Mac to start something. ——! I never was so scared in my life."

"Who is this yegg?"

"Bruner called him Slick. Slick what, I don't know."

Allen shrugged puzzled shoulders, pulled wearily against the bed. He complained: "I wish they'd hurry with that water. The only way you can keep your arm from going to sleep is stay awake and keep moving it. This is getting tough."

"I'm sorry." Hymie looked sorry.

"We'll make it."

"Hallahan would've given me a key to the cuffs but I never got the chance to ask for one."

Allen grinned: "And he never thought."

"I think he did. I told him how you were fastened and he started to take me out of the room and the hood started to go right along. I told him what Bruner said about if anything happened to the hood what would happen to you. I made Hallahan put up with him on you boys' account."

"Maybe it was best. Seems kind of funny that Hallahan didn't put a tail on you so's he could come out and crash the joint."

"I told him not to. And made him believe it ——! If he did find this place and started to take it, you boys wouldn't last a minute. Bruner'd shove you off the deep end and right now.

You know that! I told him that."

"I guess that was smart."

Bruner came in with a pitcher of water and both prisoners drank. He set this down within their reach, said to Hymie: "Time to go."

Hymie said: "If I can help, get in touch with me the same way." He shook hands awkwardly, said: "Good luck!" and followed Bruner out.

A few minutes later Bruner and the overalled man came into the room, both men carrying guns in their hands. Bruner said: "You get a break, Allen. You're going to sleep downstairs."

"What about Dal?"

"What about him? He's tough! He can take 'em."

Prentice said through clenched teeth: "I can!" He cursed Bruner with a beautiful vividness, Bruner listening half smiling and the overalled helper with rapt attention. When he stopped to get his breath, Bruner said: "My! See if you can do as well tomorrow." He motioned towards Allen. "Turn him loose." Allen said: "I'll stay here." He kicked at the man, who dodged and looked at Bruner. Bruner snapped out: "Well. You got lead in your pants?" The man slid behind Allen—Allen caught a glimpse of him from the side and ducked—and then blackness.

ALLEN WOKE UP in total darkness, his head splitting, and found himself lying on an army cot, his wrist chained to the side yet in such a position that he could sleep. The wire on the cot was not covered—the springs sagged badly—yet it was comfort compared to his former position.

From the dank odor and chill in the air, he was certain he was in the cellar of the farmhouse and as his eyes became accustomed to the absence of light he saw the gray blanks of two small windows high on the walls. Despite the pain in his head and his worry about Prentice, he finally slept—woke as the gray patches lightened with dawn.

It was very quiet for some hours, then finally, faintly, he heard movement above him—then this ceased. He tried to estimate time as it passed—tried to figure some way out of the tangle—and finally dozed again to be awakened by the opening of the cellar door and furtive steps descending the stairs.

He twisted his head and saw Schultz, tiptoeing down the stairs, finger to his lips. Schultz came over to the cot, stooped, and the handcuffs rattled and eased on Allen's swollen wrist. Schultz said: "That's better, copper! Here, take this," and passed over a blunt automatic. He added: "That belongs to that mugg that wears the farm makeup. He don't need it."

Allen sat up stiffly, holding to the gun. His left wrist, the wrist the fetters had locked to the cot, was swollen, stiff, but he ignored it, stared at the gun. He slid the breach open, saw the glint of brass and dull gleam of the lead, and said: "A-h-h!" He stood up, staggered, and weaved towards the cellar steps.

Schultz took him by the shoulder, said anxiously: "Now wait, copper! You'll feel better in a minute," but Allen shook him off. He said: "Prentice!" and started to climb the stairs and Schultz followed him.

They came into a kitchen, from this into a dining-room, from this to the front hall. Allen started to climb the stairs and Schultz warned: "Watch it! I think they're all gone but I dunno."

Allen ignored him, stumbled up. He went directly to the second door on the right, threw it open and entered, and

Schultz, after opening doors and making sure the upper floor was untenanted, followed him in, found him sitting on the floor, one arm around and supporting Prentice.

Prentice was mumbling to himself. His coat was off and his shirt hung in rags from his shoulders. His arm, where it was cuffed to the bed, was a mass of raw, swollen flesh from being chafed and bruised. The links could hardly be seen through the swelling. Both eyes were closed, one ear was torn and hanging, his face was lumpy, bloody, lop-sided, and his hair was a mass of blood over a bruised forehead.

He had plainly been very sick—his undershirt was caked with blood and vomit. He held his free arm stiffly across his lower ribs. Allen was holding him so he would not sag against his chained wrist, trying to free the arm that he held so stubbornly against his chest, saying: "Oh, Dal! Oh, Dal!" over and over again.

Schultz came forward with the key, unlocked the cuff, and they lifted him on the bed. Allen, without turning, said: "Water!" and Schultz nodded, went to the kitchen and returned with the pitcher. He put this down, shook Allen sharply by the shoulder, said: "Listen! You better get the lay." He laid a revolver on the bed, said: "His! Now listen! I think they're gone for a little while but I'm not sure for how long. See! I put that one mugg in the barn and tied him up after I seen the rest of 'em go, but they'll be back."

Allen nodded, working on Prentice with clumsy fingers. Schultz watched him a moment, said: "Doctor for him. You ain't doing no good," and Allen said: "That's right." He suddenly seemed to realize what Schultz had told him, said: "They're all gone, huh! Is there a phone here?"

"No."

"A car?"

"Uh-huh! In a shed alongside the barn."

"I've got to take him to town. Help me with him." Allen seemed to have regained his own strength, and Prentice, partially revived by the water, seemed to have a dim understanding of the situation. He struggled weakly in an attempt to sit up and when they lifted him to his feet made a faltering try at walking. He still held his short ribs with his arm and carried his head far to one side.

Allen picked up the gun from the bed and, carrying it in his hand, and helped by Schultz, assisted Prentice down the stairs and into the kitchen. They were half across the room when the back door opened and the overalled man appeared in the doorway. He stood there, framed in the light, and Allen took a step away from Prentice and shot him in the stomach. He fell away from the door, and Allen caught Prentice as he slipped in Schultz's supporting arms. He said: "One down."

They went through the door, saw the overalled man lying by the single step that led down to the yard. He was on his side, silent, hands holding his belly and his knees brought up to his hands. Schultz said curiously: "That .45 sure puts 'em down and keeps 'em there."

Allen said: "Wrong man!"

They eased Prentice to the ground by the barn and Allen sat by him, held him up while Schultz ran the roadster in the shed out in the open. Prentice was still mumbling to himself but his words were indistinct and Allen said soothingly: "There, Dal! Okey now."

Prentice clutched his arm, spoke louder, and Allen made out: "Stay! Stake-out!" He said: "No!" and Prentice, still holding his head on one side, nodded insistently.

Allen said: "You go with Schultz, then," and Prentice nodded again.

Schultz ran the car out and Allen said: "We'll load him in and you take him to a doctor. Hospital would be better."

Prentice made dissenting noises.

"A doctor then."

"Why me?" Schultz asked.

"I'm going to stay here and wait for 'em to come back."

"Hell, copper, I can't do that. I'm hot. I'm squared with you but not with the rest of the law."

"You can take him to where there's a phone and leave him." Schultz looked undecided and Allen urged: "You could phone and then take a powder. If I stake-out here I'll get the whole damn' crew."

"This bird ought to go to a doctor right now."

Prentice mumbled protests through swollen lips and Allen said: "He ain't hurt so bad that a few minutes either way'll kill him. Just phone for an ambulance and lam. You can do that."

Schultz pointed, said: "Look!"

The lane from the house to the highway ran straight for a quarter of a mile and a sedan, coming towards the house, was just making the turn. The three men were in plain sight in the open yard and the sedan slid to a stop as they watched it, swung crosswise in the road.

Allen rapped out: "Bruner!" slammed open the door of the car, fumbled for an unfamiliar starter button, but as the motor roared into life saw the car in the lane back and complete the turn and roll away. He climbed out, said in disgust: "No dice. I can't catch 'em in this crate."

Schultz said: "Good thing. They must've figured all the law in the world was here or they'd have come ahead and shot it out. You'd've looked good chasing them by yourself and them four or five. You got a break."

Prentice mumbled, trying to see down the lane with eyes he could not open and Allen said: "Load him in. I'll take him myself. They'll never be back."

"That's smart."

They loaded the beaten man into the seat and Allen turned to Schultz, asked: "Where'd you get the keys?"

"I was watching the house and when I saw that little Jew that runs the bail bond place come out here with one of the yeggs, I got smart. I knew who he was and I sent Benny in with a note to him and the yid got the keys from some copper and left them at a chili joint for me. I used my bean. I'd have busted in before but there was always somebody around and Benny wouldn't go for the shot. He hates cops."

"Where you going now?"

"Benny's waiting down the road for me with a car. I'm getting out."

Allen kicked the starter, said: "Well, I'll be seeing you."

"Like hell you will." Schultz waved as the battered car gathered headway, bawled out: "Not unless you come to St. Looey."

LEAVING PRENTICE AT the police hospital, where the doctor assured him his injuries were superficial, Allen drove to the Central Station. He was sick, sore, and very tired. As he parked the car, Captain Hallahan and McCready, another detective on the Homicide Squad, dashed up with excited questions, and Allen said: "Inside. I need a drink bad."

"Where's Dal?"

"Hospital!"

"How bad?"

"He's beat up pretty bad but the Doc says he ain't really hurt. He needs rest and quiet."

Hallahan, sputtering questions, led the way into his office and Allen took the bottle he dug out of his desk and, without waiting for a glass, took two big gulps. He coughed, choked, said: "That's better." Still holding the bottle he sat down, told of what happened at the farmhouse.

Hallahan said thoughtfully: "Good thing for you they come back when they did and figured we had the place staked. It'd been too bad for you alone."

"Maybe."

"Maybe hell. Cinch. It'd do no good to go out there now."

"You gotta send the wagon out after the stiff."

"Oh, yes." Hallahan reached for the bottle. "Take a drink and gimme that."

Allen obeyed orders. With bodily resistance lowered, the liquor was already taking hold.

"I don't quite get letting this Schultz go—"

"Had to." Allen defended himself. "We told him we would and if it hadn't been for him, we'd have been put out. Probably by now."

"Well, you could've brought him anyway."

"Would you have? I mean in case you were in the same place."

"Well, no."

"We didn't, either."

McCready said: "How bad is Dal hurt?"

"Couple of broken ribs. They had to take about twenty

stitches in his head. One ear's hurt but the Doc thinks that'll wear off. He can't see 'cause his eyes are too damn' black." Allen laughed. "He told me he felt pretty good, before I left the hospital. That's takin' 'em."

"I'll say!"

Hallahan said: "And now I got news. The news is—Russo got killed."

"How? Who by?"

Hallahan shrugged. "A guy named Keefer. There was three of these birds out of the fourteen in the cell that saw it and they claim it was self-defense. Russo, Keefer, and these three men were in the lavatory and Russo's supposed to've gone for Keefer with a shiv and Keefer's supposed to've taken it away from him and beefed him with it during the fracas. The shiv was made out of a file."

"Hooey!"

"Sure! Keefer and these three heels that claim they saw it are all broke and they'll get paid off for this and have a lawyer clear 'em on it and the charges they're booked on. Sure it's hooey. Cinch! Bruner's got fun."

"Well I'll be damned! Right in jail. Murder in jail."

"Money still talks out loud… even in jail. And these hoods'll stick to their story. They'd hang if they cracked on it and they know it. It was self-defense and they'll prove it in court. Bruner *is* smart."

Allen said: "Bruner's just the same as dead. Right now."

"Like hell!"

"He is if Dal sees him. I'm telling you."

"What about you?"

Allen's grin was evil. He said: "If he's alone *and* the street ain't too crowded."

A clerk entered, said: "Heineman wants to see either you, Captain, or Lieutenant Allen or Prentice. Any or all of you."

Hallahan looked startled, said: "Okey. Send him in." As the clerk left he said: "Now, Al! No rough stuff. I'll do the talking." Allen stared at him sullenly and said nothing and Heineman came in. He looked jaunty. He looked at Allen, asked: "Where's your partner? I hear you boys been away for a while."

The whiskey was singing through Allen's head. He bounced out of his chair, lunged at the little lawyer, but Hallahan and McCready caught him and held him. He said: "You —— damned shyster!"

Heineman held up his hand in protest. He had flinched back against the wall but as he saw Allen was harmless he came forward. He said smoothly: "Why, I don't understand. It's in the paper." The color started to drift back in his face.

Hallahan growled: "What's the act for? I know damn' well we can't prove anything against you, if that's it."

The lawyer made sure Allen was still in custody. Watching him, he said: "I'm here with a message. Not mine. My client, you know who, has asked me to tell you boys he will be out of town until I get his case dismissed. That will probably be about six months. He didn't want the police force to waste valuable time searching for him."

Allen snarled: "Where is he?"

"Out of town." Heineman smiled. "He'll be back."

"Can you get word to him?"

Heineman shrugged. "He informed me that when I wanted him, a personal in the paper would reach him."

"When you do this, tell him to stay out! That clear? Out!"

Heineman's eyes narrowed. "Is that a threat? These things

are actionable, you know."

"Try and prove anything by these boys." Allen's voice was level. "Tell him to stay out. Get me?"

Heineman shrugged again. He said: "He'll be back!" and strolled to the door. He turned there, added with a half smile: "In—a—big—way!" and walked out.

Allen watched him go, dragged a gun from his side pocket, asked Hallahan: "You got any .45 shells, Cap? This has got an empty." His voice was still, even but his eyes were glazed with the rage he was controlling. He said: "It's Dal's. He'd want it full." He paused, added: "That is, if Bruner's coming back. In such a big way."

Hallahan grunted: "What the hell! It'll be six months." He grinned wryly at Allen. "Maybe you and Dal can get something done—now your private war is put off for a while. You boys are still on the force, though a man'd never know it."

Blackmail Is an Ugly Word

Dal Prentice takes a stormy vacation—with pay

DAL PRENTICE SNORTED skeptically. He snapped: "And she didn't know this Danvers? Never seen him! And him found dead in her house!"

Captain Hallahan said slowly, patiently: "No, Dal. She knows his brother Henry Danvers, the department store man, but not Joe. Everybody in town knows Henry or of him, but Joe's been away and just got back."

Prentice insisted: "But before he went away?"

"She couldn't. Joe hasn't been here for at least ten years and she hasn't been here that long. That's out." Hallahan slewed his chair around, spoke to the man across the desk. "Ain't that right, Commissioner?"

Police Commissioner Richards was small, slight. His thin face looked worn and tired. He told Prentice: "My sister has no idea who the man was." His voice sounded worried and he kept rubbing his hand over the sparse white stubble on his chin.

Prentice narrowed his eyes, looked sullen. "Now listen! Her story is that she opened the closet door and this strange guy fell out at her, deader than hell. And that she doesn't know him. Or never did. It's phoney, I tell you. Who parked him there? Why? How does *she* rate a stiff?"

Hallahan broke in: "My Gawd! If we knew! You're supposed to be a smart copper, you tell us. He must've been planted there. That's all I can figure."

"Planted! They'd have dumped him on the street or a side road. I want to know, why plant a stiff on her?"

Hallahan shrugged.

Prentice said stubbornly: "Listen, Richards! I'm supposed to be taken off the detail and work on this. I'm supposed to hush-hush what I dig up. When this heel is found in your sister's house you kept it quiet and you can keep it covered from here on. I know that. Now why am I supposed to go on with it? What's the angle? Why not leave it drop? The papers have it the body was found in an alley, a block from there. She's in the clear, so why the quiet stuff? Is this a secret?"

The Commissioner avoided Prentice's eyes. He said weakly: "It's murder. We have a duty. I only thought it would do no harm to move the body and save myself... e-r-r... my sister, the unpleasantness."

"It didn't. He wasn't killed there or there'd been more blood. But why wasn't he left where he was killed?"

"I don't know." Richards added almost with a whine: "I was up all night seeing that it was kept quiet."

Hallahan grunted: "Me too!" The look he gave Richards was faintly derisive.

Prentice said: "Oh hell!" in a disgusted voice. "Put it another way. Unless you open up, what've I got to go on? This?" He leaned to the desk, tapped a blunt finger on a telegram. "All this says is that Joe Danvers served three years for burglary while armed, in Folsom, and that he lives in San Francisco. Or lived. I'm supposed to go up there and find out why he was put in your sister's house after he got knocked off. I don't even know whether this sanctimonious brother of his knew whether he was in the racket. Not that it probably has a damn' thing to do with it."

Hallahan commented: "Now Dal! It's hardly likely he did.

He'd know we'd dig up Joe's record if he had one. He'd be acting worried instead of so almighty righteous. When he identified the body he acted surprised because we didn't have the killers in jail."

"Maybe." Prentice looked doubtful. "And maybe he figures people would talk about him if he didn't make a fuss. He's that way. It's a break he ain't wise where the body was found."

Richards said in a worried voice: "Now Lieutenant, with the help my letters will give you, I am depending on you to keep this matter secret. That is, whatever you discover that might link my sister with this man. As far as the other men in your department are concerned, you are just having a vacation."

Prentice scowled, got to his feet. "It'll be a honey of a vacation."

Hallahan glanced at Richards' compressed lips, said soothingly: "The Commissioner's paying your expenses out of his own pocket and sending you up there. Go ahead and do the best you can. You ought to feel flattered that you're the man he picked."

Prentice snapped: "Flattered hell!" and stormed out of the office.

HENRY DANVERS OWNED Magna City's leading department store... was probably the leading man... and was noted for his lavish contributions to prohibition funds, and for a lack of these same contributions to more charitable organizations. He was cordially disliked by his fellow citizens. His secretary was cast in the same mold and had the same apparent dislike of Prentice, which bothered the detective not in the least, as he entered the reception room, sailed his shabby hat negligently along the hard bench, reserved for those with the courage to wait for Danvers, and inquired: "Is the big man in? You ask him, honey."

Honey was at least fifty. She knew Prentice from his having solicited money for the Police Widows and Orphans Fund and sniffed audibly. "Mr. Danvers is in conference but I'll take your name in, Mr. e-r-r...."

"Prentice is the name, baby. You know it just as well as I do. What you doing tonight?"

Miss Clark sailed majestically past the chuckling Prentice and into Danvers' office, to return in a moment and admit that Mr. Danvers would see Lieutenant Prentice. Her manner implied that Mr. Danvers was making an error.

Danvers' office was as spare and dry as he was himself. A plain desk, kept scrupulously clean and almost bare, and three straight-backed chairs, served to remind the visitor that it was a business office... strictly business. Prentice was as business-like.

"I've found, Mr. Danvers, that your brother Joe has spent the last several years in San Francisco. I'm in charge of the investigation into his death. I've called to ask you if you have any information that might be of help to me on this."

Danvers looked up from his desk in apparent surprise; then his pale eyes flickered away. "San Francisco! Are you sure? Joe had never led me to believe he had lived there."

"Where did he say he lived?"

Danvers' thin cheeks flushed... his voice was evasive. "My brother, Lieutenant, was a very—" he hesitated—"a very secretive man. To be frank, he never mentioned where he had lived before this visit to me."

Prentice said bluntly: "Well, that's where he lived and that's where I'm going tonight. He hadn't been here long enough to get anybody mad enough at him to knock him off. Only two weeks, wasn't it?"

"Yes. Almost exactly." Danvers drummed on his desk with nervous fingers and looked out the window to avoid Prentice's stare. "Lieutenant, I have a feeling that possibly Joe was mixed with a bad element up there." He coughed, seemed to hunt for words. "He was always… wild. I would appreciate it… in case anything is discovered… if you would… well…." He coughed again and added quickly: "I mean of course if it has no bearing on the case."

Prentice caught his glance, stared at him with hard eyes. He said: "You mean hush things up? Why should I?" in a raspy voice.

Danvers stammered: "Well... e-r-r I would be willing to... u-h-h... that is... a nominal sum. To represent me. You know."

"How much?"

"A hundred dollars."

Prentice stood up and Danvers said hastily: "Two hundred."

Prentice took a step to the desk. A big man, he had tremendous shoulders and the slender Danvers flinched as he leaned over, pounding the desk for emphasis. "Listen you! Keep your lousy two hundred dollars. Two hundred dollars!" He made a derisive exclamation. "If I find out anything about this brother of yours I'll broadcast it. See!" He walked away from the desk, away from the cowering Danvers, wheeled and came back. "This brother of yours had been three years in stir. In Folsom. It's worth more than two C's for me to forget *that*."

Danvers raised an arm in front of his face. From this cover he stuttered: "Lieutenant! It... it isn't that. I didn't mean...."

Prentice snapped out: "To hell with you!"

He started out, but turned back when Danvers called to him.

Danvers wore a placating smile. He said hurriedly: "You misunderstood me, Lieutenant. I didn't mean that I wanted to buy your silence. I want to retain you."

"I'm no private shamus. Hire one."

"Would you be interested in making a thousand dollars and that without interfering with your duty?"

The smile that Danvers meant to be ingratiating was a grimace.

"No. There's a stinger in it or you wouldn't be so big-hearted. Nerts to you."

Prentice turned his back again.

"And I'll pay a reasonable sum for your expenses."

Prentice swung around and Danvers jerked back in his chair. Prentice grunted: "I won't bite you! What's all this about?"

"Joe was my brother and I feel very bitter about his death. I want you to avenge his murder."

"I'm no avenger, I'm a policeman." He stared sourly at Danvers. "Go on with the yarn. What's the grand and expenses for? Make it a good one while you're at it.... I'm not going to listen long."

"Really, Lieutenant, I want you to find the men that killed Joe."

"I'm working on it. What's the grand for? Spit it out."

"Call it a bonus." Danvers hesitated. "And of course, to look out for my interests." He seemed to take courage, went on. "It just happens that I know Joe had money. As I am the sole heir I am interested in this and... well... Joe had no money in the local banks and I think it likely you may discover where this is. I believe this will be cash and I would like any personal property of his."

"If he didn't leave a will this will have to go through the courts."

Danvers coughed. "Well... e-r-r... I thought...."

"I get you. Hand it to you and save time." Prentice blinked his eyes, flung out: "Why in hell don't you come right out and say it? You want me to find his dough... not his killer. And what I find turn over to you instead of the D.A. Isn't that it?"

Danvers tried hard to match Prentice's straight stare, but failed. His glance dropped, and he fumbled with a paper on the desk.

"You'll look into this for me then, Lieutenant?"

Prentice grinned. "Oh sure! I'll do it. Keep an eye out for the dough. Sure!"

Danvers had regained his composure. He said coldly: "That's only incidental of course. You understand, the main thing is to find the men that robbed him of life. I feel that with your police connections you will do this before any private detective I might hire could function."

"And find the dough quicker. You're not kidding me, if you are yourself. Okey! You've hired a boy."

Prentice's eyes were hard as he stalked past the crusty Miss Clark without a glance at her. Greed was a fault with which he was very familiar, but greed about money left by a murdered brother was too far over the border-line for his approval.

IN SAN FRANCISCO, Prentice made immediate contact with Larry Sullivan of the Homicide Squad. Sullivan was red-faced, beefy, with as many years of police work behind him as had Prentice. Both men reversed the principle of a suspect being innocent until proved guilty. Both men honestly believed a rubber hose, judiciously wielded, would insure a confession in shorter time than any later method; and both backed conviction with action. Neither held any brief for criminals, yet were not averse to profiting from them in any way that did not involve the covering of any serious crime. They were fast friends.

Prentice met him in the Central Station, said: "Lo, Larry! I came to see you. I'd buy a drink if you knew a place."

"Big-hearted, huh!"

"It's business."

Sullivan said: "Come on!" and led the way to a nearby speake. Once seated at a table, he asked: "What's the beef?"

"Danvers. The yegg that got himself killed in my town."

Sullivan pursed his lips.

"All I want to know is, Sully, who he run around with and the rest of it. You knew him?"

"Too well."

"Yeah!"

"He's been working for a grease-ball named Cicco here. He was one of many."

"Who's Cicco?"

"He owns the *Club Italiano* here. Bad boy."

"Got a tough bunch, huh?"

"Just this tough," Sullivan said slowly. "We've had 'em up half a dozen times and we couldn't get a witness to appear against 'em. There was one, and we picked him out of the bay the same day he was supposed to crack to the grand jury. Tough isn't a strong enough word for these boys." He picked his words carefully. "If you get into a jam, shoot first. The department'll back you up." He added with sudden heat: "Yes, and by —— they'll give you a medal if you shoot straight."

"Nice pipples, I can see that. What I want to know most is what gal did this Danvers go for most of the time. She might be sore enough to talk a little and that'll do for a start."

"I can tell you that. The one that got the most play, the only one that'd know a damn' thing, works for Cicco in this *Club*. They'll spot you before you get within ten feet of the door as a copper, so that won't do you no good."

"If you can get me a card I can tell 'em I'm selling insurance or some stall like that."

Sullivan said: "Nerts!" derisively. "What about them flat feet? You spell six feet of copper to anybody that looks at you."

"You get me the card. I got an idea."

"What?"

"Wait and see if it works." Prentice grinned. "If I look that fly I may get over."

THE *CLUB ITALIANO* made a specialty of Italian dinners and the drinking that usually accompanied them. A little dance-floor always jammed; a floor show always risque; and a crew of waiters apparently recruited from murderers' row at the State Prison, made it a good place from which to stay away. It was very popular. Cicco was the owner, though not the nominal one.

Prentice sat by himself at one of the little tables against the wall, well away from the dance-floor, drinking Scotch he had thoughtfully brought with him and paying the waiter two dollars a bottle for twenty-cent ginger ale. The floor show closed with a flash; the girls bowed off and were shortly circulating through the crowd in their dual roles of hostesses. Dal was civil but inattentive to a very pretty blonde, but brightened when an older, tougher looking red-head honored him with her presence. The red-head nodded at the blonde who had flounced away to a table where her efforts at friendliness were meeting with a warmer reception, asked: "What's the matter with Alice? Did she get fresh with you?"

"That was the trouble." Prentice smiled genially. "She didn't. I'm no gentleman and blondes don't click, sister."

"How are you on carrot-tops?" The red-head smiled nicely. Prentice was spending money and a girl on percentage couldn't pick and choose.

"My weakness. Sit down, honey, and I'll buy a drink."

"Make it short. I gotta work till two and that's four hours yet."

"And then what? Do I meet you?"

"Say! You work too fast." She looked at him suspiciously. "What's the idea?"

Prentice covered. He hiccoughed and said: "I told you red-heads were my weakness, honey. Didn't mean no harm. I'm a stranger in town and you know how it is. Gets lonesome when you don't know anybody."

She considered. He looked like a free spender and they were scarce, yet he had an indefinable air of knowing more than he should that made her vaguely suspicious. She beckoned the waiter, whispered out of the side of her mouth: "Give me my checks on two bottles of fizz. D'ya know this guy?"

The waiter cast an eye at Prentice who was shakingly pouring a drink. "He's a stranger to me. I pick him as a copper, but the boss let him in."

"Well, if it was a tip-over this bird wouldn't be in here spending dough." She spoke to Prentice: "Listen, honey, I got to go and put on an act. Be back as soon as it's over."

Prentice agreed effusively. "That's great, Red! It's you and me for it. We'll get along."

She hurried back to the dressing-room and there stopped to put in a call for the waiter on Prentice's table. She told him: "Listen, Angelo. There's something fly about the ump-chay. Ask the big man to check up," and hurried into her costume.

Prentice had not missed the interchange between the girl and the waiter and was not surprised when a suave dark man, dressed in tux and patent leathers, dropped into the chair vacated by the girl. The stranger looked Prentice over, noting the wrinkled gray business suit, the bulge in the left arm-pit. He asked casually: "Y' havin' a good time?"

Prentice seemed quite drunk. He answered in a thick voice. "Swell! Good music, good dinner, and bad girls." His wink was suggestive.

The suave man's smile was congenial. "That's good. We've a pretty good bunch here, all right. Service okey?"

Prentice winked elaborately again, had trouble getting his face back to normal. "So far. I brought my own but it ain' goin't' las'."

"The waiter can fix you up all right. You're a copper, ain'tcha?"

"How ja know?"

The dark man smiled thinly, shrugged.

"You won' tell nobody I was here, will ya?"

"Hell, man, I don't even know who you are. All I know is, you had a card from Jerry Watkins and he gives us a play."

"Y' see, I met this Watkins this af'ernoon with a frien' o' mine an' he gimme this card. *He* knows who I am, all right."

"I don't."

Prentice leaned over the table, spoke confidentially. "If I tell you, will you keep it quiet? I won' make no trouble for you."

"Don't be silly! We're protected."

Prentice nodded sagely and during this nod his elbow slipped and he barely saved his face from the table. "Tha's th' way *I* work it. W'en a place pays off I leave 'em 'lone. Tha's jus' my way."

"That right?"

"Uh-huh!" He leaned closer, dropped his voice even lower. "Didja ever hear o' Mill Valley?"

"Some place in Oregon, ain't it?"

"Bes' little town in state. Sawmill town. We got twent' thousan' now, or damn' near. An' I'm..." He paused dramatically. "I'm Chief Police. See!"

"Is… that… right!" The dark man's voice held awe.

"Abs'lutely. Y' see why I don't wan' nobody t' know I'm here."

"I can see."

"Y' know how 'tis. Now we got a good open town…." Another labored wink. "… *You* know… th' joints payin' off an' me gettin' mine but I'm not supposed t' get out like this. *You* know."

"I know. You guys are all the same. All knocking down."

"'S good for me. I'm makin' mine." Very confidentially. "Y' know if th' council knew 'bout me steppin' like this I'd get fired jus' like that." He made an unsuccessful attempt to snap his fingers.

"I don't doubt it. I won't give you away. What you down here for?"

"Af'er a pris'ner. This guy he…."

"It don't make any difference. You're here."

Prentice was acting faithfully the part of a small-town police chief he had met while going after a prisoner. He was thankful his memory was good. He said expansively: "These little towns are place t' make dough. Jus' look at me. Now I got five kids. Tha' cos's money right there. An' I'm married. See!"

"I figured you were. With the five kids."

Prentice looked injured.

"No rib. There's dough in the little towns all right. If you got a good spot, that is."

"I gotta house tha' cos' me twent' thousan', I got me nice car, an'…." He winked again. "… I got dough, too. If I keep goin for another two years I got her made. How's 'at for money? An' I made it outta two-fifty a month."

"That's pretty good all right." The dark man dropped the subject.

Prentice stared at the floor show. "Say, ain't that red-head a honey? Wha's her name?"

"Doris Case. Nice kid." The dark man turned, glanced at the show. The red-head had just broken into her specialty dance. "I'll introduce you, Mr. e-r-r...."

"Daw. Chief Daw. I already met her. Will she step?"

The dark man grinned: "I wouldn't know," and Prentice, almost falling off his chair, shoved him playfully on the shoulder, tittered: "Naw! You would'n' know. You know how it is w'en y' get out. You're...."

"Arlo. Johnny Arlo, Mr. Daw." He stood up. "You go ahead and have a good time. If you need more liquor, the waiter'll fix you up with some good stuff."

"Appreciate it, Mr. Arley. That's th' name, ain' it? Y' know I thought mebbe 'cause I was a law off'cer I might not be welcome in here."

"Glad to have you."

Arlo left to tell the red-head: "Your big shot's oke. He's law all right but just a dumb yokel that's on the make. If you play it right he's made to order for some dough."

"Johnny, you sure? I'd hate to get rapped."

"Forget it. His name's Daw but it ought to be John J. Sap. He broke down and told all. Take your best shot."

She nodded, said: "Well... a live one..." and shrugged into her costume for her next act.

THE *CLUB ITALIANO* floor show broke at two-twenty. At two-forty, Prentice and the red-head were in a taxi, headed up Balboa Street to her apartment. If Doris had been as wary as when she started inquiries, she might have noticed Prentice was strangely sober and oddly enough, not over amorous… and that he had dropped the mantle of small-town police chief. She noticed nothing, for which Prentice was duly thankful… the characterization having been quite a strain.

In the apartment, she said: "Wait here till I go change. Then we can step out," and retired into the dressing-room giving the wide-awake Prentice a chance to examine the fire-escape running past the window and the lock on the door.

His hunch that trouble was near at hand was confirmed when, almost simultaneous with her appearance knuckles rapped on the door and someone said: "Doris! Open up!"

She looked at Prentice questioningly.

He nodded, and she obeyed and Arlo walked in, flanked by two other men. Prentice, at the same time the girl opened the door, stepped sidewise until the trio at the door were at his left and possibly ten feet in front.

Arlo stopped just inside the door, reached back without turning and closed it. He said: "Jerry come in right after you left."

Prentice said questioningly: "Jerry!" and with a rising inflection: "Jerry who?" He seemed puzzled, spoke in a thick voice.

Arlo had a thin smile on his face. He said: "Don't stall! Jerry Watkins, the fella you had a card from. He knew you, he said."

"Oh, sure. Th' guy I met this afternoon." Prentice cursed himself for not telling Watkins and Sullivan his plan—for not telling Watkins to keep quiet about him being from Magna City. But that was Prentice all over. He had thought his plan would work, and that seemed enough to him.

"Yeah! The heel that give this dick Sullivan and you his card. On the Danvers' rub-out, are you?"

Prentice's hand was inside his coat. He dropped his drunken

manner, said: "What if I am!" and cleared the gun from the clip-holster under his arm.

Both of the men with Arlo were watching the hidden hand, and the girl slipped down until she crouched, white-faced, on the floor by the davenport. The man on Arlo's right dropped his hand towards his coat pocket and Prentice rapped out: "You! Easy there! You're Bull Keegan and that mugg with you is your lousy half-brother. I seen your pictures in the gallery this afternoon. You make a break and…."

Keegan grabbed for the gun in his pocket and Prentice shot him in the chest. The heavy bullet spun him around and, as he fell, Prentice shouted: "You, Arlo! Get them hands up!" Arlo started to obey and the third man seized what looked like an opening and dived at Prentice's knees and Prentice sidestepped nimbly, leaned over and struck at his head, as he sprawled, with the barrel of his gun.

Arlo, overlooked for the moment, whipped a gun from under his coat and fired point-blank at Prentice just as Prentice half-stooped over the man on the floor. He missed. From this position Prentice shot back and Arlo dropped the gun, clutched at his throat with both hands, and fell on his face. His feet drummed on the floor and he made clawing motions with his hands.

Prentice struck the man on the floor a second time with the gun barrel and straightened with the gun covering the screaming girl. He walked to her, slapped her on the cheek, said: "Cut that! There's been enough noise without you going screwy. Where's your phone?"

Shocked into silence, she pointed towards the hall leading into the kitchen, and he grabbed her wrists and drew her with him, growling: "You ain't going to take a powder. Not now, you ain't."

He called Police Headquarters, laconically gave the address, said: "Best send the ambulance with the fast wagon. There's two stiffs and maybe three. And drag Sullivan out and bring him along. Yeah, Larry Sullivan." He hung up the phone and turned to the girl.

She said slowly, distinctly: "Why… that's… murder."

Prentice's voice was grim. "Yeah! And you change those clothes to something soberer and watch your step or you'll be in it. Hustle, you tramp."

Ignoring the frantic pounding on the apartment door, he followed her into the bedroom and, despite her protests, watched her stolidly while she donned a quiet dress and slipped into street shoes instead of the satin mules she was wearing. They went back into the front room just in time to open the door for the first of the police who crowded past the excited inmates of the apartment house clustered in the hall.

Sullivan came shortly afterward, followed by a red-faced, hulking man he introduced to Prentice as Hayes, captain of the Homicide Squad. This last looked with approval at the bodies of Arlo and Keegan and not so approvingly at the second Keegan, who was beginning to regain consciousness. He grunted: "Nice work, Prentice! Sullivan was telling me you was good. Course they started it."

"Sure! Of course they did."

"What happened?"

Prentice glanced at the girl. "Well, it was like this. We was sitting here when they come in and started to rough me up. I told 'em to lay off and the big guy"—he pointed at Keegan—

"pulled a gun and we started brawling. I had to shoot him and this guy." He pointed at Arlo.

"And what of this heel?"

The last of the trio was feebly trying to sit erect.

"Well, I knocked him out to keep him from shooting me." Prentice looked virtuous. "I was trying to keep the peace."

"Yeah! How you were. We can stick him on assault with intent, anyway." Hayes turned to the girl. "How about the twist? She the come-on?"

Prentice winked at him. "Hell, no. She's oke. Didn't have a thing to do with it."

Hayes spoke to the girl. "Was that the way it happened?"

She nodded, not looking at him. Her face was white and she stared straight in front of her. A thin trickle of blood coming from a bitten lip contrasted with her color.

Hayes turned back to Prentice. "Two down and one to go. You ain't got no authority in this man's town, either. I don't know what I ought to do."

Sullivan said: "I'll see he turns up at the inquest, Hayes. How's that?"

Hayes scratched his head. "Well, I guess it'll be all right." He stepped close to Prentice, whispered: "For —— sake! Either get that twist primed with the same story or lose her before the inquest. She acts like she don't believe you."

"Then you don't want to hold me?"

"Hell, no! Just be there at the inquest." He laughed. "Keep in touch with Sullivan and I'll give you the names of some more of these —— when you feel like brawling again."

Prentice shook the girl by the shoulder. "Listen! Le's go. I want a drink and I want to talk to you." She assented mechanically and they pushed through the crowd in the hall and downstairs. He flagged a cab, asked the girl: "Where'll we go?" and when she made a suggestion, told the driver: "Up to the eleven hundred block on Post. We'll walk from there."

THE SPEAKE WAS small and modest. Prentice stopped at the little bar, told the bartender: "Two highballs! Scotch!" and led the way to a booth.

The red-head sat down. Her voice trembled. She asked: "What was the idea in starting the shooting? It was you that started it."

"I finished it. That big heel started it when he went for a gun. Listen! I hate a hood and I don't figure to give one an even break. If it hadn't started there they'd have sanded me out on the street where I wouldn't have a chance. This Arlo was bad."

Doris said: "I wasn't married to him." Her lips quivered.

"Hell, Kid. I know you're not. You're the twist that played around with Joe Danvers. I know."

Her eyes widened. "How did you know? Did you know Joe?"

In answer he showed her his identification card.

"So *that's* why you picked me."

"Yeah! I'm after the guy that knocked off your boy friend."

"You got one, I think. Arlo was out of town, just got back today. I don't know for sure, though. How did you know who I was?"

"Oh, hell, Red! I been all afternoon at the station, looking at pictures. I knew the Keegans, Arlo, and you and a lot more. How come you worked for Arlo if you thought he bumped your sweetie? You going to give me the dope on what that rumble was?"

The shock of seeing two men killed in front of her was beginning to tell. She started to cry, at first softly, then with big tearing sobs. The waiter came back with the drinks, looked at them curiously, and as he left the booth Prentice reached across the table, lifted the girl's head from her arms and slapped her sharply on each cheek. He snapped: "All right, tramp! You going to go dramatic on me? Wake up or I'll slap you so hard you'll wobble." He cuffed her again as she looked up at him.

She said meekly: "I got thinking about the way Arlo grabbed his neck when he fell. I'll never forget that."

"You that way about Arlo?"

"I hated him. I had to work for him because I didn't dare quit. Arlo worked for Cicco."

"So did Joe Danvers. Why did Joe get spotted?"

"I'm not sure I know."

She reached for her glass, drained it in two big gulps, and Prentice called the waiter, said: "Again on the drinks."

The waiter was nervous. He said: "Listen, Cap! We're hot here. This gal ain't goin' t' make a fuss, is she? It looks to me like a crying jag."

Prentice said nastily: "Who cares what it looks like to you? When I order a drink I want it. She's oke."

Doris made peace. "I'm all right. I'm just nervous... not drunk."

The waiter went dubiously back to the bar... kept watching them.

"All right, Kid. Start in. Why did they spot Joe?"

"I'm afraid to tell."

"Of who? Quit stalling."

"You know who. Arlo isn't the big man."

"Cicco is. I know that and all about it. It's okey by me, baby, if you don't want to talk." His voice turned ugly. "You'll go down and see if you can stand the rap on this rub-out at your spot. I'm clear. With the record those hoods have got and you being mixed with 'em, you'll get the rap. Didn't I wash you clean up there? I try and play ball with you and you start to throw curves at me. Finish that drink and we'll go to the station."

"Please! I'd tell you if I was sure it was safe. We can't talk here."

"All right then. Let's go some place else. My hotel."

A man strolled past the booth and the short hairs on Prentice's neck bristled. He whispered: "Don't look for a minute. Ain't that Cicco?"

Without turning her head Doris looked, stammered: "Gawd! That's Cicco! Oh, Gawd!"

"I thought I remembered his picture."

"Gawd! My number's up."

"Would he know about the shooting yet?"

"I know he would. He probably sent Arlo up."

Her face was dirty white, make-up standing out on her cheeks in red blotches. She was biting her lip again, stopped this and picked up the highball glass, tried to drink and the rim rattled against her teeth. She set it down empty, added: "He must've been outside my place and seen us go and tailed us."

Prentice took the gun from under his arm, broke it and filled the two empty chambers, then held the gun on his lap.

"We'd better scram then. He's looking for us, it's a cinch. Some of those people in the apartment house must've told him what happened and he'll figure you put his red-hots on the spot for me."

The waiter went by and he signaled him, asked: "You got a back way out o' this bucket?"

The waiter said: "What's the idea?" in an uneasy voice. "You could go through the kitchen, I guess."

"We don't want to see a guy is all."

"What guy? Maybe I know him. Jus' what's the angle?"

"What do *you* care? You going to show me the way out?"

"Say listen, guy! The boss is out and I'm lookin' after th' joint. Ix-nay on this running around. It looks like a rumble and we're burning up now. I'm sorry, but no dice."

He turned to go and Prentice snarled: "You ——!" and his hand, holding the gun, came up over the table. "You go out in the kitchen with us. I don't want you spilling your guts too soon. You been arguing ever since I been in here and I'm sick of it. Get me, you!"

The man looked at the steady muzzle of the big gun, gulped, stammered: "Why... why sure! Yes, sir! I wouldn't tell!"

"I know damn' well you won't. Now listen. I'm putting this in my pocket but it's pointed at you. You walk ahead of us to the kitchen and through it and don't look around. Get going."

They were luckily in the back booth and their passage through the kitchen was made with no disturbance, the frightened waiter leading the way until they were half-way down the alley that led to the street, where Prentice let him go. He and the girl went on and as they stepped on the sidewalk he saw a car start in front of the speake and towards them. He caught at the girl's wrist and tried to throw her to the ground but she pulled free and Prentice dropped to the ground himself, just as the machine-gun in the car turned loose.

The girl screamed shrilly once, sagged and fell in a shapeless heap, and Prentice fired twice at the speeding car. He realized his chances of a hit were nil and ran to the girl. She coughed, mumbled: "Cicco, he…" coughed again and was still.

Prentice heard the shrill of a police whistle, then the running steps of a patrolman, gun out and excited. Prentice was cursing, still held his gun in his hand. The uniformed man shouted: "Drop it! You're under arrest!"

Prentice stopped swearing. "Sure! I would be! A bunch of hoods gun out the gal and you arrest *me*."

"Didn't you shoot? What's the gun for? Drop it, I say."

"I shot at the car."

"Car!"

"Hell… yes… car! It passed you! You blind?"

"I saw it. Did they do the shooting?"

"Yeah! There must be half a dozen slugs in the gal here and I only shot twice at the car. Get smart."

A siren wailed at the intersection below, rubber squealed, and a squad car pulled to a halt in front of the speake. Prentice identified himself with some little trouble; the body of the girl was loaded into a following ambulance, the crowd was dispersed, and the gloomy Prentice went to his hotel to figure out another angle of approach. With Cicco knowing him, and one possible source of information closed by the death of the red-head, he figured the only thing he could do would be to wait and see what a police third-degree would sweat out of the remaining Keegan brother, but he had little hope of any result from this. Cicco's cure for talking out of turn would be too fresh in Keegan's mind. What hurt was he felt himself directly responsible for the reminder… namely the death of the girl.

HE HAD WIRED Commissioner Richards the hotel where he was staying and the morning brought a wire from him. It read: *New developments Stop sister arrives San Francisco in morning Stop meet your hotel.*

He had breakfast in his room, puzzled over his problem.

His first caller was Sullivan. He came up without being announced, looked at Prentice critically, and commented: "You get action, I'll say that. What really happened last night? I'm sick about that girl getting it."

"So'm I," Prentice said gloomily. "She seemed like a pretty good kid even if she was so hardboiled and mixed with that mob. Sit down and I'll buy a drink. That Cicco is a red hot for fair."

"He is that. Keegan won't say a word and we'll have to postpone the inquest on the others because he's all marked up arguing about it. A smart lawyer'd raise a lot of hell over the shape he's in."

"To hell with him! I know damn'well I could make him talk."

Sullivan's voice was regretful. "Yeah! So could I, Dal, if they'd give me a chance, but you can't give a man the works now the way you used to. The boys'll keep working on him, though, I'll say that."

Prentice lifted his glass. "Here's to crime. Going to have company this morning."

"Who?"

"Police Commissioner's sister. The one that lives where the stiff was found. I ain't seen her yet because she was sick in bed over this deal when I left. Nervous breakdown."

"How come she's coming?"

"Dunno." He tossed Sullivan the wire.

Sullivan read it thoughtfully, said: "H'm-m. New developments. If I was you I'd sit tight and wait for her."

"I am. I have to... nothing to go on with the girl killed. I
never felt so bad in my life as I do over that girl getting the
business. If I'd worked it different it might have come out all
right. Give me that glass and I'll fill it."

"That's enough. It's morning, Dal, and I don't hit it before
noon. Tell me, what happened last night?"

"They got wise I was phoney and figured I'd pump the gal.
Will there be trouble about it?"

"Hell, no!" Sullivan laughed. "The inquest will kill the whole
thing. That Arlo had more priors than he was years old, and
Keegan was damn' near as bad. ——! I don't blame you for
feeling tough about the gal. It gets me too."

"Cicco might even have figured she was with me on the
shooting. That tommy was meant for me, too."

"He's jerry, all right. He's a smart —— Well, be seein' you."

Sullivan had not been gone more than five minutes when
there was another knock. Prentice, in shirtsleeves, glass in hand
and expecting to see Sullivan again, went to the door... saw
a very small, meek-looking lady who looked at him in some
confusion. She asked: "You're Lieutenant Prentice?" in a voice
that matched her appearance. She gave the impression that
she would be more at home in the age of bustles. Her modish
clothes were worn with a frightened air that confessed she
didn't entirely approve of them... her hair, bobbed and waved,
she wore as she might have worn a wig.

On Prentice admitting his identity she confessed: "I'm Miss
Richards. May I talk with you?" She seemed a little embarrassed,
and Prentice's appearance was excuse enough for the feeling.

Prentice came to her rescue. "Won't you come in, Miss Richards? It's perfectly all right," in a voice that was sober enough.

Plainly a little frightened at her own daring, Miss Richards entered the room and accepted the chair that Prentice tendered. He struggled into his coat, put the bottle of Scotch out of sight, and she smiled faintly at this last, said: "It's really all right. I don't disapprove of liquor. My own father…" She coughed.

Relieved, Prentice asked: "What has happened, Miss Richards? I got your brother's wire."

She ignored his question.

"Tell me, Lieutenant, have you made any progress?"

"Well, yes and no. Would you mind telling me just what happened? You know I wasn't able to see you and all I know is what your brother told me, and second-hand information is not so good. Have I got this straight? You opened this closet door and he was inside?"

Her voice was very careful. "I came home late from a bridge party. Emil, the chauffeur, let me out in front of the house and took the car around to the garage in the back and I opened the door with my latchkey. I had told my maid not to wait up for me as I knew I would be late. I took off my wrap and started to hang it in the hall closet. As I opened the door the man fell out. He almost touched me as he fell. I screamed and fainted." Her voice sounded to Prentice faintly monotonous… as if she were reciting a story she had memorized.

He shook his head, got up from his chair and went to the window. He said absently: "And then…."

"Then I called Mr. Richards and he called Captain Hallahan and the captain called the officer that walks around that district and they took the body away. To some alley, I believe."

Prentice shook his head discontentedly. He asked: "Mind if I smoke?" and lit a cigarette absent-mindedly at her nod. He argued: "It don't make sense, Miss Richards. Here's a gang killing for sure. This man was a known gangster and was shot three times in the stomach. That's typical of this kind of killing. He wasn't killed in your house or there'd have been more blood. Hallahan told me that much. He was brought there, it's a cinch. Now why? Why not tell me what you're holding back?" His voice was fretful and he scowled at her.

Miss Richards stared back at him steadily. "Please tell me what has happened here."

"Plenty! And all of it bad." He told her everything that had happened, glossing over the shooting of Arlo and Keegan but enlarging broadly on the killing of the girl, Doris Case.

The recital of the girl's death moved Miss Richards greatly. Her faded eyes flashed. "You want me to understand that this girl was deliberately killed because she might possibly have given you information about Danvers?"

"Yes. And about the men who killed him. This bunch is bad. B-a-d. The girl was really an innocent party, that's what hurts me so much."

"Why, this is atrocious! I don't see how such things can be allowed. The best thing I can do is tell you the whole story. My brother tried to shield me but I can see that will be impossible." She opened her purse and handed him a letter without further comment. It was formed from letters cut from a newspaper and pasted on cheap stationery and the envelope was unaddressed. Prentice read it curiously.

If you want your letters back watch personals in Examiner come to San Francisco and you will be told what to do remember Danvers we mean business.

He asked: "How did you get this?"

"It was put in my mail box, night before last."

"What's this about letters? What you were holding out on me?"

She said desperately: "Lieutenant, two years ago I went to Del Monte to spend a couple of months. I met a man there and, not even thinking of the difference in our ages, consented to marry him. I must have been out of my mind. I can't explain it, even to myself. I knew nothing of him... nothing."

Prentice puzzled: "I still don't see. There's no harm falling for a man if he *is* younger than you."

She flushed warmly.

"In my infatuation I wrote him things I shouldn't have written. A woman came to me and said she was his wife. I asked him and he admitted it and I gave them money. I really had to do it...." She faltered, continued: "We were to be married and I was desperately in love and..." Her voice trailed away miserably, her face was crimson.

Prentice looked at the wall, away from her, thought of Commissioner Richards and whistled. He said: "We never know. I judge you wrote things in those letters you wouldn't want the world to know."

Miss Richards was twisting her handkerchief and staring down at the floor. Her voice was almost inaudible as she answered: "I'm afraid I did. I was crazy."

"I begin to see a little light. Danvers was the man, huh?"

She nodded mutely.

"Did you give him the money?"

"First to Mrs. Danvers. She was a terrible woman, all hard and painted. Then to him. Then to an Italian that showed me one of the letters… from your description, this man Arlo. Then to Danvers again."

"What did this Mrs. Danvers look like? What color hair?"

"Red. Henna rinse."

Prentice whistled again, said: "Our Doris," under his breath. "Then you knew Danvers all the time? Why didn't your brother tell me?" He started to walk back and forth the length of the little room.

"He thought he could keep me out of it. I'm so ashamed. A married man."

"I can set your mind at rest on that. He wasn't married. This girl that was killed last night is the one that pretended to be Mrs. Danvers, I think. Though that doesn't make her death any easier to take. Did she tell you she'd sue you for stealing her husband?"

"Yes. And use my letters as evidence."

Prentice stopped in front of her.

"You say Danvers was the last to ask you for money. How much? How much had you paid before?"

"Before this last time, I had paid altogether, eight thousand. He asked for twenty thousand more and I gave him half of that the night he was killed. He gave me some of my letters."

"That's where you were instead of this bridge game, huh?"

"Yes. I met him on a road out of town. He had rented a car and I left him there and dropped in to make apologies at the party and stayed for a rubber."

"Then it was probably an hour after you left him before you got home?"

"At least two. We chatted a while at the party before I went home."

"I see. You say you gave him some ten thousand dollars for part of your letters. Why only part?"

"He said he was going to give me all of them but that he had trouble getting them and could only get part of them at a time. He said that was why he wanted the money… the man that had the letters suspected he was trying to return them to me… and that he was afraid."

Prentice said wearily: "I wish your brother had told me. Cicco had the letters, it's a cinch, and Danvers stole them back and put the slug on you for himself. Cicco rubbed him out and took the rest of them back along with the ten grand. He put him in your closet to show he wasn't fooling."

"Mr. Danvers was trying to get them back for me so I wouldn't be harmed. He had reformed and was sorry about what he had done." Miss Richards was very dignified.

Prentice looked at her in amazement.

"My Gawd! And did you believe that stuff?"

Her lips trembled. "Well… I… I wanted to." She suddenly put her head down and began sobbing and her voice was muffled by her hands. "That's why I want you to find out who killed him and punish them. He… he was the only man that ever…" She cried brokenly.

"There… there now. It'll be all right." He awkwardly patted her shoulder, staring over her head the while, then went into the bathroom and soaked a towel with cold water and gave it to her. "Put this over your eyes….You'll feel better." He poured her a small drink, commanded: "Take this. It's medicine. It'll brace you up and we've got to plan this together."

She fumbled the whiskey glass, drank… and gagged. He encouraged: "That's it! You'll feel a lot better in a minute. D'you suppose Henry Danvers knew anything about this?"

She quavered: "I hope not. Maybe he did. Joe always said he had nothing to do with his brother."

"That probably means he did. When you went to Del Monte did Henry know anything of it? Could he have tipped off Joe?"

"He might have known of it. My brother and I knew him slightly."

"Did Joe come to Del Monte after you were there or was he there when you got there?"

"After. I remember that."

"Then there's your answer. Henry told Joe you had money and to make a play for you. It works out all the way around."

"I was an awful fool, I know. I should have thought of something like that."

"You were and should," Prentice said dryly. *"Indeed* you were a fool. And I'm a bigger one to try and get your letters back. I'll be honest and tell you that if it wasn't that I think I might get my Sunday cut at this girl-killing Cicco, I'd drop the thing here. I've had no help from you or your brother."

"I'll do anything you say. Mr. Richards and I talked it over and he said I could rely on you absolutely."

"Nice of him. Now listen! They'll have to get in touch with you through the personals in the paper and till then we'll sit tight. I can't do any good angling around because they know I'm a copper. We'll work it this way." Prentice paced the floor, planned, and gave her instructions while she sat silent except for an occasional sniffle. He ended with: "And you go downstairs and register here. When we get action we don't want to run all over town after each other and I don't think they know I'm here. All plain?"

She nodded, repeated his instructions plainly, and left.

HE CALLED SULLIVAN at the station and when he came told him all that Miss Richards had told him and what he had decided about Henry Danvers' connection with the case. "He was lying to me when he hired me, you can see that. Henry knew about this ten grand and thought I might get a line on it. What he wanted more than anything else was that. He didn't care who killed his brother. And Richards! He tells me nothing except to keep quiet anything I find out. He says he wants me to investigate this murder and what he wants is the letters his sister is being blackmailed with. He wouldn't come right out and say it, though."

Sullivan said: "He wanted it to be a secret," and laughed.

"And Miss Richards is worse. I honestly think she'd rather have me find the guys that killed him than get back these letters she's scared sick about. She's sure a kick. She's nuts about the —— yet. In spite of him putting the slug on her for eighteen grand she's still screwy about him. She is, without question, the world's prize sap and I'm chump enough to go to bat with her against this team." He then told Sullivan about his plan which, when analyzed, was simple. When Cicco, after getting in touch with Miss Richards, went to meet her and collect the money he would demand, Prentice planned to break into Cicco's apartment and search it for the letters. If he found them he planned to wait until Cicco's return and regain the money Miss Richards would have paid him. If the letters were not found he intended to force Cicco to disclose their whereabouts.

Sullivan flatly disapproved and pointed out the various reasonable objections to the entire plan. But Prentice was obdurate. Like many big men, who are not afraid of getting hurt, he had fought or blundered his way through many difficult situations where the odds were all against him. His experience had given him confidence. Besides, once he had gone to the mental effort of thinking up a plan, he refused to be bothered further about it.

"I tell you, Sullivan," he said, to close the argument, "I've got the whole thing lined out. I can't miss. It's a cinch."

Sullivan's smile was wintry. "Yeah! A cinch for trouble. You got more guts than I got. Ixnay for me, starting a rumble with a red hot like this Cicco and have no more of an edge than you're figuring on. No dice. He's bad."

"I know it. It's me for it."

"Yeah! I'll be down the street in a prowl car. As long as it's just two in a car like a regular patrol, they won't get wise. I'll keep at least half a block away."

"Okey by me as long as you don't butt in and spoil my play. You'll hear the shooting if it don't work out."

"Well, I'll stand by. You phone me when the blow-off comes." He left, leaving Prentice with nothing to do except wait for the personal in the paper.

THREE DAYS PASSED—DAYS that Prentice spent teaching Miss Richards two-handed pinochle, and she consistently beat him after the first day.

He had decided the less he was on the street the safer he was and he grew genuinely fond of the little maiden lady during the enforced seclusion.

The personal, when it finally appeared, was plain. *Rich phone Capitol 2040 three Thursday,* and Prentice was at her shoulder when she called. She quavered: "This is Miss Richards. What do you want?" There was a moment's delay, then an answering voice: "Call Sutter 4927." She called this number and repeated: "This is Miss Richards." A voice said: "Yes, Miss Richards," and she asked: "What do you want?" The answer was terse. "Money! Ten thousand in small bills. We'll give you until tomorrow at three to raise the money, then phone Capitol 2040 again. That plain?"

"Yes."

"What hotel are you in?"

"The *Stewart,* on Powell Street."

"I know where it is. You phone tomorrow at three. And have the money ready." The phone clicked.

Prentice, as a matter of routine, had both phone numbers checked, finding the Capitol number to be a small Italian fruit stand, and the Sutter number a pay telephone in a drug-store. Cicco's tactics were plain—he would call the fruit store shortly before three and leave a number for Miss Richards to call and it would be useless to have the place watched. Miss Richards, following Prentice's instructions, got the money the next morning, and at three called the Capitol number again and was given a number on the Mission exchange to call. The orders given her were explicit. "Go out of your hotel and walk down Powell to Market. Cross to Market to the right-hand side of the street and walk towards the Ferry building. When a car stops for you, get in. Leave your hotel at exactly four. Got it?"

Her tiny voice quavered: "Yes."

"Go alone. Don't have a policeman with you or following

you or the letters will go to the tabloid that's fighting the bunch that appointed your brother. With the excitement over Danvers, they'll print 'em. Remember Danvers if you don't feel like doing what you're told. Is it clear?"

She said "Yes!" again.

Prentice prompted: "Ask about the letters?"

"Will you bring the letters?"

"We'll do our part. You bring the money." The phone clicked silent.

Prentice was jubilant. "We get action at last. When you get in the car, notice the men closely—not their clothes, their faces. They'll follow you from the hotel, probably on foot, and when they see everything's all right they'll signal the pick-up car. You won't be hurt—they'll let you out as soon as they see they're not followed. Are you scared?"

"A little bit." Her chin quivered. "I'm afraid to have you take this risk. Maybe it would be better to—"

Prentice interrupted firmly. "Now see here. It's all figured out. You do your part and I'll do mine and don't you worry. Did that voice sound to you like it had an accent?"

"Maybe a little. It's hard to tell over a phone."

"They must have seen you at the time they killed Danvers. You notice they didn't ask you to wear a white rose or any nonsense like that." He told her again about trying to remember the men in the car, reasoning that if she were occupied in memorizing faces and voices she would not be so apt to give way to her fear. Sullivan was notified of the hour set by Cicco and Prentice edged out the side door of the hotel.

At four, he confidently rang the bell of Cicco's North Beach apartment. There was no answering click—he expected none—

and after waiting a minute he rang other apartments until someone freed the automatic door release. He walked to the second floor, opened the door of Cicco's apartment with a pass key with no difficulty and stepped inside, locking the door after him.

The apartment was gaudily furnished but badly in need of a thorough cleaning. Empty glasses on a littered table, dust everywhere, and dirty clothes on the chairs and the floor. Dirty dishes in the sink completed a picture that disgusted Prentice, and he had the usual masculine indifference to disorder. The air was foul with the windows tightly closed.

He prowled through the rooms, methodically searching for the letters but keeping a wary ear cocked for the return of the rightful occupants. He was looking through the kitchen when he heard footsteps in the hall—then the sound of a key in the door. He stepped behind the door leading into the front room, gun out and ready, heard the front door open and close and a smooth voice say: "The old gal's got guts at that. She never made a whimper when I told her I'd give her the letters some other time. She must be simple, thinking she was going t' get 'em back."

Another voice, slightly accented, answered: "How could we sell 'em to her again if we gave 'em back now? It don't make sense. Is there a drink left?"

The smooth voice again. "Yeah! Icebox. But we're not going to stay. You go on home and I'll go down to the joint. We'll split the take now. You know—she might have a tail on us at that—it seems funny she never made a squawk. That looked like a police car down the street."

"We wasn't tailed. Angelo's drove cab long enough to lose

any copper in the world and I was watching back all the time. We're not hot."

"Maybe not, but I want to play it safe. We'll split now."

"Okey! I'm going to get that drink."

As the man stepped into the kitchen, Prentice came clear of the door and hit him on the jaw with the barrel of his gun. He heard the crunch that meant a broken jaw… knew the man was out for a long time… and eased him to the floor as he slumped. The man in the front room heard the sound of the blow, cried out: "What's that?"

Prentice stepped into the doorway, snapped: "Only me! Don't try it!" as the man grabbed for the gun under his coat. The man slowly raised his hands to shoulder height.

"You Cicco?"

The dark man nodded sullenly. "Yeah! What's the idea?"

"Oh, just fooling around." Prentice's voice was careless. "I knew that you'd want to give me the letters you and that —— on the floor out there were talking about, so I come up to give you a chance."

"What—"

Prentice hit him in the face with the gun, the muzzle striking a glancing blow on his mouth. The dark man started to slip to the floor, caught himself with an effort, and spit out blood and teeth. He mumbled something and Prentice hit him again, and he went to the floor, falling on his face. Prentice jerked him over on his back, took an automatic from the holster under his arm and sat down to wait for his recovery, knowing the man in the kitchen would be safe for some time. The man on the floor sat up with an effort, mumbled: "——! What's the idea?" His words were indistinct, had a slight lisp from loss of front teeth.

Prentice's eyes looked like agate. "I hate arguments and it looked like you was giving me one. I want those letters."

Cicco, still sitting on the floor, considered. He said as if making a discovery: "Why, you're the heel that was with that tramp Doris. Why, sure you are."

"Right! I'm the guy that gave Arlo and that hot that was with him the works. How'd ya feel about this letter business now? I was with Doris when she got it, and *that* don't rest easy. Do I get the letters? I'd just as soon fix you right up, don't think I wouldn't."

Cicco said hastily: "——! I ain't got 'em."

"But you can get 'em."

"I swear I can't."

Prentice raised the gun.

Cicco's eyes widened. He looked past Prentice for a second and as he did, someone reached past Prentice's shoulder and struck his hand, the hand holding the gun, with a blackjack. As his paralyzed right hand loosed the gun, Prentice made a desperate grab for it with his left. He caught it, but as he spun around the sap landed solidly back of his ear, and he slumped in his chair, balanced a moment, then sagged to the floor on his side, motionless.

Cicco was still sitting down. He said: "Nice, Angelo, nice. I didn't hear the kitchen door open at all."

Angelo was short and swarthy. His nose had been broken and badly set, both ears had the formless appearance that typifies the ham fighter. He growled: "There's a prowl car parked halfway down the block and as I put the car away I seen it. I figured something was phoney and come in quiet. Who's this?"

"It's the heel that did up Arlo and the Keegans so pretty.

He's all washed up now. But we can't do him in here. Get some rope or something to tie him. When he snaps out of it, we'll walk him to the car and ride him for the bump-off. We oughta hurry."

"He must've hit Andy mighty hard. I stepped on his hand when I come in and he never made a peep. I waited on this guy the night he made the play for Doris."

"I heard him hit Andy. Then he come in and backed me up." Cicco felt of his mouth. "I never said a word to him and I lost the front of my teeth."

Angelo looked at Prentice curiously. "He's a tough-looking baby."

"He *is,* too. He's through now." Cicco got to his feet, staggered, and hurriedly sat down. "The —— hit me twice and I can't walk yet. Get that rope, will you?"

Angelo looked in the kitchen for something to tie Prentice up with and came back in the front room. His voice was complaining. "There ain't nothing here. We'll have to just watch him."

"I'll watch him all right." Cicco retrieved his gun from Prentice's pocket. "You go out and see if you can get Andy to snap out of it."

Prentice was lying on his side, knees drawn up into his stomach. Cicco leaned over and slapped him in the face. Prentice groaned slightly, drew his knees up more, and Angelo, in the kitchen, called: "Is there a drink in the place? If I can get a drink down Andy, I think he'll snap out of it."

Cicco answered: "In the ice-box," reached down and slapped Prentice again and Prentice jerked over on his back and kicked out with both feet, catching Cicco squarely in the belly. Almost with the same motion he was on his feet and reaching for his own gun on the floor. Cicco was knocked out by the force of the blow and crashed into the littered table and from there to the floor.

Angelo heard the commotion and came running in, whiskey bottle in one hand and tugging at his gun with the other. Prentice, his back to him and stooping for the gun, heard him coming and turned and fired in one movement, but, off balance and still partially dazed by the sap, missed him and hit the whiskey bottle, spraying glass and whiskey all over the wall.

He steadied himself and lining the gun on Angelo's stomach fired again and Angelo wavered and sat down, both hands gripping his middle. Prentice took the gun from Cicco's lax hand, searched Angelo and took another from him, wobbled in the kitchen and dragged Andy into the front room. Andy was still out. He went back in the kitchen, walking steadier now, found another bottle of whiskey in the ice-box and brought this and a glass of water in the front room, sat down, took a big drink out of the bottle and looked at Angelo. He said: "All right, egg! Curtains for you unless you get to a doctor. Going to tell me things?"

Angelo groaned: "Oh ———! I got it this time."

Prentice's voice was calm. "You got a chance if you get to a hospital and get patched right now. You're going to talk or die right there on the floor with me watching you. It's your dice. You say what you want. ——— sake, mugg, I put that slug high enough and far enough to one side so you *could* talk."

Angelo groaned again and muttered in Italian.

"And talk English, you heel. I didn't get that last crack."

Angelo looked at him with pain-filled eyes. "What you want to know? Get a doctor!"

"You tell me where this guy keeps his letters and you'll have a doctor in five minutes. You don't, and your number's up."

"Oh ——! Please! I talk! He's got a cache in the *Italiano*. There's a safe in the wall besides the one on the floor. All the stuff is there. Get a doctor."

"You sure?" Prentice was suspicious. "What about the combination?"

"He's got combination in—book—pocket. Please—please get me—doc—" Prentice went to Cicco, searched and found a leather-backed notebook. He looked through this, held it where Angelo could see. "This it?"

Angelo moaned and nodded.

Prentice said viciously: "Then I'll tell you. You got it right in the gut from a .45. You ain't got a chance. What in hell did you think I was shooting at—the moon? —— you, you'll work this blackmail and girl killing, will you!"

Angelo started mumbling in Italian. Prentice watched him sourly, listened to the mumble die in intensity, took another drink and walked to the phone on the wall. He lifted the receiver, said: "Police Station," heard footsteps in the hall, then a pounding on the door, and reached over with one hand and unlocked it, still holding the phone.

Sullivan walked in, followed by another man in plain-clothes and Prentice grunted: "Where were you when the fireworks started?" and into the phone: "Just a minute." He gave the phone to Sullivan. "It's the station. I was just going to call for the ambulance. I gave up looking for you."

Sullivan looked at the three men on the floor, spoke briefly into the phone and turned to Prentice. "Another Arlo, huh! We started as soon as the shooting did but had one hell of a time getting into the joint. Everybody was afraid to open their door. Are they dead or just playing dead?"

"Just playing." Prentice pointed at Angelo. "This grease-ball here won't be playing very long, though." He walked to where the packet of money Miss Richards had given Cicco was lying in the wreckage of the table. "I know where the letters are and I'll bet there'll be more than the bunch I'm looking for there. Ain't you curious?"

"Where?"

"This *Club Italiano* spot that Mr. b—— owns. I suppose we'll have to get a warrant?"

An ambulance siren sounded outside and a police surgeon and two internes came in. The surgeon knelt by Angelo, shook his head. "Not a chance. He won't last three hours and I doubt if he comes to. What happened?"

"He played too rough and I didn't want to play."

"He won't play any more."

Angelo and the others were still unconscious as they were loaded into the ambulance and sent to the emergency hospital, with the man that was with Sullivan riding along as guard. Prentice and Sullivan watched the ambulance drive away and Sullivan suggested: "Le's go. It'll take about ten minutes for the warrant after we get to the station. Judge Thomas won't ask any questions if I tell him there's a blackmail angle… he's been paying off himself, unless I'm out."

MISS RICHARDS' LETTERS were found in the wall safe at the *Club Italiano*, along with many others, all neatly enveloped and filed. There was an odd lot of jewelry from a Market Street stick-up that Cicco had never been suspected of having had a hand in, and thirty-odd thousand dollars, in large bills. Prentice, alone with Sullivan in the office, calmly proceeded to count out eighteen thousand of this, hesitated a moment, then added another thousand. Sullivan watched him curiously but came to life with a violent: "Hey! What's the idea?" when Prentice pocketed this.

"It's for Miss Richards. She's paid this bunch of boys eighteen grand and her brother's paying the nut on this trip of mine. That's what the extra's for. I'm not trying to chisel it… you can be with me when I give it to her."

"But man! You can't do that! That'll have to be prorated among the people that've paid off. You just can't take it like this."

Prentice faced him with a snarl. "I can't do it! By God, I am doing it! Now listen! I break the damn' case and I'm going to see the old girl gets out alive on it. What the hell! Who knows about the dough but you and me and if it hadn't been for the old gal you'd still have this bunch in your hair."

Sullivan considered, slowly grinned. "Well, there's something in that. What about the beef Cicco'll put up?"

"To hell with him! I'm the one to beef. You coming in before I had a chance to work him over. You're going to put me in the cell with him and give me a break before I leave town. To hell with him! Who'll believe him?"

"I could pretend I never saw this."

"You never saw a thing then. Let's see if there's anything but letters in the old gal's envelope. I'll give 'em to her, and I bet she goes screwy."

The first letter in the packet proved to be from Henry Danvers to Joe Danvers and advised Joe that a certain Miss

Richards would be at the *Del Monte Hotel* and that she was the one they had talked of. It was dated approximately a month before the first of Miss Richards' letters to Joe. Sullivan looked at it and whistled. "He was in on the frame and they kept this for proof so's they could keep him in line."

Prentice's face was grim. "I've had him picked as a wrong one all the time. He's going to pay me that grand for looking after his interests, as he puts it, and then I'm going to give this letter to Richards and see what he'll do with it."

"He won't do one damn' thing. They never do. He'll shut up and thank heaven his sister's out of it. You see."

"Well, it makes me a cinch to collect the grand he promised me. I can blackmail on my own side, now."

"You can, all right." Sullivan grinned. "And you will, I'll bet. More power to you."

They left, to take the money and letters to Miss Richards. She was very grateful. After Sullivan left she turned to Prentice.

"They—my brother told me that you were a very hard man, Mr. Prentice, and I can't see how you could be otherwise, with the work you have to do and the terrible men you have to deal with; and you certainly give such an impression. But I have discovered something which I do not believe they even suspect. That hardness, which is very real in trouble, is only a surface hardness over a very noble, self-sacrificing, generous heart. At least, it has been that way to a helpless little old lady who has been sorely in need of just that sort of friend."

Dal blushed all over the place, until he managed to think of an excuse to leave and stumbled out the door.

PRENTICE WAS BACK in Magna City a month later,

being forced to wait and testify in the state's case against Cicco, Keegan, and the broken-jawed Andy. All three men got long sentences, though the killing of the girl, Doris Case, could not be proven. The stolen jewelry on top of the conclusive evidence of blackmail was sufficient to put them away for almost as long a time as even the vindictive Prentice thought proper. Cicco complained bitterly about the shortage of money found in the safe, but having no proof as to the actual amount this had amounted to nothing.

After reporting to the Commissioner, Prentice went to Danvers' office and was announced by the acidulous Miss Clark. Danvers rose to meet him, said: "I trust, Lieutenant, you have carried your quest to a successful conclusion."

Prentice grunted and sat down. "Well, that depends on what you call success. I got the hoods that killed your brother all right. I killed three of them and the other three got twenty years. How's that?"

"Then of course you found the money my unfortunate brother left?"

Prentice looked at him blankly. "I'm sorry, Mr. Danvers, to have to be the one to tell you this. Your brother was a blackmailer, and any money he had was obtained in that way."

Danvers coughed. "Blackmail's an ugly word. Joe may have done things… things he shouldn't have done, but the money he left had nothing to do with that."

"I don't agree. The people he robbed have a moral right to every dime."

"But not a legal right. If they care to make a claim and the court upholds them, of course I'll have nothing more to say."

"You knowing they wouldn't do a thing on account of scandal. That's a good stall." He added bluntly: "It don't make a damn' bit of difference anyway. I didn't find any dough but I found his killers and I'm after my money. The agreement was a thousand dollars an' expenses and I spent another two hundred."

"Can you prove that you got the killers?"

"The men now in jail testified that a man named Arlo did the actual shooting. And that Arlo was accompanied by a man named Keegan. I killed them both in self-defense.

"And this man Arlo was the man that killed poor Joe?"

"I said so, didn't I? Arlo held the gun but Joe committed suicide when he put the cross on the heels he was with. He was a dirty blackmailer and he got just what was coming to him." He stood up. "Now that you know that, what about my dough?"

"We had a tacit understanding, Lieutenant, that you were to recover the money that Joe left. I must refuse to pay you unless that money is found. You have nothing to show there was any agreement between us."

Prentice said slowly: "Then you refuse to pay me?"

"I certainly do."

Prentice took a step towards the desk and Danvers pressed the bell for his secretary. He glared back at Prentice and when she came in, said: "Please stay here for a moment, Miss Clark. I want you for a witness in case this man gets violent." To Prentice. "You come in here with a wild story about my poor dead brother and expect money for it. I will not pay you a cent."

Prentice walked to the door, turned back and faced Danvers and Miss Clark. He said: "Okey by me! You do as you think best and so will I. I'll be seeing you."

He reached in his pocket and got the letter Henry had written Joe about Miss Richards. Holding it so Danvers could see and identify it, he asked: "Did you have the girl friend there write this or was it personal? I found a bunch of stuff like this but I forgot to tell you."

"Why—what's—what's that?"

"A letter. I thought the D.A. might be interested so I saved it out." He turned again.

Danvers' face paled. He cried out: "Wait! Miss Clark, I won't need you." Prentice stood to one side as she left the room and Danvers asked: "Where'd that—"

"I held it out, I said. I had a hunch you wouldn't pay off."

Danvers' face was white and sweating. He said: "Why this is blackmail," in a sick voice.

Prentice mimicked: "Blackmail's an ugly word." He waved the letter. "I bet the D.A.'ll think so too. I want my money."

"There's nothing I can do but pay it. I can't have a scandal." He pressed the button again, told Miss Clark: "Make Lieutenant Prentice a check for a thousand dollars and bring it to me to sign."

Prentice said: "Twelve hundred," softly.

"I mean twelve hundred, Miss Clark."

She brought the check in, Danvers signed it, but Prentice waved it back. He said: "And I want it certified. I like to be a nuisance."

He waited in silence for the half hour she was gone, studied the check when it came and slipped it into his vest pocket. Danvers said: "That'll all, then!" Prentice jerked his thumb at the door, said: "Send the gal out," and Danvers said: "That's all, Miss Clark." He watched her leave, said nervously: "May I have the letter now?"

Prentice stood up, crossed to the desk. He put his hand in his pocket, Danvers extended his own hand across the desk for the letter, and Prentice jerked him by the lapel of his coat half across the desk. He brought his fist up from his pocket viciously, then twice more. Danvers slipped down on the desk, blood running from a broken nose, and Prentice looked down at him, said softly: "That is the only sort of medicine that will do a blackmailer any good," and went out.

Miss Clark was at her desk. She looked up and he stopped by her, blowing on his knuckles. He reached in his pocket, took out the letter, told her: "Tell Mr. Danvers that I'll return this note he wrote me the next time I come up for a donation to the Widows and Orphans Fund. Tell him he'd better hold out a nice bit for them, too." He went to the door, threw back over his shoulder: "You'd best wait until he's back to work, though. He'll be home for a few days, he was telling me."

He ambled towards the elevator, said under his breath: "Until they patch up that schnozzle of his anyway." He looked very happy.

Dal Prentice Thinks It Out

Set-up this month—solution next month

FOUR MEN WERE in the one-room cabin, Lieutenant Dal Prentice, a medical examiner, a fingerprint expert, and Jones, the man whose call had brought the officers. Or rather five men, counting the dead man in the chair in front of the fireplace.

Prentice, staring soberly down at the body, noted that the man's head rested on the back of the chair, that both arms were hanging lax and that a revolver was lying on the floor directly below the right hand. He saw a blue hole in the right temple. He asked: "This was Albright?"

Jones' voice was steady. "Yes. J.C. Albright. He lived by himself here. I was his only friend, so far as I know."

Prentice waved at the body, at the gun. He said: "I'd like to know the time of death and I'd like the gun printed, boys." He turned back to Jones. "You say you found him?"

"Yes, I was on my way into town and was within a few feet of the door when I heard the shot. I was so close, that's why I came in and found he'd shot himself."

"Nobody could've run past you then, huh?"

"I don't see how they could."

Prentice examined the back door and found it bolted. The two windows also were fastened on the inside. He asked: "You been anywhere since you called?"

"No. I thought I ought to stay right by the phone, until you came. I'd like to go now though, as I am late for my appointment."

Prentice nodded: "In a minute!" and walked to the police

doctor who whispered: "It's either murder or suicide. Probably murder, as there are no powder burns." He added: "Dead about half an hour. Death was instantaneous. If that helps you any."

The burly detective looked at his watch, said: "That checks with the time he called in," turned to the print man who was studying the gun under a glass. The man looked up from this, said: "The gun's bare, Dal. No prints at all." Prentice turned to Jones.

"Thought you were pretty smart, guy, didn't you? Thought your best bet was to stay right here and fool us, eh?"

"What do you mean?"

"I mean you've sewed yourself right up with this kill in two different directions. You've proved it was murder and you've proved you did it. You're under arrest."

What were Dal's two points?

Solution:

1. The dead man could not have wiped prints from the gun.
2. By Jones' own testimony and the locked back door and windows, he had proved that only he and the dead man had been there at the time of the shooting.

www.ingramcontent.com/pod-product-compliance
Lightning Source LLC
Chambersburg PA
CBHW031218020726
47499CB00002B/629